We Saved Ourselves, Kinda

We Saved Ourselves, Kinda

Larry Arrowood

Woodsong Publishing
Seymour, IN

We Saved Ourselves, Kinda
Larry Arrowood

2023 All rights reserved.

We Saved Ourselves, Kinda is a historical fiction. The book is based on events from the author's childhood; however, the names, characters and tales are the product of the author's imagination and are used in a fictitious manner. Any resemblance to actual persons, living or dead, is purely coincidental. This book is a rewrite of a previous book, *They Came To Save Us*, by Larry Arrowood.

ISBN 978-1-961482-00-5

Published by Woodsong Publishing
Seymour, Indiana

www.woodsongpublishing.com

This is the author's thirteenth book. He may be contacted via email: larryarrowood@mac.com

Woodsong Publishing additional books are available through Barnes and Noble, Amazon, or the readers preferred online book supplier.

" … Save yourselves from this crooked generation."
Acts 2:40 ASV

Table of Contents

Preface

If "silence is golden," my family would be filthy rich. For some undisclosed reason, we didn't need to talk. We only talked out of necessity, with one disclaimer: we also talked when we were angry, but that doesn't necessarily fall into the category of necessity. Necessity has its unique category. For example, if the bowl of biscuits gets stalled on one end of the table you ask, "Would you pass the biscuits, please?" That request is out of necessity, but then again, it could be out of anger if someone is hogging the biscuits. Either way, we were not usually inclined to communicate very much.

This family trait left me with some frustration when I discovered significant tidbits of information on my own, but by that time it was too late for it to matter. Like, no one bothered to inform me that an ancient, warriors' path snaked a few miles from where we lived. I found that piece of history much later in life, when I ran across a copy of a Kentucky map, commissioned by President George Washington, hanging on a wall in an antique shop in Edinburgh, Indiana. It was marked as plain as day: warriors' path. And when I placed my fingertip on the spot of my upbringing, it almost touched that ancient trail. Why was this important? With Cherokee blood flowing in my veins—another bit of info someone failed to share with me—that would have been important if I had gotten into something like, say, politics. Apart from politics, I might have appreciated hiking that trail in homemade moccasins as a reenactment of my unknown ancestors.

I'll never quite understand how the fascinating story of the "blue skin" Fugate clan eluded me for almost sixty years. They lived but a few hollers over from us. My wife discovered the saga of these folks when we did research for a novel I wrote entitled Troublesome Blue. The Fugate lineage carried a rare gene pool that left some of them with a blue skin-tone. I later discovered a Fugate tombstone in the Arrowood Cemetery—a cemetery named after my ancestors, but it was a cemetery that I didn't know existed until I took a trip a few years back doing some genealogy research. For some reason I never thought to ask my parents "Do we have a cemetery named after our family?" So, no one bothered to tell me this bit of genealogy.

This don't-ask-don't-tell trait left some unknown events that effected my childhood, while it left some events so sketchy that the detail pool is murky at best. I have many memories that are somewhat flawed, and at age seventy-something, they are fading fast, and as one of our famous statesmen once said, "That dog-gone, pony-soldier mishap down in Scottsdale, California, really affected me when I was a boy growing up in Pittsburg, Arizona," or something to that effect, as best I can recall his speech.

I readily admit my fleeting years piqued interest to discover my past. And Mom was in a nursing home, dying, and I assumed she might be taking some nuggets of interest to the grave. Dad had already passed away, and he had talked less than Mom, so I'm sure lots of tidbits were forever lost at his passing, like the role he played in the war in the South Pacific and how the kamikazes attacked his ship, and him witnessing—from a distant ship—the signing of the treaty that ended the war with Japan. He never bothered to mention his medals, or the acclaim ascribed to his ship: the USS North Carolina—the most highly decorated warship of its time. So, with Mom dying, I hastened to learn more about my roots in the heartland of Appalachia Kentucky. And I needed to affirm some of my memories: a one-room schoolhouse, two floods that displaced us (the last one uprooting us entirely and landing us in Newport, Kentucky, a rowdy little town across the river from Cincinnati), long-ago neighbors scattered like feathers in the wind, an old mule named Maud, and other stories I'll share in this book. I stayed by Mom's bedside so long as she would share. And true to character, her sharing mostly was a response to my questions. Like the time I asked about my recollections of a beautiful, white horse that grazed in the field a short distance from our house. "Do you remember that horse?" I asked. "Why, sure, I remember her. She wuz yur daddy's horse. He rode her whiles he delivered the US Mail." Dad was a mailman? Like the Pony Express? And no one bothered to share that little bit of trivia with the first-born son? "That wuz a fast horse," she continued, "the fastest in the community. Yur daddy gave others a head start, but that horse always overtook'm." I must confess, that information almost made me mad, for as a youngster, I had walked past that racehorse almost every day and never knew she belonged to me. And the story about Dad delivering mail? It was definitely off the government records. I'm assuming the real mail carrier hired him on the side as a substitute.

Now, some folks today might describe my family as being dysfunctional. Surely it couldn't have anything to do with Mom and Dad dropping me off at the monthly schoolboard meeting and waiting in the car while I went inside to recite a poem about two roads snaking off into a yellow woods, or something to that effect. Evidently, my teacher had nominated me for the task. In retrospect, maybe we were a tiny bit dysfunctional: a mite antisocial at times, especially if we weren't related to someone. And, no, I can't recall them asking me how things went with the schoolboard recitation, nor did I feel the urge to voluntarily tell them. Our explanation is that we just didn't see the need to always talk about everything. And I suppose we didn't consider our life all that interesting. So, sad to say, because of that minor, family idiosyncrasy, my recollections may be somewhat flawed, and I may have to fill in some blanks for the pages ahead, but I'd like to share the stories as best I can.

This book is a work of fiction with bits of truth scattered

throughout. It is partially true because most of the places, events, and people are real. Still, it is fictional because it is told as seen through the eyes of a child: a memory that is flawed, not necessarily purposefully (though I filled in some blanks—okay, I filled in a lot of blanks to try and make the stories come alive) but because of my immature and imagined perception. Through the eyes of a child, little is often viewed as big, and gloom is sometimes viewed gleefully. And when perceived by a child, rumors—and sometimes lies—are not processed through a filter of truth. I used some childhood names of literal people, for they were my neighbors. Still, I scrambled some names, because after all these years, I kind of forgot whose name should be associated with what event. I confess up front and beg anyone who knew me as a boy to not be offended at my imperfect perceptions and dwindling memory. Then again, some of you might want to thank me because I fiddled a little regarding what I could have said. I hope you enjoy! And laugh some!

Chapter One

Copeland

Indian Summer brought unseasonably warm weather to the Cumberland Plateau. Fallen leaves hinted that winter was not a distant intruder; frosts had already turned the persimmons into a squishy brown, and a squashed pumpkin or two littered the landscape, leftovers from a recent Halloween ruckus. Milkweed seedpods dangled in the breeze, opened by the elements to expose the cotton-like content that escaped to float cloud-like on the wings of the morning zephyrs. The gentle breeze rustled stubborn leaves that clung obstinately to life on the pin oaks. Two buzzards waltzed on the winds of first light, celebrating another dawn. Though majestic in flight not unlike the eagle, their terrestrial mannerisms give them a bad rap: hunchbacked, baldheaded, and roadkill connoisseurs. A flock of geese, in a rugged "V" formation, suddenly appeared from the bottomland where they had spent the night, attracted by the kernels of corn that had fallen through the cracks of the harvest sled and the mouth of an ornery, old mule named Jack. The geese flapped their wings vigorously to maintain altitude as they cut through the fog rising from the river. The leader squawked orders, and the message resounded throughout the column, all the way to the rear. And then they were gone.

A stillness lingered: a serenity one breathes in deeply and exhales slowly. It was a stillness that had lingered thousands of years before the first Cherokee ventured into this land in search of bear, beaver, bison, and a host of animals that roamed this mountainous region. It was a serenity that remained still, except for the occasional calamities that visited the few inhabitants of this mist-veiled valley.

A lone whistle of an approaching passenger train broke

the silence of the tranquil morning. Black smoke billowed from the engine stack, forming a tell-tale outline in the sapphire sky as it traced the path of the L&N Railroad which hugged the ever-winding mountainside along the North Fork of the Kentucky River.

****

A young couple, hardly in their twenties, with suitcase and tickets in hand, stood silently by the railroad tracks, awaiting the train. By her unbuttoned coat and protruding stomach, it was apparent she was heavy with child; therefore, it was obvious to where they were traveling. The nearest doctor was fifteen miles away in the sleepy town of Jackson: too far by mule for an expectant mother and too risky not to get there before labor pains began. This young woman declined the assistance of the obliging midwife. Too many stories loomed of a frightened husband delivering his own child because the midwife couldn't get there in time, or a snowstorm prevented her arrival altogether. Giving birth in Appalachia was risky business, and too many headstones identified the graves of children whose date of birth and death were the same. She did not want her child to become another statistic.

"Thank there'll be a room fer us at the hotel, Delmar?" she asked.

"Don't thank there'll be any problem findin' one this time of year, sweetheart," her husband replied. "You ain't feelin' like Mary and Joseph ar' ya, Fairlean'?" he asked, his brow furrowing a faraway expression. "No room at the inn. What a turrible fix they wuz in! But the good Lord wuz lookin' out fer'em."

"You just kain't always per'dict these thangs," she expressed her anxiety, but Delmar did not respond. "Shore am glad Doc Lewis opened his office in Jackson, fixed-up with that birthin' room and all," she continued as she glanced in the direction of the approaching train.

Doctor Lewis' office was located on the ground level of the Jackson Hotel, across the hallway from the barbershop. Several hotels welcomed mothers in waiting. Delmar planned to check them into one of Jack Lovely's Restaurant and Hotel efficiency apartments until their second child decided to arrive. It would have been more convenient to stay at the Jackson Inn, but Jack Lovely's place was more in line with their wallet.

They cringed at the whistle blast of the approaching black, Baldwin locomotive as it rounded the curve by the Strong's place. Delmar hastily inhaled a couple drags from his hand-rolled Prince Albert cigarette, dropped it to the ground, and twisted it into the cinders with the toe of his government issued boot. Though a veteran of the US Navy and five years removed from the Pacific Theatre, his features still resembled those of a couple teenagers waiting to catch the train to the nearest high school, also located in Jackson. The local, one-room school only went through eighth grade. That's when most students from their community entered the work force, but a few continued their education at the High School in Jackson. The train was their only means of getting there.

The morning sun peeked over the horizon and reflected off a weather-beaten and bullet-punctured sign that identified this tiny spot on the Kentucky state map: Copeland. No population mentioned. No slogan. Simply Copeland.

Delmar helped Fairlean into her cramped seat aboard the passenger train. Climbing over her feet, he half-fell into his seat as the train hissed a long sigh and lurched forward. The steel wheels spun slightly and then gripped the rails, moving forward ever so slowly, then faster and faster with a cadenced clatter as each wheel clanked at the connecting joints of the metal tracks. The train chugged along, billowing smoke and bellowing a warning at all road crossings and at an occasional child who waved wildly, enticing the engineer to engage the piercing whistle.

Delmar scanned the advertisement promoting an 8MM home movie featuring Hopalong Cassidy in "Bar 20 Rides Again," passing time more so than being interested. Movies were as foreign as a limousine, for he owned neither a home-movie projector nor a television. He dozed momentarily, but a sudden change in the coach's lighting snapped him into reality as the passenger train entered the Dumont Tunnel a short distance out from Jackson. A groan from his wife startled him.

"Ar' ya havin' pain?" he anxiously inquired.

"No, dear, 'twas only a dream. I was dreamin' of a baby boy, cott'n white hair and purdy as a picture. You thank that's what he'll be? A boy? I want'em to be a boy, Delmar, fer you."

"Whatev'r tis, Fairlean, t'will make me mighty happy. You just rest a bit more. We'll be thar soon enough."

The middle of November found Delmar anxiously pacing the floor of the tiny efficiency apartment in Jackson. Two weeks had passed since they disembarked the passenger train and took up temporary residence in town. He picked up a sports magazine for the umpteenth time and scanned the headlines: Ezzard Charles KO's Freddy Beshore; Nick Barone, defeats Joe Louis by a decision. The military had awakened his curiosity for boxing. The headline announcing the Ben Hogan United States Open Golf Championship did not interest him; golf was a rich man's game and sounded boring to him—not to mention that the nearest course was probably a hundred miles away. A new, white, V-8 Ford, with chromed hubcaps and a dazzling hood emblem, was parked across the street, and that caught his attention and did interest him. Someday he would own a car, but not necessarily a Ford, perhaps a Rocket 88 Oldsmobile. But right now, he would settle for a baby and a used rocking chair. He needed to get back to work. The efficiency apartment, at $2 a day, seemed awfully expensive. He didn't yet have one of the newly invented credit cards. He paid cash. At the minimum wage of seventy-five cents an hour, it would be rough going this year, especially with a new baby and all. He was more than a little worried, but he was happy his wife was having their second child, another chance for a boy.

His young wife sat in a chair by the window, watching two pigeons on a roofline across the street. The reflection of her face expressed a pang of sadness.

"You missin' home?" Delmar asked.

"I got another young'n and a dog to care fer, Delmar. And the hogs kain't feed themselves," she said.

"Yur family will take care uf that. Surely it won't be long now." He tried to comfort her. "How ya feelin'?"

"Same," she sighed.

Sleep came uneasily. A strange growth on her abdomen had appeared with this pregnancy. She was concerned enough to talk to the Lord about it. She had pondered the story of Samuel's mother of the Scripture, and she considered how Hannah vowed to give Samuel to the Lord because he was a miracle child. A tear trickled down her cheek. "If'n he's a boy and if'n he's healthy, I'll give'em to the Lord," she blurted out.

"What's that all about, Fairlean?" Delmar asked.

"I wuz just a'thankin' out loud," she answered.

The pain began the next day at 5 a.m. The hurried trip down the street to the doctor's office offered a distraction and thus some relief. At 10 p.m. the child finally came; a seven-pound, cotton-white-haired boy. A Douglas Crockwell illustrated calendar hanging on the wall of the doctor's office showed Thursday, November 16, 1950. With some luck, the child would make it into the twenty-first century—life expectancy was on his side at 68.2 years. His young mother would never hear about Dr. Spock's Baby and Child Care, with lots of hugs, kisses, and permissiveness. Her son would be raised by the age-old guidelines of the hill people; a bit cold and rigid, with a "spare-the-rod-and-spoil-the-child" mentality. They spoke little about love, but it abounded— like dandelions in springtime—within the family clan. Nothing mattered more than family.

"Let's call'em Larry," Fairlean whispered, exhausted from seventeen hours of labor. "And I'd like to giv'em a middle name, too, Monroe, after my Daddy and after that singer, Bill Monroe. You know he wuz born in Kentucky?"

"Larry Monroe t'will be just fine, sweetheart, mighty fine," Delmar said, smoothing back her sweat-soaked hair from her brow. "And that wuz a president's name, too."

A half-dozen names chosen that year would someday be familiarly spoken by the hero-adoring fans born this record-breaking decade for births—the baby boomers were arriving. Lionel Richie, Jane Pauly, Mark Spitz, and Stevie Wonder were already snuggling in their twenty-five-percent-more-cotton Pequot white sheets and eating their Gerber Baby Food. None knew that the others existed, or that they would someday be famous household conversational pieces. But none of the babies born that year brought more joy to a couple than the joy this poor, hill-country couple experienced this day.

***

They laid Fairlean and her newborn on an army-green cot and hoisted it onto the train baggage car for the ride home. Delmar, beaming with parental pride, grasp the iron handrail and deftly swung into the baggage car and sat down beside them on a wooden crate stenciled on the side in black letters: Prest-O-Lite Hi-Level Batteries. An hour later the train rumbled to a screeching halt in front of their white, clapboard house, an uncommon depot. How neighborly of the engineer! Fairlean's younger brothers, just out of school for the day, delightfully helped to unload the cot and its cargo. They hesitated alongside the train, exhilaration showing on their faces as they stood next to the idling, massive machine.

"Wanna hold'em, Fanny?" Delmar said to Fairlean's younger sister, Fannie. She picked up the baby and cradled him in her arms.

Neighbors quickly gathered to examine the newest arrival to their community and wait their turn to hold him. Oh, the marvel at the miracle of birth!

Delmar offered the conductor a tip, but he adamantly refused as he clambered aboard his idling engine. "Wouldn't thank uf takin' yur money, Delmar," he said.

Fannie got rather poetic, holding the baby. "Ten fangers, ten toes, two yurs, and a pointed nose," she said. Laughter erupted at such impromptu poetry.

A cool breeze blew gently. Its hint of a coming fifteen-inch snow went unnoticed. Smoke drifted upwards from the chimney in the middle of the roof of the Arrowood home. Their dog, Bounce, laid on the front porch wagging his tale against the attack of the last of the year's nagging gnats.

Delmar called to his mother-in-law, who stood in the doorway, holding his smiling two-year old. "Joyce Marie been a good girl, Lottie Belle?"

"Shore has, Delmar, cept she's ready fur ya'll ta be home."

Delmar bent low to the cot and whispered affectionately into his wife's ear, "We're home, Fairlean. We're home."

Copeland was the place they'd call home for the next thirteen years. And this senerio would be repeated five more times.

Chapter Two

The General Store and US Post Office

A raggedy man in his late twenties sat on the front porch of the only store within miles. A front-porch fixture at the general store, which doubled as a US Post Office, his clothes were faded and filthy, and they revealed recent patches that may give another year of wear. He eyed a familiar face approaching the store, and his adrenalin rushed when the middle-aged man dropped the butt of his cigarette onto the ground, but he cringed when he crushed it into the soil before mounting the steps.

The man gave him a cordial smile and said, "Mornin', Sidgel.

Mornin'," Sidgel said and quickly turned away his gaze.

The man opened the screen door and stepped inside the store, which smelled of a combination of linseed oil, wax paper, pickle juice, and dead mice. He stepped cautiously across the hardwood floor, for the grimy film of linseed oil could be a mite slippery.

"Mornin', Ida Mae," the man said.

"Mornin' Fulton," Ida responded.

"Where's Sidgel living, now that his folks are gone?"

"Not sure," Ida said. "Show's up here alot, sometimes afore sunrise."

"I'm needin' to take the mornin' train to Jackson," Fulton said.

"Our groceries not good a'nough fur yur taste?" Ida asked. She smiled as she retrieved a train ticket.

"You know better'n that, Ida Mae. Needin' some items

you just don't got hur."

"That wouldn't be a new pair uf work boots, would it?" she asked, looking down at his scuffed brogans.

"You know me like a book, Ida Mae. And I'm a'needin' some parts fur my plough and such. Got a couple months to get ready fer the spring plowing."

Ida Mae opened the wooden cash box, took out change for Fulton's twenty-dollar bill, and recorded her first transaction for the day. "Hurts me to take your money, Fulton," she said with a wide grin. "But it takes a mite of fuel ta turn them iron wheels, and the commission uf the ticket sells helps keep this store open."

Fulton showed no response to her attempted humor. "Bill up yet?" he asked.

"He'll be along shortly. Needin' ta talk with'm 'bout somethin'?" she asked.

"Nah, just wantin' to say howdy. Teachers and preachers shore got life easy not havin' ta get up early to slop the hogs and all," Fulton said, straight faced.

"Course he don't get no winters off like you bigtime farmers does," Ida countered.

Fulton laughed as he slipped a rubber band around his wad of money and stuffed it into the front pocket of his denim overalls. He glanced out the window at Sidgel. "Wonder if he's had breakfast?" he asked.

"Don't know," Ida said as she started preparing a sack lunch of thick sliced bologna for her husband and their teenage son, Shoog. Shoog was a student at the community's one-room school; her Bill was the lone teacher.

"Could you make another one of them sandwiches fur me," Fulton asked. "Cheaper hur than in town."

"And tastes better, too," Ida said. "Mayonnaise with that?" she asked.

"Sure. And add a smidgen of mustard." He glanced out the window again. "And could ya make one fur Sidgel?"

"Sure can," Ida Mae said. "By the way, you got some mail yesterdy, but nobody come by ta pick it up," Ida said as she reached under the counter, pulled out a stack of mail, and thumbed through the envelopes.

"Who from?"

"Now you know I don't nosey inta everbody's mail, Fulton. But I thought it important cause it's from the county commissioner's office. I just happened ta notice that."

"Might be good news, Ida Mae. Hopin' ta get us a bridge built across the river. Right hur at your store is the perfect place to get it built. Might bring you a few more customers from across the river."

"Would be nice, Fulton, real nice. This store could use some extra cash, especially with all the credit we gotta carry fur ar people hur, till they get a paycheck."

"I know, Ida Mae, I know. And that's why I'm pushin' ta have the bridge come almost ta yur store's front door."

Chapter Three

The Teacher

K nown by most in the community as Mr. Deaton, he carried a worn, leather satchel filled with books. Always one to be prepared, he cradled a black, folded umbrella that doubled for a cane as he leisurely lumbered the two-mile trip to the schoolhouse. His unconscious, cadenced steps caught every-other creosote-soaked railroad tie. It seemed a long time he had made this same trek, perhaps too long. But time, like speed, was not something that mattered much in Copeland. The Indy 500 up in Indiana where his relatives had moved to, with impressive speeds, meant little to a community that had neither a road nor vehicles. And the locomotives that traversed the winding rails through this community could neither attain nor sustain high speeds on the incessant curves carving their way around the hillsides. Perhaps someday he would purchase one of those cars coming out of Detroit, but that seemed a distant dream. However, he could relate to Kentucky Derby winners like Middle Ground, and his jockey, Mr. Boland, for the highlanders of his community prided themselves in their fast horses—and mules. Such trivia existed in Mr. Deaton's memory, for he was an avid reader, and he devoured the newspapers out of Cincinnati, Frankfort, and Lexington, that arrived weekly in a US Mail pouch dropped off from the passenger train.

Young Shoog Deaton followed a good piece behind his dad. He was proud of his father yet resented the association: he found himself wanting to blend in with the other students. He was pushing manhood, but boyish antics still tugged, pulling him in two directions. Yesterday he had a conversation with his father about what kind of occupation he wanted to pursue, but today he kicked rocks and occasionally flung one

23

at a flock of swooping sparrows along the tracks.

Smoke drifted lazily from the soot-covered flues of wood-burning, kitchen stoves. Doors opened on squeaky hinges and a line of children streamed from the houses perched on stilts. The stilts served an important purpose: they elevated the houses above the occasional floodwaters of the North Fork. They also made room for a root cellar for potatoes, and they offered storage shelves for Ball jars full of canned goods.

Strains of Good Night Irene drifted from a squawking radio, the words hardly distinct above the static. A dog barked a welcome and trotted out to meet him. "Mornin', Spot," Mr. Deaton greeted the dog. "Ain't got biscuits fer ya today. Maybe tomorrow."

With the unseasonably warm weather, he would dispense of building a fire in the woodstove at the back of the classroom. That would save firewood for another day. He hardly noticed the chatter of the children as they fell in line behind him, like apprentices of an ancient rabbi. Neighbors, many of them his former students, waved and called out a hearty "Howdy, Mr. Deaton."

The monthly paycheck he received was meager wages for his years of service. Still, he felt fortunate when compared with others in the community. His salary, combined with his wife's income from their grocery store and her being the post-mistress, made for a decent living. And this neighborly comradery was sufficient payment. Daily. Most everyone respected him. He smiled and waved back at the familiar neighbors. "Good day, to ya," he shouted. More than not, he called them by name.

Local folks called his wife Ida Mae, but they called him Mr. Deaton, a respect long given him for his role as the community schoolteacher. Such respect was sometimes more akin to reverence demanded by the hickory stick he kept over the lintel of the front entry to the schoolhouse, but that same stick had made him some enemies. Strange how the Bible verse didn't always work: "Spare the rod, spoil the child." He hadn't figured that out in all these years as a teacher. Some students just didn't take to correction, like zebras don't take to riding. They're destined to run wild.

Chapter Four

The Mail Carrier

An aging man on horseback overtook Mr. Deaton and his entourage as they rounded the curve nearing the schoolhouse. The man had a long history of delivering mail to the hollers surrounding Copeland—rain or shine. We assumed he was one of the few horseback mail carriers left. The once popular but now long defunct short-lived Pony Express was created from an entrepreneur spirit built around speed. Copeland's equestrian route existed because of necessity rather than the need for speed, for there was no other way for the mail to be delivered, except by foot. However, the rough terrain wore out a man's shoes and his feet rather quickly. The distance he had to cover necessitated a bit more stamina than his walking pace, so he rode his horse on this daily trek. He traveled to places where motorized vehicles had never ventured, nor would they venture for years to come, for lack of bridges and traversable roads made it impossible. He carried mail that arrived daily on the morning passenger train. Ida Mae sorted the mail for the locals and gave him the rest to be delivered to eager faces on multiple hollers. The letters in his saddlebag, and packages stuffed in bulging burlap sacks tied behind the saddle, would be delivered by nightfall. The postal service was the community's primary source of communication with a distant and unfamiliar world. No telephones existed, and radios lacked good reception.

"G'mornin' Mr. Deaton," he called out, waving the reins in his left hand. His right hand rested unconsciously on his colt forty-five that hung from his belt.

"Mornin' Greenberry. Ridin' a little light ain'tcha?

"Yep. Got nary a one uf them catalogs ta d'liver taday.

26

Shore am glad. But that don't make the people happy none."

Greenberry rocked a rhythmic sway in the squeaky, leather saddle. The horse's hoofs made a steady thump on the worn, cinder path which ran alongside the railroad tracks. The horse's slower gait signified he recognized another long day ahead. Greenberry had been accused of occasionally catnapping along the way, but no worries, for his horse knew the route well.

Chapter Five
The Schoolhouse

The schoolhouse perched on a knoll of yellow-clay earth overlooking the railroad and the North Fork of the Kentucky River. It occupied a piece of property once part of the Noble farm. They were a more well-to-do family in the community of not-so-well-to-do families.

Mr. Deaton sat at his desk and reread the letter that had arrived from the Breathitt County Board of Education. They needed an up-to-date report: How many students? Grade levels? Condition of books? Number of usable desks? Repairable desks? Additional comments?

There had been talk of a swinging bridge across the North Fork to connect their community with the newly built road. That would make it possible to acquire additional students from the other side of the river, but more than likely, the authorities would have his students cross the river and catch a bus to a school farther away. Progress pleased him; still, it saddened him. He placed the letter inside the top drawer of his desk and turned his attention to another school day and the sounds of playful students outside.

Walking to the front of the classroom, Mr. Deaton held ajar the weather-beaten door to the paint-deprived building. He clanged the brass bell he kept on his oak desk, announcing the start of the school day. Students filed in and took their assigned seats at the double desks, youngest to the oldest from the front to the back. He made a mental note of each student and gave Shoog an aggravated glance when he, late as usual, raced into the classroom, trying to get to his seat before his dad returned to his desk. Shoog scrambled over the back of the bench behind Billy and Fred Brewer, brothers who were one grade apart, grades seven and eight, and they were his best of friends. All heads turned to view the routine scene. Fred gave Shoog a sideways smile. He was careful not to facilitate Shoog's antics, for he'd been on the receiving end of Mr. Deaton's hickory stick a few times, and it was no cakewalk.

Roll call followed, with students responding "here" when their name was called. As usual, noone responded when the name, Jack Costello, was called out.

Mr. Deaton picked up his red-letter edition, and flipping through the pages, read aloud from the writings of Dr. Luke: "But love ye your enemies, and lend, hoping for nothing again...."

The door hinges squeaked as Jack slipped inside and sauntered across the room. Jack seemed to carry a chip on his shoulder, and he definitely carried a sharp knife in his pocket. Mr. Deaton cleared his throat, noticeably irritated.

"Think you could git up a mite earlier fer school, Jack? If'n you want a job other'n shuckin' corn in the bottoms all day, you best sharpen yur mind the way you sharpen that knife of yur's."

Jack said nothing. He turned his back on Mr. Deaton, stomped to his desk, and fell hard onto the slatted bench, knocking books to the floor. Mr. Deaton continued to read aloud: "Be ye therefore merciful, as your Father also is merciful. Judge not, and ye shall not be judged: condemn not, and ye shall not be condemned: forgive, and ye shall be forgiven...."

The pledge of allegiance to the flag and prayer to the Almighty God followed.

Chapter Six

The Sickness

Our neighbors to the right of us were the Kings. Kelly was the daddy, and he was sick with a cough and getting worse: almost violent at night. He vowed to stop smoking, but his nerves bothered him when he tried. He needed to visit the doctor in Jackson; however, that would be an expense he hadn't planned for.

Some folks said he acquired the sickness while serving some time in prison, as if that made it different than other sicknesses. But no matter where he got the sickness, he was a wonderful neighbor. He was married to Beulah Mae, and like ours, they were a large family. But unlike us, his family had to deal with the sickness.

My mom was at Jackson having another baby. Being the good neighbors they were, the Kings offered concern, cause lots of babies seemed to come down with sicknesses. They checked on us most every day. Beulah Mae's unborn child was kicking wildly in her womb. She and my mom were keeping close to even in having babies.

Yes, as much as we hated to admit it, and I'm sure his family was embarrassed that we all knew, Kelly had run with the wrong crowd sometime in the past, and that got him into trouble with the law for a while. But he'd gotten baptized, and his name was on the church membership roll, so that changed most everything except the sickness. But unlike his sin, which the good Lord took care of, he didn't quite know how to get made whole from his sickness. The chronic cough just wouldn't go away.

Chapter Seven

The Fishing Hole

Life appeared simple along the North Fork. Dogs loafed on the front porches of a dozen houses scattered along the meandering river. An elderly grandmother, clothed in a faded, cotton-print dress, and shielded from the sun by her crinkled bonnet, hoed weeds from a patch of sweet corn. A child cradled a raggedy doll as her "bubby" pulled her in a worn Radio Flyer along the cinder path paralleling the train tracks. A large orange and brown monarch fluttered over a patch of milkweed, flittering from limb to limb.

It was a lazy day and I wanted nothing more than to go fishing. I was nigh on to six years old and had my own pole. Dad made it from a cane he cut down by the creek that bordered our property to the east and flowed into the North Fork that ran back of our house. Dad had good intentions when he cut the cane pole, but he was seldom home long enough to take me fishing. And Mom refused to let me go fishing alone. No amount of pouting, or threats of running away from home budged her stubborn will.

Our house was sandwiched between the North Fork and the L&N Railroad Line running from Hazzard to Jackson and snaking the curves of the river. Of all the places along the hundred and sixty-eight miles of the North Fork, it was a known fact—at least to us—that our property bordered one of the best fishing spots. It was the best because the water ran deep along our property. Much of the river flowed shallow in the summer season; conversely, our fishing hole always remained deep.

Mom had her reasons for denying me fishing rights. A raging North Fork once took her under, and she narrowly escaped. For some unknown reason to us, and perhaps herself,

31

she viewed the river's dangers as payback for anything sinful she had ever done. She constantly fretted about one of us kids falling into the water and drowning. Second to that fear was the concern of one of us cutting a foot on a broken pop bottle while wading in the creek but especially wading in the North Fork. It was a misnomer to call my family "barefoot hillbillies," for Mom hardly allowed us to go barefooted, even in the house.

"Kain't I go barefoot some, Momma?" I begged.

"It ain't good fer you. Yur cousins went barefoot and it caused'em ta have flat feet and now they kain't go inta the army," she explained, and added, "What would I do if'n you cut yur foot off with yur Daddy away working and me not knowin' when he'll be home?"

We wondered about that, not about Dad being away, nor about what Mom would do, but about having to walk around with one foot missing until Dad got home. So, we always wore shoes, and Mom continued to deny me fishing rights in the best spot on the North Fork.

My negative thoughts drove me near to desperation. "The summer is passin', but hur I am just sittin' around lettin' all this opportunity to fish go to waste," I murmured to myself. "How kin I improve my skills without going fishin' once in a while?" I concluded that living along a river doesn't make you a fisherman any more than living by a church makes you a saint. I had lived by both for five years and hadn't become either.

Tommy Lee Spicer defied the odds about fishing but not necessarily sainthood. Even though he didn't live along the river, somehow, he was still the best fisherman around. I suspected he was born with a pole in his hand, cause he caught fish when others couldn't. Behind his back we kids called him Tommy Lee the flea. No particular reason other than it rhymed, but it seemed like something you didn't call a grownup to his face.

Though we lived along the river, we rarely ate fish, probably due to the time it would require sitting for hours on end trying to catch enough fish to feed all five of us kids, plus the six adults that frequented our table. That would be Mom, Dad, Aunt Fannie, Uncles Billy and Fred, and Grandma Brewer. Uncle Verdie was in the army by then, so he no longer counted, though he used to live with Mom and Dad before I was born. Anyhow, we never developed a taste for fish; instead, we preferred chicken, for they were in abundance running around in a fenced area behind our house, and they were much easier to catch than the fish swimming loose in the hundred and sixty-eight miles of the North Fork. And even if we caught a mess of fish, it took more time to scale them then it did to pluck a chicken. And two chickens were sufficient to feed us; conversely, two fish would have started a fight at our table. Mom somewhat used that argument against me going fishing. "We got plenty uf chickens. Why do we need them smelly fish? We kin raise chickens ourselves and they hain't near as hard to catch as fish," she said. I tried to use the argument of free food as a reason for me going fishing. We didn't have to feed the fish, but we had to feed the chickens morning and night. She never gave in to my reasoning nor my begging.

The way Mom preferred chicken over fish, I didn't really understand why she got so upset the day Tommy Lee came walking across our yard carrying a strand of fish from our fishing hole, where he had spent the night fishing. It was a day long in coming, but sure to come, at least some folks were saying, though it resembled most any other day to me. Tommy Lee never offered to share his catch, but he did like to brag. For some reason, though some things are hard for a five-year-old to reason out, his fish stories often smelled fishy. This particular morning, Mom was in no mood for a braggart, especially one who had caught his fish sitting on our riverbank.

Tommy Lee held up his string of catfish and asked Mom, "Whatcha thank uf these beauts, Fairlean?"

"I thank yur'r next thang to a thief, Tommy Lee Spicer, fishin' from ar riverbank," Mom snapped.

"Whatta you care if'n I catch yur fish? Y'all don't fish none," Tommy Lee reasoned.

Mom barked, "If all the good-fer-nothing-scoundrels around this community would git thar lazy bones a job and do a real-ta-goodness honest day's work like my man, they wouldn't have time fer loafin' on the river bank." .

She continued to hit him square between the eyes, not with her fist, nor the churn-handle she was holding, but with words—adjectives, verbs, adverbs, and a few words that got me into trouble if I used them at the supper table. Boy, was she ever ticked! I was enjoying the dialog, for it was fun to see Mom riled up at someone other than myself!

Tommy Lee changed the subject quicker than a beagle-chased rabbit in a cabbage patch changes direction. "When's Delmar a'comin' home," he asked.

"What'cha wantin' ta know fer," Mom questioned. "You needin' yur beans hoed?"

"Nah. Just wonderin'," he said, as he hastened across our yard.

Mom momentarily stopped churning; her hand held a firm grip on the handle. I thought for a moment that she was going to go after him with the churn handle as her weapon. It seemed she acquired that trait from the Brewer side of the family: either quiet-natured or explosive, with nothing in between.

Tommy Lee mumbled something about his bad back and skedaddled down the road, purely defying the bad back he claimed. That seemed the wisest thing Tommy Lee could have done at the time—leaving instead of arguing with a riled-up woman with a churn handle in her grasp. Mom was a little touchy about any man in our community who didn't work but fished all night, slept all day, and drew his government check. I don't think she was jealous of the lifestyle, only that she felt he was on the lazy side. To her, fishing and welfare seemed hypothetically impossible, even hypocritical. "Work for welfare" seemed more compatible terms; she felt handouts bred laziness. She justified her sensitivity since Dad had to be away for days at a time working—she missed him immensely and admired him profoundly. And when Dad came home from work, he still had lots of work to do around the house. So, he seldom had time for fishing, even though the best fishing spot belonged to us.

To set the record straight, Mom did let me go fishing by myself—once! It was a hot, humid day in August and life was slow.

" Momma, kain't I go a'fishin' taday?" I asked.

"Too yung ta go fishin' by yurself, son."

"I'm almost six, Momma. Floyd Bowling is six and his momma lets him go fishin' alone."

"Floyd Bowling's momma kin do what she well pleases, but I ain't her and you ain't him."

"Shucks, Momma. I'm bored outta my tree."

"Told you not ta use that word, son. Too close ta cussin'."

"Sorry, Momma. But kain't I go just this once?"

"What'll I tell yur daddy if'n you drown?"

"Hain't gonna drown," I argued.

"I'd feel better if'n yur daddy wuz hur."

"You know Daddy don't never hav' time ta take me fishin'."

"Don't you talk mean 'bout yur daddy, specially whiles he's away working ta put clothes on yur back." She sure was protective of Dad.

"Hain't talkin' mean, just sayin' he hain't got time whenever he gits home. Too busy workin' the garden and fixin' stuff. Come on, Momma, please. I kain't stand another day not goin' fishin'."

After much wheedling away at her misgivings, she finally acquiesced. "Go ahead, but if'n you drown'd, it's my fault and I kain't never fergive ma'self fer it."

Elated, I sprinted to the shed and retrieved my pole—for she might change her mind if she suddenly recalled any child having ever drowned in the last fifty years. Once at the water's edge, I baited the hook with a worm I'd gotten from under a rock, and delightfully dangled it into the crystal-clear water, that is, in the six inches of shallow water a hundred yards upstream from the real fishing hole. For Mom's final stipulation demanded, "You kin go just this once, but stay away from the deep fishin' hole."

Though somewhat disappointed, I reasoned that fishing in shallow water was better than not fishing at all, and who knows, maybe there were mother fish who also instructed their children to stay in the shallow water away from the deep fishing hole, especially with Tommy Lee hanging out there.

It just didn't seem fair to me for neighbors to fish at our fishing hole when I couldn't. So, I dreamed about the right of passage, when I would be old enough to fish without permission, and I would fish from the bank of the deep water at our fishing hole.

I sulked about not getting to fish most of the summer. The falling of leaves signaled the startup of school: always after Labor Day. I was still five but chasing six come November, going into the first grade, and frightened. I was somewhat apprehensive about having Mr. Deaton as a teacher, and I wondered how he could teach me anything with all eight grades and forty students in a single classroom. But then again, Mom had him as a teacher, and she could read and write and do math. Still, tales by the returning students about the big hickory stick he kept over the doorway frightened me. So, I anticipated school like I did losing a baby tooth—the terror of pulling a tooth was balanced by the nickel I always found under my pillow the next morning.

Notebooks were scarce; we mostly used the chalkboard. Standing at the chalkboard, chalk in hand, and hand resting on the board like runners kneeling at the starting line, adrenalin-charged students waited for Mr. Deaton to call out the math problem or spelling word, and sometimes he asked for the capitol city of a certain state. Competition motivated: for a beginner it was exciting, but it was also terrifying. Repetition, whether doing or observing, sharpened. Perhaps this is what Mr. Deaton envisioned with his "abeunt studia in mores" philosophy—practices zealously pursued pass into habits. And Mr. Deaton assured us males that our continued practice of tardiness—a habit he attempted to break with his zealous use of a hickory stick—could become a lifetime of habits. I also learned that all competition wasn't necessarily good.

On one particular day while standing at the chalkboard, a paramount combination of fear, excitement, and neglect besieged me. Having drunk three, full dippers from the water bucket during recess, I failed to allow myself enough time from play to go to the outhouse. This, in conjunction with the anxiousness of the competition at the chalkboard, an emergency arose. The "urge to go" overwhelmed me as I stood there in front of the class trying to trace the sentences: See Spot go. Run, Spot, run. See Spot run. Maybe a subliminal message from the combination of words sent me over the edge and contributed to the most embarrassing event of my childhood. The enemy rushed in like a flood, the bladder surrendered, and water soaked all the way down my britches, forming a sizable puddle around my feet on the hardwood floor. I attempted to saunter nonchalantly back to my seat as if nothing was amiss, but the snickering made that impossible, and the tears trickling my cheeks was a dead giveaway. I bowed my head, humiliated and afraid. The snickers subsided as Mr. Deaton rose from his chair. I envisioned his reaching for his hickory stick, and fear griped my heart as I heard him walking toward me. Oh, how I hated school. I wished I could be like Tommy Lee and just fish my life away.

"Ya best go on home, Larry," Mr. Deaton said rather kindly. I reluctantly raised my head from the desktop and looked at him. "Just tell yur momma I thought it best ta send you home early," he said and walked back to his desk.

He didn't scold and humiliate. Perhaps this wasn't too bad after all. I gathered up my Roy Rogers lunch kit, with its ten-ounce thermos bottle and "Polly Red Top" stopper, and I headed home.

Surprisingly, I found the house empty. Where could Mom be? I wondered. Then I wandered out to the back yard, saw my fishing pole propped up against the smoke house, and got an idea. Why not go down to the fishing hole? After all, I'm old enough to be in school, and surely that makes me old enough to fish at the hole.

The worn and narrow path descending to the water's edge proved steep for a five-year-old. Slipping and sliding, I fought for footing to keep from plunging into the water. My fishing line became tangled, but there was no need to undo it, for Tommy Lee's poles were all there, neatly propped up over the water, and held in place by Y-shaped sticks that resembled oversized slingshots stuck into the ground. The lines dangled tantalizingly in the water, desperately needing someone to check on them. I fished for what seemed like hours but caught nothing. Sensing it wise to keep my clandestine operation a secret from Mom—and Tommy Lee—I sneaked back to the house and found her in the kitchen.

"Whatcha doin' home so early?" she asked.

"Mist'r Deaton sent me home cause I wet ma pants, Momma. Got scare't half ta death at the chalkboard tryin' ta trace some words."

"It's okay, honey. Most ever one does that thang at least once in a lifetime. Don't cha feel bad a'tall."

Mom gave me more affection that day than I generally received from her. Such sympathy rather surprised me. I wondered about her statement, "Most ever one does that thang at least once in a lifetime." I assumed the once in a lifetime excluded babies.

I hung around the kitchen and watched Mom cook supper, hoping for some more sympathy. None came, but she did comment in a sort of querying way, "You shor' do smell like fishin' worms."

"Wonder why fer?" I mumbled, as I sniffed my shirtsleeve.

After Mom's awful ruckus with Tommy Lee, and maybe him suspecting someone was checking his fishing lines, he moved his poles a few feet downriver and fished from the bank of our neighbors, Laney and Tari Peters. They weren't quite as sensitive as Mom. Still, Tommy Lee tossed his line upstream into our fishing hole. Fulltime fishermen may be borderline lazy but not necessarily crazy. They know where the good fishing is; furthermore, for fishermen, where there's a worm, there's a way. I continued to sneak and check Tommy Lee's lines and was beginning to view myself as a pretty-smart fisherman—and hooked. But then something happened that redirected my interest.

Chapter Eight

The Visitor

A young woman—attired in a light-blue suit, patent-leather shoes, and a matching tam—stepped off the morning passenger train. She shielded her eyes from the glare of the bright, June sun and searched the audience for a friendly face. All she saw was inquisitive stares. She struggled with her luggage, as the train, puffing tiredly, pulled away from the station. She gazed longingly after it until it became a distant sound. A couple of curious youngsters ventured slowly to where she stood. Her warm smile bade them welcome; they reflected the same.

"Needin' some hep ther' ma'am?" the older boy asked.

"Yes sir, Mr ...."

"Joshua Ray, ma'am. Friends call me Josh. This hur's ma brother, John Daniel. Goes by Dannie at home. Kin we hep ya some?"

"Yes, thank you," she said, glancing at her luggage. My name is Nancy York. I'm looking for a place to stay a few weeks. Is there a hotel or boarding house close by?"

"Ain't no sech place round hur a'tall, Miz York," Josh said.

"It's Nancy."

"Yes, ma'am, Miz Nancy."

John Daniel studied the conversation in silence.

"Who set ya a lookin' this way anyhows, ma'am?" Josh questioned as he arranged her luggage in an orderly fashion, with the larger ones on the bottom and the smaller ones on top. He studied the luggage with admiration, having never seen anything quite so fancy. "We ain't really got no place fur visitors 'cept family who comes sometimes. They just stay with rel'tives."

"You mean to tell me there is no place for a traveler to room or board?" she asked. Her pleasant smile dimmed.

"Got that right, Miz York, I mean, Nancy," Josh answered.

John Daniel stood half hidden behind his brother, with his hands stuffed into the pockets of his faded overalls. His burr haircut stood straight out from his head, like a frightened porcupine. His blue eyes captured the color of Nancy's blue suit. He instinctively scratched the calf of his lanky, left leg with the toes of his dirty, bare foot.

"You best talk ta Ida Mae Deaton. She's the woman in that store right over ther'. She kin pro'bly hep ya if'n anybody kin. Don't pay no mind ta the man on the porch. He's kinda touched." Josh nodded toward the store where a man sat on a wooden, pop crate drinking from a soda bottle.

Nancy walked briskly toward the store, glancing at the sign that indicated it doubled as the Copeland Post Office. On the front porch a napping dog opened his eyes, stood, moved a few feet, and laid down again, still in her path. The straggly dressed man leaned lazily against the wall and stole a glance at her but seemed to eye her with contempt as she stepped around the dog. She smiled at him as she pushed open the screen door and hesitated while her eyes adjusted to the dimly lit room. She instinctively pressed her hand to her nose. What a strange odor! She had never smelled anything quite like it.

The storekeeper stood behind the counter; her backside pressed against the shelves that lined the wall. She swayed from side to side against the shelves as if an attempt to scratch her back. She stopped abruptly as Nancy entered, her expression revealing a hint of embarrassment.

"Come right on in, young'n," she said. The passageway of about three feet between the counter and shelves barely gave room for her hefty physique. Goods lined the shelves behind her from floor to ceiling. She cleared her throat and smiled a welcome to the stranger. "Mornin', Miss. Ain't seen you 'round these parts afore. What kin I do fer you?"

"I assume you are Ida Mae," Nancy said.

"That'd be me alright. The boys told ya?"

"Yes, Josh directed me. I am needing a place to stay, but it seems I might have a bit of trouble finding it," she said, mustering a determined yet unconvincing demeanor.

"Don't worry yur purt, little head none, child. We'll find a place fer ya a'fore bedtime. Now, what did you say yur name wuz, Miss?"

"Nancy. Nancy York. I'm from Cincinnati."

"Cincinnati! I wuz in Cincinnati once with my husband. We went down ther' ta buy some hardware fer the store. What an awfully big place! What brings ya up ta our part of the country?"

"I beg your pardon, but Cincinnati is north of Copeland, so I traveled south to get here. Shouldn't here be considered down instead of up?" Nancy queried, but quickly wished she could retrieve her words. Exhaustion was taking its toll, she assumed, for she was on edge.

"We just always say down ta Cincinnati," Ida Mae answered.

Nancy had just received her first of many lessons to come from the hill folks. She failed to consider their concept of geography. Elevation, not direction, matters most. Everything is up if you are coming to the hill country; down if you are leaving. From up here you look down on the rest of the world around you. This was the Appalachians—the Cumberland Plateau. She was in the hill country, closer to the stars and the sky, where the air smells of lilac, daisies, and wood smoke. The land was still unpolluted by factory emissions and the sounds and fumes of automobiles, quite unlike her city home in the Ohio Valley.

Nancy had boarded the evening train at the Union Station in Cincinnati only yesterday. Her mother fought back tears as her dad rattled off last minute reminders. "You'll change trains in Lexington. Don't forget to pick up your luggage. Call us as soon as you arrive." Her dad was proud of her but naturally concerned. This assignment was far different than classroom lectures. "Probably necessary to fulfill college requirements," he had said as he conceded to the project.

"Do you have your tickets, dear?" her mother asked.

"Yes, Mother." Her tone somewhat scolded her mother's protective demeanor.

In retrospect, if her parents had known the circumstances—no room, no restaurant, and now she assumed no telephone—they would have objected more than they did. And at the moment, the yesterday adrenalin rush of her college project vanished rather quickly.

"What brings ya up hur, child?" Ida Mae asked.

Nancy faintly heard the question as she retreated from her thoughts. "I'm a college student. I'm doing a research paper on the poverty-stricken Appalachian people."

Ida Mae cleared her throat louder than necessary and fidgeted with an apron string, her disapproval minutely detectable on her face. The silence was obvious.

"I'm sorry. That was a poor choice of words," Nancy apologized as she stumbled for less offensive words. "Let me start over. I'm doing research on the culture of the Appalachian community. I'll be here most of the summer, and I desperately need to find a place to stay." Her exhaustion was clearly visible in her voice and on her face.

Ida Mae squeezed from behind the counter and waddled over to Nancy, who at five feet two inches and weighing in at one-hundred twenty pounds, looked rather petite beside Ida Mae, who placed a calloused hand gently on Nancy's shoulder.

"We'll find ya a place, Miss. Don't cha worry none." Ida paused, staring contemplatively at the ceiling, where a hundred flies stuck to a couple strings of fly-paper. She tapped her pursed lips and said, "Think I know just the place, if'n ya don't mind a little work. Fam'ly up the road could use a young gal like you ta help out a little with the child'ern. The daddy's away workin' alot. 'Bout half a mile up the tracks, first house on the right. Tell Fairlean, that's the lady uf the house, Ida Mae Deaton sent ya."

"How many children do they have, Mrs. Deaton?"

"Couple or so. You'll like'em."

"Thank you very, very much, Mrs. Deaton. You have been so kind and helpful."

"My pleasure, Miss Nancy. And you can call me Ida Mae, like everyone else does. Oh, and don't give no mind to Sidgel on the front porch. He's kinda diff'ernt, but he won't bother ya none."

When Nancy stepped outside the store, Sidgel tossed her another glance but pretended to be asleep. Joshua Ray and John Daniel stood waiting, already holding her luggage, looking pleased as punch with themselves for such thoughtfulness.

"Wher we a'goin'?" Josh asked.

"That way," she pointed. "First house on the right."

"That'l be the Ar'woods," Josh quipped.

"Oh, really?"

"I know all five uf their child'ern," Josh answered.

Nancy mumbled under her breath, "A couple or so?" She glanced over her shoulder to see Ida Mae standing on the porch, smiling and wiping her hands on an apron.

"What's that, Miz York?" Josh asked.

Nancy did not answer.

"That five don't include ther' mommy and daddy," Josh said. He added with pride, "The daddy, Delmar, he fought the Japs in the war. Brought home some medals fer his fightin'."

Josh rattled on, but Nancy was not listening. She spent the half-mile trip reflecting on her immediate situation. She had envisioned this assignment quite differently: a self-contained, private room with plenty of time to write and enjoy nature as she interviewed the hill people. Instead, she was on her way to live with a family of five children. Oh, well, she thought, maybe this will help my grade.

A mangy dog galloped to meet them. John Daniel knelt to greet the dog. "How ya doin', Jiggs?" he said, as he rubbed the dog's fur and picked at an over-ripe tick clinging to a floppy ear.

Four plump faces with inquiring blue eyes lined the front porch. A boy and a girl peeked through the banisters, while a tow-headed lad and a smiling lass looked over the rail. A gaunt mother, nearing thirty years of age, Nancy guessed, sat rocking a baby. She hesitantly stood as they approached.

"Howdy, Fairlean," Josh said.

"Howdy, Josh. Dannie. You boys doin' okay?" Her face remained stern.

"We're okay, but Ida Mae sent Miz Nancy hur," Josh nodded with his head toward Nancy, "to stay with y'all fer the summer."

At the mention of Ida Mae, Fairlean's drawn face softened. She fidgeted with a lock of her long, brown hair.

Nancy smiled and raised her hand to silence Josh so she could speak for herself. "Mrs. Ar'wood ..."

"Yes, Fairlean Ar'wood," the young mother responded. "This hur's all my yung'ns.

"Hello." Nancy acknowledged the children who stared intently but silently at her.

"Mrs. Deaton, Ida Mae, the lady at the store, sent me ...."

****

That's how I first met Nancy York. As I looked over the banister, she stood there before me, pretty as a charcoal-colored picture over the mantle and looking as innocent as a new-born lamb. I loved her at first sight and spent my days trying to figure out how the age difference could work out. Her project lasted all summer as she worked alongside us in the garden, washed dishes, diapered the baby, and sat with us in the evenings counting fireflies and talking about our lives. She inquired as to what it was like living in the mountains and shared what it was like living in the big city. At night she took out a pastel-colored notebook in which she wrote what I assumed were her thoughts about us and our conversations. She blended well into our family as she filled in hundreds of blank pages those summer evenings. She seemed such a perfect fit. I never considered her leaving; it seemed she would want to stay with us, forever.

Chapter Nine

The Rock

Sunbeams peeked between the sheer curtains and awakened me long before I wanted to get up. I lingered in bed, for it seemed I should remember something but could not. The distant whistle of an approaching train motivated me to get dressed. I yanked on my jeans, rolled up the pant legs, and grabbed a t-shirt as I rushed to the front porch to wave at the engineer and conductor.

Morning dew sparkled like diamonds scattered across the countryside. A fog blanketed the North Fork, like the grogginess that dulled my brain, so I determined I'd better plan something exciting for the day. I decided that after breakfast I would climb to the top of the hill and visit coffin rock. It was at that moment that I saw her, and my foggy brain cleared in a heartbeat. She sat perfectly straight in the front-porch rocking chair, her dark hair pulled back off her forehead and flowing across her shoulders and down her back. Looking out across the distance, she seemed not to notice my lingering stare, and even if she had, I couldn't think of anything to say.

"Good morning, Larry Monroe." The words flowed from her lips like the calm and refreshing waters of a spring: unlike Mr. Deaton's gruff voice which seemed murky and choppy like the raging waters of the North Fork during flood time.

"Mornin', Miz York," I squeaked out the words.

"I wish you'd call me Nancy."

"Mornin', Nancy." I tried to think of something impressive to say but couldn't. "How'd you know ma full name?" I blurted out.

"Your mother ...."

The noise of the passenger train drowned out Nancy's last line.

"What'd you say?" I yelled.

"Your mother told me last evening, after you had gone to bed," she repeated the sentence loud enough to be heard above the noisy clanking of the train. "She also told me you were six years old, finished the first grade the youngest in your class, and made right good grades. Good marks," she corrected herself with a smile.

Nancy sure could make you feel good about yourself, I thought. "See ya later," I said as I leaped two steps at a time and ran to the tracks to watch the train as it rumbled toward the station.

The train couplings clanged together as the engineer decelerated for the Copeland stop. The brakes screeched a long, shrill sound; metal moaned, and air-hoses hissed. The locomotive lunged, then braked again, and eventually the hunk of steel stopped. A stream of smoke and steam surrounded the engine, giving an illusion the train was on fire. The train had no sooner come to a stop than it gave its hurry-up warning, a loud blast from the air-horn, a notification to any potential passengers. I knew the routine by heart and could repeat verbatim the commands of the conductor as he hastened the passengers aboard. The engineer released the brakes and the train jerked forward, slowly gathering speed.

When I returned to the front porch, Nancy asked, "I was wondering if you and Joyce would accompany me today as I get acquainted with your community? I asked your mother for permission, and she consented."

I already had plans for the day. I wanted to view coffin rock with my own eyes. The community folklore abounded with tales about the rock, and I couldn't get them out of my mind. I had planned the entire school year for this summer to be my inaugural visit. I wanted to see it, to trace the outline formed by the bloodstains, and view the Indian head carved in the stone. Then again, I could visit the rock tomorrow, I thought, since Nancy needs my help today to introduce her to our neighbors.

"Reckon I'd like ta go with ya, Nancy," I said, rubbing my nose profusely with the back of my hand. My nose seemed to always itch when I talked to adults, especially strangers.

"Good!" She smiled. "We'll get started after breakfast. I'd like to help your mother do the cooking. On second thought, maybe I can learn from your mother how to cook." She laughed at herself.

"You'll be needin' some firewood," I said. "I'll fetch some."

"That is very thoughtful," she said.

I glanced momentarily at her, stared instinctively up the hillside toward Coffin Rock, then clambered down the steps and hurried to the woodpile.

Chapter Ten

They Came

I wasn't sure how Nancy heard about us. It puzzled me that she chose to come to our community; still, it thrilled me. Mostly only kinfolks came from far away to visit with us, like our cousins, the Copes, from over Booneville way. Yet, there she was, a total stranger a few days prior, now like family, eating every meal with us and sleeping in my sisters' room with them. She had her place at the table opposite Mom, and we kids vied to sit next to her. She expanded our world daily and encouraged us to open our world to the outside. But she sure used some highfalutin words. During supper one evening she commented, "How ironic that your county, Breathitt County, though isolated from the world, has made it into such national newspapers as The Chicago Tribune, The Washington Post, and The New York Times."

"What duz ironic mean?" I queried.

"Sort of like the two don't go together," Nancy explained. "Like poison ivy growing in a flower garden. It's out of place. Would you like to see some of the articles?"

We gathered around her as she pulled newspaper clippings from a folder and read aloud. The writers of the articles talked about our "over-zealous taste for revenge" and "underprivileged state of poverty"—which we interpreted as too much feuding and too little food. The writers used adjectives we weren't accustomed to: unreclaimed savages, affrays, barbarism, consanguineous marriages, anarchy, and mobocracy. Nancy explained to us the meanings of the words. I wondered if she believed what the articles said about us.

"Surprisingly, in national papers, you are written about as much as cities like Lexington, Louisville, or Kentucky's

Little Chicago—Newport," she added.

Wher's Newport?" I asked.

"It's a rowdy river town opposite Cincinnati, where the Licking River flows into the Ohio. Got itself an infamous reputation. I've been there," she exclaimed. "It is a rowdy place indeed."

With all the bad things strangers wrote about us, it's a wonder anyone outside our own ventured into our highlands, especially young Nancy York. The articles portrayed us as ruffians, and here was Nancy, living among us and writing about us. Perhaps she would set the records straight. We were none of those things they had written, though perhaps we were in days gone by, but things had changed.

Breathitt was our county. That's mostly how we identified where we lived: by the county more so than the town. Our county was named after a Kentucky governor that nobody around seemed to remember. I had never been outside our county, except the time we visited our cousins in Boonville, over on the South Fork in Owsley County.

Throughout the summer weeks, Nancy engaged Mom into conversation more than anyone else I knew. Mom, who generally was mum with strangers, and didn't have much to say to friends, except when she got upset, told Nancy lots of stories about our community—stories we had never heard before.

"We call our county Bloody Breathitt," Mom said, "cause men prefer guns from a distance over talkin' out ther' problems face ta face. Many a man has been ambushed from a distance, like my rel'tive, Captain Bill Strong."

I'd never heard that story before, but Mom was right about shootings. I remember Jeff Spicer and Edgar Spurlock meeting on the Haddix Bridge. Each fired at the other and both took bullets; neither survived. I stood on that very bridge once, visiting relatives, trying to imagine the shootout, and wondering why they shot each other. It was a "savage concept of honor" we were accused of, and to some degree, maybe they were right.

Mom continued, "In a two-year period some yurs before I wuz born, 'bout twenty-seven men died as vengeance tore apart what wuz generally a calm land. The days leading up ta 'lection day have a way of revealing the worst of demons in a man, as if politicians are the lords of the universe. Lections and booze are bad bedfellows." Mom talked incessantly while Nancy scribbled in her notebook. I'd never heard Mom talk so much in all my life, except maybe when she was condemning the gossips at the church we attended or fussing over Tommy Lee Spicer fishing from our hole.

"One uf ar' rel'tives, wuz shot and kil't on lection day," Mom commented sadly, staring regretfully at the hillside. "It wuz a senseless thang. Left a fam'ly fer his wife ta raise alone. Seems like lection day don't do us no good a'tall, no matter who gets 'lected."

Nancy was one of the few people to come with our genuine interest in mind—or at least it seemed so. Others had come and gone for decades, but their own interest seemed to be the main motivation. Nancy became one of us, going to church on Sundays, playing games in the evenings, and catching fireflies at night. We viewed her differently than the others.

Others came as strangers and left the same. They came first for the virgin timber—tall, mature, and plenteous—which they stripped, leaving the hills barren and exposed to the elements. Afterwards, King Coal and his court reigned, striping the native highlands of her dignity and leaving soil on her hillsides bare to the elements. The former misty-morning mountaintops, majestically crowned with jewels of dew, with valleys clothed in downy fog, and rolling meadows bedecked with flowering lei, succumbed to saws and axes, and the erosive means of logging and mining—with personal scorn for the land. Such disregard for nature left men with a residue of blackness that stained the soul with despair, but worse, it coated their lungs and shortened their life.

The clever companies bought mineral rights from generational landowners who couldn't read or write or understand anyone owning the land except God—but the promise of enough money to pay the spring taxes on the land tempted too many into placing their "X" on a page filled with confusing terms, which suave lawyers explained with promises of fortune. The conglomerates gave little but took much—then left. The sun that once shined bright with promise on our "ole Kentucky homes" dimmed with the prosperity of foreigners who did not even care to own a home in our beloved highlands.

Though Nancy generally asked the questions, one day Mom asked Nancy, "Did you git gover'ment help fer yur schooling, Nancy?"

"No, not from the government, but I did receive a scholarship from the school. That helped a lot," she said.

Mom looked beyond Nancy towards us when she asked that question. Perhaps she had us in mind with that query, but then she continued, "Maybe some folks look ta the government fer more than they should. Still, no matter how much schoolin' you git, there's only so much demand fer specialized people in ar' community. We already have two doctors in Jackson, and we have ar' local schoolteacher and a barber. And the cost fer so much schoolin' raises the amount uf money we ar' willin' ta pay fer services—or kin afford ta pay. Why pay the educated barber a dollar fer a haircut when my Delmar'll cut yur hair fer twenty-five cents ev'ry Saturday morning? And he does it on credit if'n yur're broke, and fer free if'n yur're down on yur luck. Better still, you kin do some horse tradin' with him most any day."

Nancy listened contemplatively. We were glad to hear Mom talking so much for a change. Nancy brought a spark to the mundane of summer evenings, especially when the mosquitos were too hungry for us to venture outside.

Mom continued, "Take fer example ar' neighbor, who happens ta hav' a license ta barber 'cause he went ta Frankfort and got some schoolin'. He threatened ta report my husband fer barberin', but the folks round hur like the way my Delmar barbers, and he's cheap. Which'un do ya thank the people ar' gonna come to? The educated barber, or my Delmar?" Mom asked.

"Your Delmar," Nancy answered as she broke out in a smile.

"Right. And so, the fellars said to ar' local barber, 'Delmar don't charge fer his haircuts. We just tip'm a bit fer his trouble.'

Nancy's notebook filled up rather quickly, but we couldn't comprehend ourselves being that interesting. She wrote nightly and seemed to not care that we noticed, and we trusted her with our thoughts and feelings.

We expected Dad any day. We wanted him to meet our new friend. He generally came home at least every other weekend. Though inconvenient, most of our men worked away but drove long distances to get back home, for roots grow deep in Appalachian soil. The soil, though full of toil, gave us life. We were poor, but we had food so long as the crops didn't fail. We felt blessed; ours was a bumper crop most every year. In fact, in all my years, I never heard of any person in our community dying from starvation, like they do in the big cities, especially with all the Mason and Ball jars of canned fruits and vegetables everybody kept stored under their stilted houses and the Irish potatoes kept all winter in the root cellars. We could have fed another community about the size of ours from the canned goods we threw away every summer—leftovers from the previous canning season—as we needed the jars for the current harvest. Still, charity and pride often conflicted in the plateau.

"Are you voting this year, Fairlean?" Nancy asked.

"No, prob'ly not. Too much bother going ta the polls and all with the child'ern," Mom answered.

"What do you think of the politicians on the ballot this year?" Nancy asked.

Mom responded, "Don't know most uf'm. Know a few locals. Probably General Eisenhower will become president, 'specially since he won the war and all. We ain't 'ginst Washington politicians; it's just that we already have enough uf ar' own right hur' at home ta deal with."

"Like whom?" Nancy asked.

"Well, there's the local commissioner always willin' to assist the needy with commodities like cheese, canned meat, and powdered milk. He don't mess with no red tape and such. Those that need help ask and generally receive, kind of like Jesus said in the Bible. Our family receives some help during hard times. My Delmar sometimes has a week or two of downtime when a coalmine closes, or a construction project finishes. Ther' ain't no lazy bone in his body, so he always finds another job, but he ain't the least bit too proud ta bring home a box of government commodities if'n the cupboard is a bit bare—or a neighbor is in need."

I enjoyed evenings sitting on the front porch, swatting mosquitoes, and listing to Mom and Nancy talk. During those summer months with Nancy as our boarding guest, I gave no thought to her leaving. No one in our family had ever left before, except Dad, but it was short term and he always returned. Life had not yet prepared us for departures, except for serving our country in the military and some that went on to heaven; rather, our experience revolved around arrivals. Mom was expecting, again, number six.

That summer the county commissioner found funding for the materials to build us a swinging bridge to stretch across the North Fork to the recently built road, but only if we furnished the labor—for free, of course. Dad joined in to help. It was dangerous work, spanning two heavy-duty cables across the river and assembling the floor, section at a time, working their way across, suspended fifty feet in the air. We all gathered to watch the progress, eager about our first bridge.

Our welfare program consisted of an opportunity to work. It seemed like a good deal, neighbors working together for a common cause and each needing the other for survival. And when you were really in trouble, say like a speeding ticket to one of the few who own a car, my Uncle Verdie swears the Justice of the Peace, whom I'll not name, would fix the ticket for two bucks and half a pint of whiskey—the two bucks were for court costs; we assumed he drank the whiskey. But I should caution you that Uncle Verdie swore about a lot of things before he got religion. Mr. Deaton said the reason Verdie was so windy was because he was born in the month of March. Now I didn't quite know what that meant, but I have had a kite or two completely blown away by March winds, so I figured Mr. Deaton meant Uncle Verdie was endowed with a high degree of imagination.

We walked with Nancy daily to the post office. She always looked forward to letters from home, so much so that I sensed a tinge of jealousy in myself. After one such letter she announced, "I'll be leaving in a few days."

"So soon, child?" Mom responded.

"It has been a wonderful summer for me. I will never forget my experiences here, living with your family and in your community. I'll always hold you dear in my heart. But I need to return home and prepare for my fall, college semester."

Her abrupt announcement stung me worse than a bumblebee. I ran from the room to my hideout underneath the house. I could hear them talking above me, but they could not see me. Our house sat on stilts, creating a storage space underneath the house. It was little more than a crawl space for adults, but I could stand upright. Rough sawn lumber placed vertically surrounded the entire house, which offered me privacy, but I could peek through the cracks. This was my fort, my castle, and my seclusion. The spider webs kept girls from venturing in, but they sometimes caught me in their fearful grip. Peeking through the cracks, I could see what was happening in the small world around me, but the world could not bother me here. I pondered the downside of having guests, and how if you never had a visitor you wouldn't have to say goodbye. All in all, the good times of having company outweighed the sad times of departure.

Nancy York was not the first to come and go, but she had seemed different. Others had come, always wanting to be our neighbors from a distance. But we had long ago developed neighbors that were always in hollering distance and always ready to lend a hand. Even if we were not on good speaking terms, a neighbor in need stirred the slumbering soul and awakened compassion. It brought our Christian charity, like cream, to the surface.

Others came to save us, but their salvation seemed conditional. They never really liked us for what we were but for what they could make us. We were merely projects. Their salvation demanded change; a change we were reluctant to accept. It was a price too high even for the highlanders of eastern Kentucky. We were true Americans: white Anglo-Saxon Protestants—not necessarily able to put it into those words. We called ourselves Kentuckians, with a flavor of our own traditions, mixed with some carryover from Scotts, English, and French ancestry. Aide-toi, le ciel t'aidera—translated: help yourself and heaven will help you. And we added a line: don't depend too much on outsiders. We couldn't say any of those French words back then, but we lived by that philosophy.

Time and distance isolated us from the many new and varied ideas flourishing in the rest of the world. With generations of learning in the art of self-sufficiency (bordering on pride and superstition), we were mostly unaffected by the civil rights controversy brewing in other parts of the country. No black folks lived in our community, so mostly the accusations of discrimination didn't affect us one way or the other.

I was surprised when I heard that my relatives—the Strong's, on Mom's side of the family—had slaves in the years long past. This family secret remained a closet skeleton for years. William Strong had brought them from Virginia in 1801 and settled on the North Fork in Perry County. Actually, our Kentucky homeland used to be called Kentucky County, Virginia. One of his slaves was down by the river washing clothes on a scrub board when news arrived that a boy from Kaintuck had made it to the White House and had freed all the slaves. She threw up her arms, lifted her face to Almighty God, and exclaimed, "Thank ye God, we's free at last." At least that's how it was told me. And I'm told my relative, William Strong, freed his slaves and joined the Union forces where he became known as Captain Bill Strong. He was heavily involved in the "Red Strings" during and after the Civil War. The "Red Strings" were the opposing forces against the Ku Klux Klan. But it seems Captain Bill also used his position to murder Confederate sympathizers in our county. The jury's still out in my family regarding Uncle Bill. We're beginning to lean toward him being a rabblerouser more than a patriot.

How ironic that the government was still trying to save us, the poor folks whom prosperity passed and poverty formed a palisade too formidable for us to transcend. Evidently, we viewed our life and our land differently than the government regarded us. We called it Canaan Land; still, our Canaan had its giants to conquer. We were working on them, perhaps too slowly for outsiders, so, they came to hasten the cause. But we were unconvinced they had the right answers. Could they improve upon, or even match, what we counted as the blessings of the Lord: a roof over our heads, food on our tables, and clothes on our backs? And the good Lord was generations and a host of annual revivals ahead of them, though some revivals were questionable, as you will later discover in this book.

I don't mean to imply that all who came were bad and selfish. Dedicated missionaries found our community decades earlier, and they were the kindest people to ever visit. They brought in barrels of used clothing, taught the children to read and write, but they also taught us what was right and wrong.

Mrs. Myrtle Kessinger and Miss Carrie Stoffer worked as missionaries at Haddix. They did all kinds of unselfish acts to lessen the pain but also to liven the mundane. Take for example the Christmas play they planned. They worked on this project for weeks. It was the talk of the community. But too many things are beyond our control—call it fate or whatever. After the final practice, as kids were exiting the building, all excited about the upcoming performance, Miss Stoffer fell off the front porch where banisters were being repaired. Some grownups carried her to her home and laid her on the couch. Mrs. Kessinger knelt beside her. The children gathered around weeping. Miss Stoffer lay there smiling, her work done, those caring little faces her reward. She lovingly looked at them and spoke ever so softly, "See you in heaven," then she died. Folks said it was a broken neck. Both her life and her death exemplified her faith. She didn't just talk about a resurrected Christ whom we had to see through the eyes of faith; she lived and died revealing attributes of the Christ of her faith.

Some itinerant missionaries visited our school about once a month. They gave us tiny New Testaments with a page on which to write our names, and they encouraged us to memorize Scriptures. Even the most uninterested among us learned to quote John 11:35, "Jesus wept." And they taught us the meaning of the Scriptures by the lives they lived. They gave much but expected little in return; they came with little but left our coffers fuller than before.

What the missionaries taught us about Jesus remained long after they were gone. Their teaching gave us a unique perspective to life. Take for example, the basics of life: food and water. They cared about nutrition and safe drinking water, but they also taught us that in the worst of conditions we could eat from the everlasting bread of life and drink from the fountain that never runs dry. Clothes? They shipped in donated clothes by the boxes, but they also shared that Jesus covered us with His robes of righteousness. Their lessons lingered: "...love your neighbor as yourself...love your enemy...lend to those in need...." And we were better because of them. So, we hesitated in getting too excited about promises of a better life made possible by politicians. When you'd already been "a tast'n Christ's heavenly manna," pity and promises from political strangers paled in the abundance of inward peace you already knew. And since some were fudging on whether or not our heroes of the past were even Christian, suggesting George Washington never really prayed at Valley Forge, and Abraham Lincoln's prayers were a political ruse, and stuff like that, their offer of a secular salvation seemed rather insignificant. It was like offering us a lunch box in which to carry our peanut butter and jelly sandwiches, instead of our usual brown, paper poke, as if the taste was in the container. Our paper pokes seemed just fine. So, needless to say, we were suspicious. They came anyway.

Chapter Eleven

The Secret Meeting

The climb proved exhausting but the view worth the effort: breathtaking. For the first time I saw my community from a bird's eye perspective. The houses looked like miniature monopoly pieces, and my neighbors resembled ants scurrying about. The North Fork, though obviously there, was obscured by summer foliage. My destination, Coffin Rock, lay just ahead.

I was still angry at Nancy York because she was abandoning us. But it would probably be good to be shed of her, to be on my own again, to do boy things for a change, rather than tagging along after a nosey woman snooping around in other people's business. Exploring the rock would be a welcome reprieve.

Years of folklore of Indian legends surrounding the rock made me curious, yet cautious. Some said it was a place where the Cherokees made human sacrifices and that the blood of victims left a strange stain upon the rock. I had doubts, for they also said I came from one of the rabbits hopping around on the hillside overlooking our house. I knew better about the tales of where I came from, because Mom and Dad always went to Doctor Lewis' office in Jackson for a new child. And I doubt they had rabbit cages in his office; rather, I suspected they had baby beds.

I turned left off the worn trail, cautiously approaching the rock, for who knew for sure that no Indians remained hiding out somewhere, awaiting another Tecumseh uprising. If the white man could hide his moonshine still for years on end, why couldn't an Indian hide his teepee? Still, no full-fledged Cherokee had been seen in these parts for over a hundred years—ever since President Andrew Jackson's Trail of Tears scooped them up like a rogue does a neighbor's bee-colony, and armed guards hauled them off to no man's land. And it seems our government didn't care if thousands died along the way so long as the survivors could serve our whims. But that was way back in the early to mid 1800s; though I heard some remain in North Carolina, for a relative had visited Cherokee, North Carolina, and said they talked to some real Indians with feathered hats and all.

Mr. Deaton had told us about the Indians and the Trail of Tears. Some in the class thought it was just fine what the president had done. I had mixed feelings about it, for some said we had Cherokee blood on both sides of the family. No one had solid proof, just word of mouth. But even if I wasn't Cherokee, something seemed mighty wrong with how we did things to them.

I slowed my pace. Just ahead the rock loomed formidable, standing sentinel over the valley these many years, though I had never seen it. And now, surprisingly, it wasn't nearly as big as the yarns told me, but true to the rumors, it did resemble a coffin. One corner looked like a head, surely an Indian head, for we would have known if one of our own had carved it. The chin pointed in the direction of the North Fork. Maybe that was proof it was used by Indians, for they could have paddled their canoes along the North Fork and gone all the way down to Tennessee or over to Chillicothe, Ohio, by way of the Scioto River.

I climbed onto the rock but froze in my tracks. In the center of the rock was the blood, just like the rumors, but it was not an old bloodstain; rather, it was fresh and real. Red and thick! Blowflies swarmed it. I immediately felt sick at my stomach.

Something terrible has happened here, I thought. Perhaps a crime has been committed. Somewhere nearby there might be a body. Or maybe the person was wounded and had crawled off to hide in the bushes, perhaps needing help. Or the murderers may have hidden the body. I wondered what should I do.

I don't know how long I stood there staring at the blood, before a noise startled me back to reality. The sounds of the forest are many, but each has its place. An out-of-place sound in the forest is like a sinner sitting on the front pew in church. Sinners sit on the back row, not on the front. A sinner on the front row spells trouble; he either wants a handout or else he's drunk.

My senses piqued from a sound carried upon the breeze. Was it a deer stepping gingerly? A squirrel scurrying through the leaves? A wolf stalking its prey? No! The sounds I heard were out of place. I slipped from the rock, slid into some underbrush, and waited. That's when I realized my hands and knees and head and most every part of my body was shaking uncontrollably.

Time passed slowly, like the melting icicles dangling from the cliffs by the Strong's place, just beyond our house, hidden from the spring sun for a month or so. I wasn't sure if my shaking body was the result of the blood on the rock or the unknown sounds growing closer and louder. They came quickly, like they knew I was there, and they needed to prevent me from seeing the blood, but they were too late, for extra saliva—that comes just before you throw up—was filling my mouth. I had already seen the blood. I wanted to run, but it was too late. I was trapped.

I heard the crunching of leaves, the snapping of fallen limbs, and the scraping against the briary thickets that snagged their pantlegs. Crouching lower in my hideout, I pulled my shirt higher around my face, which was already buried in the leaves. I could hear their heavy breathing caused by the climb, and I strained to see their faces as they ascended the rock and sat down in a circle, cross-legged, Indian style. That seemed weird. Masks hid their faces, but I could tell they were not Indians, for they wore baseball hats, though one hat did identify as an Indian tribe.

One of them finally spoke. "If'n anyone tells, they're gonna pay. Understand?" Evidently, he was their leader.

"We're all in this thang t'gather," he warned. "Kain't nobody back out now."

The speaker sat with his back towards me. I listened intently but could not make out all his words. The others hardly spoke, and when they did, it was mostly in agreement with the leader.

Sweat trickled down my forehead, and the saltiness stung my eyes. A bee buzzed around my head, while a mosquito buried its sucker deep into a vein in my right arm. I smacked it into a bloody mess, and the scene of the blood on the rock flashed before me again. I felt queasy, and more saliva formed in my mouth. My nose itched.

A sudden commotion caused the leader to stop in mid-sentence. All stood and waited in silence—obviously anxious. Another masked person crashed through the brush towards them, waving frantically; evidently, it was their lookout.

"Som'ons a comin' up the hill right over thar," he yelled, pointing in the direction of the same trail I had taken.

"Foller me," the leader commanded.

They scrambled through the brambles in the opposite direction of the approaching intruder, faster than a rabbit chased by a hound dog. I could hear them yelping a good hundred yards off as briars slashed their arms and pierced through their pant legs. I waited in the underbrush, anxious, yet curious.

A bedraggled Sidgel Diddle meandered up the path. He carried a brown, paper sack in one hand and a walking stick in the other. He stopped at the rock, laid the sack atop it, propped the stick against the side of the coffin, took out a pouch of tobacco, and rolled a smoke. Obviously exhausted by the climb, he clambered onto the rock and inhaled deep and long on his cigarette. Smoke rings drifted upward as he allowed puffs to escape his lips, like a catfish blowing bubbles.

I couldn't hold out much longer in my cramped and motionless position. I wondered how long he would stay. Had he seen the blood? Perhaps I should come out of hiding and pretend that nothing was amiss. Or I could tell him that I had nothing to do with the blood, that a bunch of hooded fellows did it. My head spun. This all was too much for a six-year-old brain, so I just stayed in my cramped position trying not to cry.

After a while, Sidgel gathered his belongings, inhaled one last, long drag from the cigarette, and flipped the butt onto the ground. He left without a second glance. A minute or so passed when a stream of smoke drifted upward, and a fire quickly spread in the dry leaves. I waited until he was a good way off before springing from my hiding place to stomp out the flames. I needed to put out the fire, but I wanted to get out of this place before the masked fellows returned.

Branches slashed at my face as I dashed through the brush toward home. Mom stepped out the front door just as I rushed into the yard. "Supper's ready. Find yur sisters and brothers fer me and wash up," she commanded.

"I'll do just that, Momma." I was out of breath. She noticed and seemed to toss me a curious glance but said nothing.

The table was spread with steaming hot roasting ears, sliced tomatoes, half-runners floating in grease, fried potatoes, and creamy cold slaw—all gathered from our garden. Someone handed me the bowl of tomatoes. Somehow, they seemed redder than usual and much juicier. Joyce picked up a container and squeezed catsup all over her fried potatoes. My eyes blurred, for all I could see was the blood covering Coffin Rock. My stomach convulsed.

"Are you okay, Larry," Nancy asked.

I didn't answer; instead, I leaped to my feet and ran from the table.

As I sat on the front steps holding my stomach, chatter continued in the kitchen. It eased the pain somewhat to know that Nancy York cared about me, or else she wouldn't have asked how I felt. Then I heard Momma say, "I declare, he's whiter'n a ghost. Must'uf caught something. Joyce, go fetch me the castor oil."

Just the thought of another spoonful of castor oil and I felt better immediately. Like some were saying, it truly was a miracle cure.

Chapter Twelve
The Community

I brooded over the thought of Nancy York leaving us, but my anger had subsided, and I eagerly accepted her invitation to go with her to visit more neighbors. By now I was more sad than mad about the abrupt announcement of her departure, for I reckoned she didn't realize how attached we had gotten to her.

Nancy worked feverishly talking with our neighbors, wanting to learn all she could, both about our past, and our present. She was curious about why we used a lot of fictitious names instead of their real names.

"Cause ever'body knows ever'body by ther' nicknames" I explained. "Shoog, Buggins, Tallies, Fidder, Foggie, Bannie, Corn, Bug." I rattled off a list like Mr. Deaton doing rollcall every school morning, except he used our real names.

"But why do you use nicknames instead of their real ones," Nancy questioned.

"Don't ever'body have a nickname?" I asked.

"Not everyone." Nancy said with a smile.

We mostly did. Mine was corn, given to me by my uncles because I could eat my weight in corn-on-the-cob. We had nicknames for reasons even we sometimes forgot. And they were sometimes generational. Take for example the Tallies. We called them that because their grandpa was Italian. The nickname happened years ago because the local's found it easier to call them Tallies—short for Italian—instead of stumbling over DePasquale, or whatever their name was when they first arrived off the boat. And so, three generations later the name still stuck. But then again, who knows why we called anyone Shoog? But we did. A nickname was not being disrespectful, so long as the person didn't mind. We were in the same boat in some way or another regarding nicknames: we all had them.

We felt tolerable to one another but being tolerant didn't mean we were without an opinion. And owning an opinion is not criminal so long as you don't bring emotional or physical harm or pain to those who beg to differ. But a character flaw needed challenged like a flogging rooster needed de-spurred.

We knew a lot about each other because we walked by each others' homes often, not because we were exercising for health reasons or planning for a mini-marathon; rather, walking was our primary form of transportation. Part of the journey was the anticipation of chatting with a neighbor. Dad and Mom celebrated their eighth wedding anniversary before they owned a car. In fact, just like others counted time by anno mundi and anno urbis conditae, we, too, dated events by A.D. and B.C. But our initials stood for "after dinner" and "before cars."

Our community, though without a road, was fortunate to serve as a depot for the L&N Railroad. We rode the passenger train to Jackson to do major shopping and eat at a restaurant. In '53, while the rest of the world sat glued to their television sets, watching the flickering black and white images of Britain's new monarch, Queen Elizabeth II, we sat on dynamited bolders eagerly watching construction crews build our first road.

Unfortunately for our community, the authorities decided to build the road on the opposite side of the North Fork and our houses. This immediately changed the social status within our community. Before the road came through, others were low on the totem pole because they lived opposite the river from our community, which boasted the train depot; conversely, after the road came through, we were less significant living on our side of the river, especially after the depot shut down. Langley and Julie Davison became overnight socialites, though I doubt they realized it—they just happened to live on the wrong side of the river until the new road changed their property to the right side of the river. After school-consolidation happened, the location of the new road forced us to trek the railroad track to the swinging bridge at Copeland and wait for the school bus: quite inconvenient in the frigid February weather. Conversely, the Davison family waited in their living room until they heard the bus whining and groaning as it followed the bend along the North Fork. While we bemoaned our frozen toes, at the sound of screeching brakes, they came running with coats still in hand.

Our community hardly noticed a recession; not that we had an abundance. We were already accustomed to doing without most conveniences. Folks continued to rotate the same few dollars that had been around since ... well, since B.C. (before cars). I suspect every dollar bill in our community had most everyone's fingerprints on it. And I doubt that any of it ever got sent back to Washington to be replaced; we Scotch taped it instead.

The natural lights of creation and the surrounding sounds of nature determined wakeup and bedtime more so than a clock. The rooster awakened us, and the hoot owl reminded us it was bedtime. A.D.—after dinner—we sat for hours on the front porch, counting lightning bugs and talking about whatever. When someone appeared in the distance traversing the railroad tracks or the cinder path, they were the conversation piece for the evening. As they came into view, the game of "who wants to be a millionaire" began.

"I bet'cha a million bucks you kain't guess who that is," someone challenged. And the game continued until the neighbor was within speaking distance, when it then turned into the game of "Q and A."

"Howdy," someone would say. There was no particular order as to who spoke first, and howdy wasn't a question. Though an abridgement of "how are you doing," for us it was simply the equivalent of hello: to which you responded, "Howdy."

Our "howdies" were followed by a question: "How y'all doing?" Of course, this was a question which needed an answer, and the answer also solicited a question. It makes for a longer conversation to ask an open-ended question. I much later learned this in a college counseling class. We were actually doing college-level communication without a college education.

And so came the answer to our open-ended question: "Purdy good, and how y'all doing?"

"Same," the other person said.

"That's good," came the reply.

From there the conversation branched off into subjects such as the weather, the possibility of a flood, or whatever the year's almanac predicted. We were using the FORD-method (family, occupation, recreation, dreams) long before some ingenious communicator formulated the acronym. The dialog ended with something like, "We'll be a seein' ya." Some of the more religious folks added "if'n the good Lord be willin'."

After our neighbor passed hearing distance, we were left with enough fodder to feed our curiosity and to spend the evening speculating.

"Wonder wher' they been?"

"Reckon wher' they're a goin'?"

"Kain't 'magine this time uf day."

"You wonderin' why they're alone?"

"Yes, I wuz. You, too?"

"Yep."

I'd like to think we were the good-Samaritan-type neighbors. We knew if their children were sick with the croup or needed clothes. We cared if they went to church or not. We attended each other's going-away parties when someone moved to the city or one of our boys went off to serve his country, which was more often than not for our eighteen-year-olds. We gathered daily at the only store, which also served as the post office. We eagerly awaited as Ida Mae sorted the mail and handed it out, one letter at a time, calling every name aloud. We stood around the potbelly stove in the winter or sat on the front porch during the summer, reading the mail and sharing the news—the good and the bad.

Each morning we waved to Greenberry Turner as he rode horseback to the distant hollows to deliver the mail. My Dad, at 17 years of age, substituted for Greenberry as a United States mail carrier, perhaps one of the youngest mail carriers ever, with a Colt .45 strapped to his hip, astride what he boasted was the fastest horse in the community: a gray mare named Molly. I doubt the US Government ever knew about this arrangement, but it didn't seem to matter to anyone in our community as long as the mail got delivered. Mail was never returned due to an insufficient address, for Greenberry knew where everyone lived. If the mail made it to Copeland, he delivered it to the right home.

Laney and Tari Peters were our closest neighbors to the left. Mom really loved them: they were more like parents to her then neighbors. For years Tari served as a horseback librarian—delivering and picking up books in the outlying hollows. Being a reader, she was real smart. We visited with them often during the warm months. While the adults talked on the front porch, I once removed a rusty horseshoe from an aged bush in their front yard. Eager to share my discovery, I carried it to the porch to show off my treasure.

"Wher'd you git that horseshoe, son?" Mom asked.

"Stuck in that bush over ther'."

"Lord'y hav' mercy child, you've done gone and moved it fer the first time sense it got put ther'," Tari lamented.

"Put it back this minute afore I whup you fer it," Mom demanded.

I never was sure why the ruckus over a horseshoe,

perhaps something to do with it being placed there by a relative just before they went to be with the Lord: perhaps a departure sign, for we were into signs. If a bird tried to fly into your window, or you dreamed of muddy water, or your right hand was itching, it was all a sign: death, company, or good fortune. Maybe the horseshoe was a personal thing with Tari, like a thrown shoe while delivering the inaugural edition of *Gone With The Wind.* Anyway, quite shamefaced, I replaced the shoe to its sacred spot and sheepishly sneaked away to consider my sin. It's difficult to shed oneself of the guilt of sin from an unknown source. I sure hope that particular scolding didn't leave some sort of subliminal scar on my conscience: like being afraid of horses or librarians or bushes. Who knows what opportunities I've missed if that was the case.

Ours truly was a wonderful community: close, caring, and cooperative. But though we didn't realize it, we were obsolete compared to the changing world not too distant. In the towns, cobblestones had long ago replaced their graveled roads. And in the cities, asphalt was replacing cobblestones. Ironically, in an even more modern trend, some were removing the asphalt from cobblestones in an attempt to return to more original. All the while, we were still admiring our new road to which they occasionally added gravel that was coated with a tar sealant. During hot, summer days, the tar bubbled, and we ran our bicycles over the bubbles to hear them pop. All in all, we realized the need for modernization, but the one thing we couldn't quite comprehend was that trucks were outpacing trains. That just didn't make sense when we considered how many trucks it would take to haul a trainload of coal from the Cumberlands. And one of our happy times was counting the train-cars loaded with coal, so modernization was messing with our moods.

Occasionally, a plane flew over our community. And we heard about the Russians launching a Sputnik, starting a race to the moon, which was absolutely impossible, and we debated such.

Catalogues kept us up on changing styles and home improvements. By "kept us up" I mean we saw pictures of what others were wearing and what color schemes were popular on the walls of city homes. All that was intriguing, but one thing that made no sense to us at all was why front porches were being moved to fenced back yards.

Yes, the world was changing around us. We hated to admit it, whether we liked it or not, but we, too, were destined for change, however slow in coming.

Chapter Thirteen

The Feud

The local feud started one day when my sister, Brenda Sue, and I, walked along the railroad tracks with Lloyd and his younger brother, Mike. We were on our way home from the store. They were trying some newly acquired cuss words that seemed to be inappropriate in front of my little sister.

"No cause to use such words in front uf my sister, Lloyd King," I said.

"What cha gonna do 'bout it?" He challenged my rebuke.

"I'm ganna whup you fer it, if you don't stop," I responded. And by now I was getting angry at him.

"You might try," he said.

And I did try. Arms and feet flayed, dirty fists jabbed, and fingers intertwined with hair. It looked more like two people tangled in a parachute tumbling towards destiny than it did a fight. Barking dogs joined the ruckus. Brenda Sue grinned with glee, after all, it was her honor being defended.

The fight began on the tracks, continued all the way to Lloyd's front yard, paused for a moment when he threatened me with a chunk of coal from the cinder bucket on the front porch, resumed when he missed his target, and ended at the front door with Lloyd safely inside. I figure I won the fight, since I was the maddest and he run off inside his house, so I started to leave. Right then Lloyd cracked the door and yelled out, "Chick'n!"

I stopped flatfooted, wheeled around, then thought better than to go inside the house after him, for we weren't allowed inside the house without permission. I went on home to find Brenda Sue recounting the fight, word for word. This was one time that Mom excused my fighting, "Cause fightin' fer good is right. That's why our boys went off to Europe and Japan: fightin' fer honor of what is right."

Very early the next morning, Lloyd was pounding our door to death. It woke up the whole house. Mom answered the door and found Lloyd standing there, all frantic and scared. Tears formed streak-marks down his cheeks. His eyes, puffy and bloodshot, looked like he'd been beat up. It scared me to think I had done all that damage the day before.

"What's a matter, Lloyd King?" Mom asked.

"My momma needs help real bad," Lloyd said, wiping his nose on his shirtsleeve.

"What fer?" Mom asked.

"It's the young'en. He's bad off."

Mom rushed over to find Beulah Mae sitting in a rocking chair holding her baby, crying and praying for the Lord to spare him. Kelly was having one of his coughing fits on the front porch. Mom cradled the baby in her arms, and that is where he died.

The sickness caused concern about contact, but Mom's compassion over-rode caution. With the strange sickness in their family, they sent for Doctor Cornett, from Jackson, who made house calls when someone was really bad sick. He looked the situation over and flat out asked, "Who in this house has tuberculosis?" That's when Kelly had to go to the sanitarium in London, Kentucky. He eventually came home, but I don't think he was ever able to work after that.

The feuding never quite ended, but we always came to some kind of truce. Neighbors need one another, so we didn't dare stay mad too long.

We once discussed in a Sunday School class about the Good Samaritan. Seemed folks back in Jesus' day were having trouble knowing who their neighbor was, so He tried to help them figure that out. They finally did, and it wasn't the likely one. But when the Sunday School teacher asked the class who our neighbor was, I didn't have to think twice.

"It's the Kings," I said.

"Why?" she asked, just like Jesus always asked questions.

I couldn't quite explain it to her, I just somehow knew.

Chapter Fourteen
July Fourth

Daybreak produced a crimson glow on the clouded horizon. The eve of July Fourth dawned hot and stuffy.

"Gonna rain taday," Mom said during breakfast.

"How ya know, Momma?" I asked.

"You never heard yur daddy recite that sailor proverb, son?" she asked, rather surprised looking.

"I hav', Momma," Joyce chimed in. "Red at night, sailors delight. Red in the mornin', sailors take warnin'."

"Kain't tell rain that away," I said.

Whether it was true or not that it was going to rain, we still took to our visiting that day. There were a few neighbors Nancy hadn't yet visited, in particular, the Prathers. We hesitated in taking Nancy inside their fence. They were an elderly couple who lived in a house built high on the hill overlooking the store and post office. They came from the old country, wherever that was, and still spoke with a strange accent.

"Do ye hav' any mail fere me, Ida Mae?" Natalie would ask in an accented tongue of broken English spoken faster than we could hardly think.

The Prather's mostly stuck to themselves, except to get their mail and buy groceries. Their children had long since moved away to the city. I never met their children, but I think they had gotten a college education which, more often than not, necessitated moving away to find work in one's profession. Jobs were scarce in the Cumberland Plateau during the fifties, especially for the college educated.

Vincent Prather mostly went by the initials V. C., but I don't know what the "C" stood for. Sometime in the past, he was a watch repairer whose use of the King's Language, "by golly," according to Momma, bordered on profanity. Uncle Verdie, the talkative one in our family, knew a lot about most everyone. He told me that V. C. had his coffin already made, kept it in his house, and delighted in showing it to the faint of heart and curious of mind. I'm not sure if the casket was to prank, or if he was just being prepared.

A wire fence isolated his property, which was unusual for our community. Whenever a neighborhood pickup game sent a softball flying over his fence, we were afraid to retrieve the ball. We automatically suspended the game until a birthday or Christmas landed one of us with a new ball, or we got lucky and found one in the driftwood along the North Fork.

Some thought V.C. stood for "very cruel." After all, he was the one with a coffin in his living room. Further, he once gave my Uncle Verdie his first bite of "chaw'n" tobacco, as Uncle Verdie called it. Maybe Verdie wanted to get even, but was afraid of V.C., so instead of doing anything of a retaliatory nature to V. C., he gave me my first chaw when I was five. He told me it was candy and worked best if I'd chewed fast and spit often. "But don't swaller yur spit," he added. How kind of Uncle Verdie!

"Ain't as bad as they seem though," Joyce commented as we slowly entered the gate to the Prather property."

"How's that?" Nancy asked.

"Well," Joyce began, "on Christmas once't, Mr. Prather delivered a sack uf toys to ar' house, includin' a few used balls. I guess because ar' fam'ly wuz large and growin'. Or maybe he wuz rememberin' when he wuz a young'en. And maybe the V.C. stands fer "very carin'" instead of "very cruel"—least ways durin' that partic'lar Christmas."

"How observant," Nancy responded.

"Joyce always wuz a bright one," I said. I knew, for Mr. Deaton passed her two grades in one year because she was so far ahead of the others in her grade. I was proud of Joyce.

We survived the Prather visit, but we automatically walked faster as we approached Sylvania Spicer's house.

Nancy's interest piqued. "Why are we going so fast."

We didn't dare say why, we simply skirted around the issue and kept walking. The real reason? We thought she might have the curse, like some of the people in the Bible: cursed with a disease. She had a huge goiter on the front of her neck. We weren't sure how she got the curse, but folks said Matilda Fugate was a witch, so maybe she had caused the curse. Matilda was buried beneath a pine tree on the Noble farm. Folks wouldn't let her be buried in the regular cemetery. Some said she used potions and stuff. She was always collecting herbs and making those potions. She used to deliver babies, but folks got scared of her.

Nancy started to say something, I assumed another lecture, which she was prone to do when she was displeased with us. So, I blurted out, "She's got a curse. And Matilda Fugate wus a witch, and maybe she cursed her. And that young Ulysses fellar wuz a warlock. That's a man witch. Died at age twenty-one. He ain't buried with the reg'lar folks and neither is Matilda. All kinds of evil markin's on Ulysses' tombstone."

Nancy did not respond, though I could tell she was displeased and disagreed.

As we passed Sylvania's house, sure enough, she sat on the front porch smoking her clay pipe. Now, some neighbors wondered aloud why a church-going woman indulged in such a habit of pipe-smoking. But that was one vice the pulpit vacillated about condemning, and neighbors tolerated it, and children like me simply wondered how it tasted. And you could see the goiter on her neck. That was proof enough that she had the curse.

"Did ya see her goiter?" I asked Nancy.

Nancy challenged my logic. "The goiter is probably caused by a lack of iodine in her diet. That's why store-bought salt is better for you than the salt Sylvania probably has used for years. I assume her salt came from that local abandoned salt pit you told me about and doesn't contain iodine necessary in our diet for thyroid hormones."

We had never heard such before, and we didn't totally understand what she said, but maybe she was right. It could have been the lack of something in the diet that caused a goiter and not a curse. I have to admit, that was refreshing to hear.

The social layout of our community resembled a wagon wheel, with the general store and post office as the hub, and the hollows and branches as the spokes. Nancy spent a lot of time at the hub, collecting her mail, buying us Royal Crown Cola's for five cents a bottle, if you didn't take the bottle from the store, or else promised to return it. She sure had a lot of money. While we drank RC's on the front porch of the store, Nancy drank in the tales of the people, ever curious.

Our last neighbors to visit were the Costellos. We were concerned about taking Nancy up Copper Head Hollar where they lived: the name tells most of the story, but there was another reason. While cursing caused a lot of over-use of lye soap around the church-going community, cursing had a few compatriots at the Costello residence. The Costello's lived in the same house where my mom and dad first set up housekeeping. It was here that Uncle Verdie—the same tobacco-chewing mentor mentioned earlier, but when he was much younger—got into serious trouble with my mom. While chasing the baby chicks around the yard, and whether on purpose or accidentally—we will never know for sure—he killed one. We recite his explanation at every family reunion, to his consternation. To my mom he explained, "Rooty kill't the doody." Translated, it meant the rooster killed the baby chick. But for some reason, no one believed his story.

The Costello's were a large family of eight kids. Young George was near my age. We went to school together and were friends, but his older brother, Jack, was an ornery one. I was always afraid of Jack. He was one of the mean eighth graders from our one-room schoolhouse. The official name for our school was Washington School. I assume the school was named after President George Washington and not Booker T. Washington or George Washington Carver, since there were no colored folks in our community. Then again, it could have been named after Martha Washington, though I don't remember anyone ever mentioning it. There is a fancy inn at Abingdon, Virginia, that was named after the first lady, and it got its name while it was a ladies' college, the inn later retaining the name. So, it is possible our school was named after Martha. A statue in front of our school would have helped identify the character of its namesake—too much is sometimes taken for granted. Nowadays, a few college students have some strange idea of tearing down the statues of our founders and progenitors because they were not perfect. We sure could have used one of those statues. And we would have been quite proud to have President Washington adorning our landscape.

Mom had graduated from Washington School. Joyce and I were following suite. Mr. Deaton always liked our mom; he reflected such in the way he treated us. Though we wanted life to go on forever the way it was, we knew they were closing some of the one-room schools and busing students to big schools with lots of students. We didn't give much thought to our school closing; rather, we busied ourselves with our summer guest.

We were dead-tired from our all-day excursion, especially the trip to the Costello's place. July 4th eve found us hanging out on the front porch of the store, listening to Nancy go over her notes as we sipped from our pop bottles. She wrote so much that day that she had to buy another spiral notebook.

"Never sold so many notebooks," Ida Mae commented.

Nancy let me select my own peppermint and licorice sticks. The neighbors at the store, though usually as socially awkward as a twelve-year-old who's grown ten inches over the summer break, were pleased to pose for a picture with her, especially since they heard she was leaving soon.

"Miz Nancy promised we'd be in her scrapbook," Ida Mae told them. "Ar' ya shore you ain't writin' a book 'bout us, Miss Nancy?" she asked.

Nancy only smiled.

Our conversation turned to the weather, for the wind had picked up. A storm threatened. Dark clouds rolled over the hilltops, dropping heavy atmosphere into our valley; an uncanny cool and darkness prevailed. The day's activity came to an abrupt halt as we hastened home, hoping to beat the rain.

Mom was right about the weather with her "red in the morning" saying. It came in torrents, with driving rain and a wind tossing tree-limbs all over the yard. Hailstones the size of marbles beat hard against the cornstalks, like grandma beat her quilts hung out on the clothesline. The corn had been knee-high by the 4th of July, but now it lay flat as a flapjack on the stovetop. We stood on the front porch and told Mom about our day's adventures, speaking loudly to be heard over the pounding rain. She tried to listen but seemed preoccupied by the storm, probably only thinking about the corn crop.

"You worrying about the corn, Momma?" I asked.

"What's done's done and ain't nothin' we can do 'bout it," she said.

The rain subsided, but we didn't venture out into the water-saturated yard. We sat on the porch and talked, and as the evening wore on, Nancy took more to lecturing than interviewing. She seemed troubled that folks didn't take kindly to modern science, nor give much heed to programs for progress, so she was hoping that our family would be more open to her suggestions. But we didn't quite know what to make of her insinuations that we suffered emotionally and intellectually from our isolationism: she even hinted that our one-room schoolhouse was a form of isolationism. She suggested things that would make life safer for us: like outhouses and pigpens located farther away from the wells. Such suggestions were downright silly. "Why walk a mile to slop hogs when you can throw food to'em over the back yard fence?" we argued. She even voiced her approval of the consolidation of the numerous one-room schoolhouses, ours included. Somehow, Nancy seemed connected to a plot. I didn't want to think that about her, but she shore got nosey at times.

When I thought this way, I wanted to run off and be alone. I thought again about Coffin Rock, about the blood, and about the club. I wanted to go back, but I was scared. Still, I felt a drawing to go back. Curiosity? Adventure? Freedom? I didn't for sure know why, I just did.

As twilight snuck in, a bottle rocket suddenly shot skyward and exploded into a hundred colors. In a matter of minutes, the sky blazed with celebration. Somewhere in the distance, someone lit off an M-80, followed by a whole pack of smaller firecrackers.

The explosions illuminated a lone figure, walking briskly on the railroad tracks, coming our direction. Joyce recognized him first. "It's Daddy," she exclaimed.

Joyce and Sue bounded down the front porch stairs and sprinted to meet him. He dropped his suitcase and gave them a bear huge, long and tight. Mom came running out of the house to check on the commotion. When she saw Dad, she cupped her hands over her mouth, and cried.

Doyle, sitting on the front steps, stripped to a cotton diaper, looked up at Mom and announced, "Da'da home."

Chapter Fifteen
A Game of Marbles

The sun reflected a brilliant gold on lingering clouds, its beams beckoning me to mosey down to the store to see what the other fellers were up to. With Nancy York gone, I had extra time on my hands. Plus, I was trying to shake off the mulligrubs about Dad leaving again to go work up north. I thought, it sure is a nice day for marbles. So, after breakfast I asked, "Kain't I go down ta the store fer a while, Momma?"

"What fer?"

"Just to see what's hap'nin."

"You ain't gonna take yur marbles ar' ya?" she asked.

"Ever' body else'l have ther's," I argued.

"Suit yursef, son. Ain't no skin off'a my hide. But don't cha come a'cryin' ta me fer more if'n ya lose'em."

I ran to my room and retrieved a shoebox of marbles from under my bed. Running my fingers along the contents, I admired the colors and forms: transparent swirls, onionskins, end-of-day, pop-eyes, corkscrews, and cat's-eyes. Some were cracked and others chipped, but all were round. That's what mattered most. I scooped up a two-handfuls and stuffed them into the pockets of my jeans.

Our marble games did not win friends and influence people; conversely, they made enemies and created distrust. Still, the challenge of the game drew us back. The game of marbles in the 50's was an important competition to prove one's skill. We played in front of the Copeland store in an area where the grass succumbed to the hundreds of callused knuckles and knees and the thousands of cat-eyes and log-rollers that attacked the same spot vigorously throughout the summer. Contenders—some with shoeboxes full of prized, multi-colored marbles—came to compete; most left after discarding the boxes and stuffing their few remaining marbles into their pockets. Shouts of "you fudged" or "you moved yur marble" created frequent scuffles.

Entrepreneur Berry Pink of Marble King envisioned every boy in America having at least fifty marbles. Some of us had less, always going back to the store for more, but losing them quickly to the sharpshooters. Even the government got in on the act, with Congress passing legislature to protect the marble industry in America from "those copycat Japanese imports." But the government didn't protect me from the champions in our local community.

I went to the games as often as I could talk Mom into letting me, but mostly I watched, for I was a novice: too young to compete with pros like Danny Haddix and Joshua Ray, who showed little mercy to novices like me. After the older fellows finished their games, I used the scuffled playing field to practice for the time when I would be a contender.

The first game was usually for practice, though it sometimes inaugurated a fight as contestants argued whose marbles belonged to whom at the end of the practice game. The rest of the games were for keeps. I watched enthusiastically, studying each style.

"Got any marbles, Larry?" Josh asked. "We need another play'r."

His invitation surprised me, for they usually didn't let me play, as I took too much time aiming and such. The request hung tantalizingly in the air, dangling in front of my fear of losing like a carrot before a wild rabbit.

"Hain't got but'a few," I said.

"Afraid ta join with us?" he challenged.

The dare could not go ignored; my eight-year-old-manhood was at stake. I accepted the challenge, slipped my hand into my pocket, and pulled out a fistful of beauties.

"Let's play a game of five's and fer keeps," Josh insisted.

We counted out five marbles apiece, placed them into

the square drawn in the dirt, and lagged to see who got to go first. Josh lagged a slow and easy underhand toss toward the line drawn in the dirt about ten feet from the marbles. Danny lagged an aggressive, straight-as-an-arrow shot with a backspin that stopped the marble on a dime, a hair's breadth from the line. I went last, and the marble slipped off my fingers, about an eleven-inch shot.

"Shucks," I blurted out. That was so close to cursing that I didn't dare say it in front of Mom, but it gave me a sense of belonging when I used it in front of the fellows. "Redo!" I yelled. "It slipped outta ma fingers."

"Sorry 'bout that, Larry. Slips count." Josh chuckled.

Josh angered me for not giving me a second chance. I wanted to get even, but he was the far better player.

Danny won honors, so he let go an airborne shot from behind the lag-line that dropped deadeye into the middle of the twelve-inch square, scattering marbles everywhere. The shot sounded like a .22 rifle ricocheting through the river valley. Five shots latter he had cleaned house, except for one lone marble. His backspin settled inside the box, causing him to lose his turn.

Josh went second. He knelt on one knee, aimed a cock-headed bead, and misfired just as I asked, "Wher'd ya git them scratches, Josh?"

"Ain't fair!" Josh protested. "You interfered with ma' shot with that dumb question."

His hands and arms showed noticeable scratches all over. Josh seemed as protective as a cornered coon. I tried to imagine him with a mask over his head, sitting on Coffin Rock, cross-legged and looking silly. Was he one of them?

I protested, "Ain't no dumb question, it's just a question. Couldn't help but notice them scratches all over yer hands and arms. Cat scratch ya?"

"It ain't none'uf yur nosey business, but no, didn't get clawed by no cat," he shot back.

"Don't need ta git so riled up 'bout a few scratches lest'n you got something ta hide," I countered.

"And you should keep ta mindin' yur own business a'fore you git yur nose busted," he said. And then he kicked his marble halfway to the store.

It was my turn to shoot. I knelt while Danny stood there looking down at me kind of strange, like he was surprised I asked Josh that question. My marble missed.

Danny's next shot finished the game.

I was minus five marbles, humbled by my loss, and now possibly in danger for revealing a secret I should know nothing about. Perhaps I should tell Mom about the club and Josh's scratches. No, I thought, for if I do, she'll never let me go up to Coffin Rock again. And I was already itching to go back up there and check out the bloodstain in the middle of the rock. I wondered again who the masked guys were. Josh sure did act mighty guilty.

Chapter Sixteen

King James

Dad came home early Saturday morning, so we would go to church come Sunday. When Dad was gone, it seemed too great a task for Mom to get us ready by herself, march us up the tracks to the church house, then corral us for a couple of hours in the hard, slatted-wood benches. And with Dad not there as a balance, she was liable to get into a spat with one of the gossips. But with Dad home, all that changed.

We had our share of preachers, but I was partial to my grandpa: some called him Preacher Arwood, but most referred to him as Preacher Charlie. Preacher Spicer was another good preacher, but the two were definitely in contrast with their style of sermon delivery. Take for example how they used some of the questionable words of Scripture: like the Bible word for donkey, which was a cuss word in our home. Grandpa was more on the reverent side, always weighing those cuss words of the Bible and trying to find an acceptable substitute. He did right well with his vocabulary, except when he got mad at Jack, his old mule, but even then, he just yelled a lot, but he never used a questionable word in the pulpit, even though some Bible verses did.

Not so with Preacher Spicer. He was different than Grandpa in that he used those Bible words that I wasn't allowed to use. If it existed in the King James, he did not hesitate to use it in or out of the pulpit. He was quick to point out that snake handlers were dumb as an asinine, using the shortened version and sometimes prefacing it with jack, referring to the beast of burden of course, just like the Scripture does. Ants weren't just pesky insects; they were pesky pismire ants. Again, he used the shortened version of Scripture, just like it was in the good old King James.

I must admit that I struggled with Preacher Spicer's vocabulary. He used words I didn't dare let Mom hear me say, words reserved for playing marbles or when you were in a scuffle on the playground and needed to feign courage. But there he was, a preacher, using them like they were as common as a cold. Only later did I learn his shocking vocabulary was correct. Actually, it was a carryover from the old language, simply a shortened version; however, I doubt Preacher Spicer knew their origin. To him it was acceptable colloquialism because it was in the Scripture. Since his theology was irrefutable by a six-year-old boy, in time, acquiescing my doubts and overcoming my fear of the Lord and Mom—mostly Mom—I developed my own set of Bible cuss words and assumed a lot more cuss words existed in the King James than I should have.

At the supper table one evening I used one of my newfound terms. I hadn't meant to do it, but the oilcloth covering the table stuck to my arms as I sat too long leaning on it. That was good reason for me to keep my elbows off the table, even though I knew little about etiquette. I felt we had sat a little too long without leaning on the oilcloth, and since the conversation had died down and needed livened up, or else supper needed to be over, I propped my elbows on the table, looked over at Mom, and exclaimed, "Shore is (expletive) hot today, ain't it, Momma?"

Mom's head jerked back, kind of like the hog jerks when Dad shoots it between the eyes with his .22 rifle so we can butcher it. Her ears perked, like a spooked horse. An eternal silence reigned for a good five seconds before she exploded. "Whur in the world did ya hur sech kind uf lang'age, yun'n? Yur Daddy don't use them kind uf words, and you shore ain't gonna use'em either in this house." And I assumed she meant anywhere else.

I tried to explain, "Preacher Spicer uses them words, 'cause they're in the Bible. And if'n they're in the Bible, it shore is alright with the Lord. And if'n it's alright with the Lord, it should be alright in ar' house."

A dozen eyes bored holes through me, like I had just desecrated the sacred book, even though my objectionable language was from the book they were defending. I wanted to defend myself, but the look on Mom's face told me in no uncertain terms that the issue was closed, the judge had proclaimed the verdict, and punishment awaited the unrepentant.

Humiliation descended into my soul and certainly upon my face, reminiscent of the scattered, ash-like frost on a crisp fall morning, though a slight smile on Uncle Billy's face warmed the chill a bit. Emotions swelled and tears wet my shirt as they dripped off my nose and chin. I tried to finish my cornbread, but it tasted of lye soap. That was the first and only time Mom ever heard me cuss. Of course, she wasn't with me twenty-four-seven.

An evangelist later reinforced my argument for more liberated language when he read one of those cuss words from a passage of the Old Testament. But he had come too late to redeem me from the wrathful warning of Mom and the stoic stares of a table full of siblings shaming me for desecrating the sacred book at our dinner table. Evidently, the evangelist spent less time than he should have preparing for his sermon, or he was "waitin' fer the anointin'," or was just trying to collect his thoughts, for he read right into one of them Old Testament cuss words, something about what a man does to a wall. The boys broke out in a wave of snickering that rocked up and down the pews the remainder of the service, especially every time one of them looked at the other, which was but seconds apart. The older women blushed redder than rouge and wouldn't look at the evangelist the rest of the service, either keeping their eyes shut as if in meditation, or else fixated on the picture of Jesus hanging behind the pulpit. Some of the men nodded, as if in affirmation and not wanting the preacher to feel too badly about his blooper: that is until their wives poked them in the side with an elbow.

The evangelist, noticeably shaken, tried to correct his error by quickly reading beyond the Scripture that caused such commotion.   Catastrophically, the word appeared again a few verses later. The waves of snickering from the boys went from above average to tidal wave; it would have sustained a surfer for an hour—which is about how long the sermon and snickering seemed to last. The blushing women scolded Pastor Charlie with their eyes, their expression pleading, "Kain't ya do something with this cuss'n man of the cloth?" But my grandpa had gotten passive in his old age, and he found it difficult to take the bull by the horns. He picked up a songbook and flipped its pages, as if looking for a closing hymn.

Some Bible translators choose more euphemistic terms for the before described cuss words, but hill folks were accustomed only to the old language—and that was the translation the Gideons were giving to us in school: the good old King James. "Old tis better 'cause it has been tried and tested," some argued. "Even the devil himself has had time ta scratch and poke about fer errors but kain't find nary a one."

Even a humiliated evangelist, quoting those words from the Bible, did not change their minds about the good old King James. "If t'was good 'nough fer Paul, tis good 'nough fer all," echoes in my memory.

Church folks still carried their worn-out Kings James Bibles to every service, cuss words and all, and sinners kept right on getting saved. But Mom never acquiesced her rules: no cuss words in our home, no matter what the preacher says from the pulpit.

Chapter Seventeen
The Unforeseen

The fifties started the second half of the game of the century; time to evaluate, recuperate, and make fewer mistakes than the first half which saw two, world wars. But the Korean Conflict soon shattered the hope for peace when communism invaded the penninsula. The UN team came out determined; however, determination is sometimes deterred by the unforeseen. In this case, it was 300,000 Chinese troops pushing back, leaving millions of casualties. A few lines drawn in the sand became the barrier between communism and freedom. So, while some boys were returning home, others were leaving for Germany and Korea to serve as peacekeepers.

Major events unfolded around the world: Churchill retired as Prime Minister of Britain; Peron was overthrown as dictator of Argentina; Lego's were invented. These didn't affect us, but we had our own events materializing. For starters, a train derailed in front of our house while we were playing in the yard some thirty yards away. The conductor saw Mom frantically waving and pointing at the train, and suspecting something terribly wrong, pulled the emergency cord. It shook the engineer a might, the sudden breaking of the train while he had the throttle thrust forward, but it saved the train, and maybe lives. What a sight watching those huge, steel wheels digging into the cinders, throwing rocks, and chewing up crossties! Mom was considered for an award. Her finger-pointing—warning us of the impending danger—got the attention of the conductor. We could surely have used that money, but someone else collected it instead. Perhaps they needed it more.

Further in the unfolding events, our dog, Jiggs, got run

over by a train, cutting off a couple legs, and so he had to be euthanatized: that's a word we didn't know. One of my uncles put him down with a bullet instead of a needle.

More importantly, uncertainty reigned as to the future of our local school. Mr. Deaton decided to retire and talked about moving up north to Indiana. We could understand him retiring, but we couldn't comprehend him moving away. We talked a lot about his recent altercation with young Jack Costello. Some folks figured that experience was the straw that helped him make up his mind about retirement.

It all happened so quickly and unexpectedly. On a day like any other—long and uneventful, but full of potential, Jack sat underneath the schoolhouse during an entire recess, whittling away on a stick of hickory. The schoolhouse was built on stilts and the shade underneath was inviting but sometimes invited trouble; it was a good place to connive, and Jack did some conniving that day. The piece of hickory in Jack's hand slowly took on the resemblance of a dagger, which he tucked under his belt. Knives had to be kept in your pocket, but a wooden stick for carving could be stuck in your belt in plain sight and easy to retrieve.

Mr. Deaton clanged the brass bell to end recess; Jack thought otherwise and came waltzing in late. When Mr. Deaton tried to correct him, a fight ensued, and it ended with the wooden dagger buried in Mr. Deaton's upper left arm, close to the heart. It bled profusely, like maybe it had entered the heart. Mr. Deaton remained standing in front of our terrified class, noticeably shaken as he attempted to clog the flowing blood with old newspapers that he kept for us to read. And he tried to calm with words the rush of blood through our pounding hearts. Such a frightening sight was more difficult to erase from memory than it was to erase the slate chalkboard. Lots of yelling continued between Jack and Mr. Deaton.

"You'll leave this school ground immediately, Jack."

"I'll leave when I'm ready ta leave and not a second afore."

"Now, I said, and never come back!" Mr. Deaton demanded.

"Whose gonna make me?"

A couple of the older students slowly stood. They walked toward Mr. Deaton. For a moment I thought they were siding in with Jack. Instead, they just stood there beside our teacher, stern faced. One tried to help stop the blood flow.

"Please, Jack. Git yur books and leave, now," Mr. Deaton pleaded, but Jack hesitated. "Now," Mr. Deaton repeated.

Jack stomped out, leaving his few belongings behind.

In retrospect, I assume Mr. Deaton's insistence that Jack leave immediately was partially due to his concern of the response to this incident by his own son, Shoog (actually, William Goble Deaton, II), who was about the same age as Jack. There was sure to be another fight when Shoog found out, but Shoog, an only child, was probably no match for Jack, and especially Jack's knife. Shoog, as usual, was late himself from recess. Older students acquired this habit, which was difficult to break—even with the hickory stick Mr. Deaton kept above the lintel of the main entrance. I suppose this was a subtle warning to all who entered, but the older students would just as soon take the licks across their bottoms and enjoy a few extra minutes of play than sit on their bottoms on the hard wooden chairs all afternoon. So, many times after lunch they came in late or did not show at all. Mr. Deaton resisted arbitration with students in those days; still, tardiness continued. And Shoog was tardy again this recess. That was one time it was good that he came in late: probably the only time he didn't get in trouble for it.

I pitied Jack, bent on feeding his propensity to fail and starving his potential to climb out of the barrel of bitterness in which ill fate had birthed him. With one, wild-cat slash of his wooden knife, he severed a link to a better life. But I think he perceived that hickory dagger was somewhat payback for the hundreds of stripes he had received from the hickory switch belonging to Mr. Deaton. Yes, I pitied Jack, but I also feared him, because if he could do that to a grownup, what could he do to a little kid like me. So, in a way, I was glad to see him go.

I felt embarrassed for Mr. Deaton, standing there with his clean, white shirt all bloodied and torn, his pride frayed a bit also. Both Jack and Mr. Deaton seemed to have lost that fight. Jack probably wanted to be expelled; hunting, fishing, and gallivanting around the countryside seemed a mite more exciting than learning how to read, write, and cipher numbers. Jack never came back. Mr. Deaton retired at the school year's end.

Chapter Eighteen

Miss Terry

The approach of another school year proved quite trying. Who would replace Mr. Deaton? We waited anxiously as the school officials in Jackson debated on closing our small and outdated Washington School. But our school opened again with a new teacher, and we were delighted.

We busied ourselves learning from flash cards with Miss Marsha Terry, from over Cane Creek, where my great-grandparents, John B. and Eliza Lewis lived. Miss Terry was young, full of life, and beautiful. The latter somewhat distracted us boys from our learning skills. And when she pitted the boys against the girls in vocabulary contests, the girls mostly won, but we had our excuses, mainly, we let them, or so we argued during recess. Truth be known, the girls seemed to have a knack for word memorization. I think they call this some type of right brain advantage. We boys definitely seemed wrong brain disadvantaged. To further complicate our wrong brains, we didn't use phonics back then, just rote skills. I still struggle with a lot of words, like "chimley" instead of "chimney." And is it "I want some corporation" or "cooperation?" My best friend and I got into a heated discussion in college over his making fun of my use of "encouraging corporation among ourselves." He teased, "We're not a company, Larry. We're a class." Moreover, I find myself saying certain words with an accent that is a dead give-a-way of my roots, just like I was learnt it—I mean, just like I was taught.

The mid-fifties was full of notable events. It was the closing of some old chapters and the beginning of new ones: Albert Einstein died, and the Mouseketeers debuted on TV. Mr. Deaton was gone, but Miss Terry moved right in to take his place. I was partial to Miss Terry, and things were running smoothly. Then a few weeks into the school year came the sudden and horrible news: they were closing our school and busing us to another school about twelve miles away. Miss Terry made the announcement on Friday; I never saw her again.

The new school, located in the community of Quicksand, made us feel like foreigners, and we were certainly outnumbered. The building formerly housed the Breathitt County High School, but the county built a new high school at Jackson. Though disappointing to have our local school shut down, the school at Quicksand had its advantages; it boasted a classroom for every grade and a low teacher-pupil ratio. The school board explained how consolidation was more economical for the taxpayers, and we could have a ball team, better qualified teachers, and more opportunities. We believed them.

The Quicksand Elementary School perched on the top of a barren hill overlooking the community. The Ed Comb's store was located at the bottom of the hill. The school bus couldn't climb the steep incline to the school, so it dropped us off and picked us up near the store. We walked up and down the hill, eating our candy bars, which we purchased at the store before and after school. Ed Comb's store had a much better variety than our local store in Copeland, and I was partial to the Zero candy bar, which Ed supplied.

I don't remember any of the teachers' names in that big and better school, and I doubt that any of them remember mine. Taxes kept on climbing, so Dad had to work harder, and I was too little and too afraid to contribute to the ball team. The best I could do was loose in the annual marble contest, though I did almost win the Maypole King and Queen contest once. I lost because a local student ran home and collected a few more pennies—after the parents had counted the totals and found him to come up short of my jar, which seemed a bit unfair. It was too far for me to run home; further, I had probably collected all the pennies we had in my home. In contrast, I'll always remember my first-grade teacher's name at the one-room Washington School, and if I should meet him today, I am sure he would ask, "How's yur mom and dad doin', Larry?"

There's a lot of talk now-a-days about community: whether political, social, or religious. We have the community drug store, the community bank, and the HMO's of the medical community. The church is no longer a congregation; it, too, is a community. Fortunately, I grew up in an environment society currently seeks; ironically, society endeavored to save us in the '50's from that community environment.

I hear talk that consolidation may have been a mistake— something about *"mole ruit sua"* (it collapses from its own bigness). If it was a mistake, I can't help but wonder how differently life might have turned out if they had left us alone at the Washington School. I doubt we'll ever know for sure.

I wondered if Nancy York had anything to do with our school closing. But I didn't linger long there, for I had finally gotten her out of my craw, and I was well beyond sulking over her and her opinions.

Chapter Nineteen

Death

G randma Brewer died during the winter of my second
school year.   I think I grew more that year than all the
previous—not in height but on the inside. The growth was
painful, like the tearing down of a landmark to erect a library.
It was hard getting used to. You are pulled by both the past
and the future. Seems like we lost a lot in a short while that
year, but life went on.

Death, like geography, is hard for seven-year-olds to
comprehend. And I definitely struggled with understanding
geography; therefore, needless to say, I struggled with
understanding death. Unless you had done some traveling,
which I had not, it was difficult to visualize how huge the
world was. As far as I knew, my community took up most of
the world, though Nancy York said otherwise. I reasoned,
how can fifty states of varying colors, shapes, and sizes fit
on a single-page map when my community alone could not
fit on that same single page? Surely there were a few more
communities as big or maybe even bigger than ours? And
how could a thread-size, blue line scribbled across a page
called a map, represent a river that touches the soil of at least
ten states, beginning way up in Minnesota and stretching for
more than a thousand miles all the way down to the Gulf
of Mexico? The river flowing past the back of my house
was bigger than those rivers on the map, but it wasn't even
shown. Geography was confusing. And so was death.

With only the experience of life, it was difficult to
understand when Grandma Brewer died. I didn't comprehend
all the emotions. Why all the ruckus? She'll eventually wake
up.

I asked Dad, "Why does she just lay thar on the bed, not

movin' or nuthin'? Why don't she wake from'er nap like she always does?"

Life I could understand; death was awfully confusing.

Friends and neighbors from all around gathered in as if for a church meeting, but it was no ordinary gathering, for many were crying, and the rest were silent. I cried too, not knowing why, it just seemed I should. Fulton Noble and my dad built the coffin in the back yard. We kids played nearby, occasionally offering a quizzical glance but somehow knowing questions were out of line. Isabelle Clay prepared the body for burial—for free. She carefully lined the wooden coffin with white satin shirring and covered the body with a shroud of the same material. I later learned this act of kindness was her contribution to many a family in our community.

Grandma Brewer took sick January 5th on Aunt Fannie's birthday. She died January the 13th on Uncle Fred's birthday. It was a Sunday. They buried her the next day on Uncle Billy's birthday. How coincidental these events would occur on the birth dates of her children—if life and death ever fall into the category of coincidence!

Grandma's dog, Bounce, died that same day after howling all night as Grandma laid in a comma. Bounce had belonged to us, but on a visit from Grandma, she and Bounce bonded so well that Mom gave him to her. Grandma and Bounce became best friends—reciprocating needs, I suspect.

Many neighbors attended the viewing. We appropriately called it the layout; the deceased was laid on a bed, table, or temporarily constructed platform of rough-hewn lumber. The layout incorporated an emotionally-stirring church service. There were certain folks who specialized in singing for funerals. The community knew who they were and always expected them to sing. The funeral singers were more than willing to perform—to me they seemed a little too eager. If you were not sad before you came, you would be before you left—the funeral singers saw to that.

Grandma Brewer's was the first of a host of funerals I attended. Each is etched in my memory: the sermons, the songs, the seriousness. At Grandpa Charlie's funeral the singer tuned the guitar after the group was announced to sing. They sang *The Grass is Greener on the Other Side*, tuned the guitar a little more, and chose another song that was sadder still: something about begging the undertaker to drive slow.

During the layout, many talked about everything except the deceased: the garden, the children, the quilting, but not the deceased—awkwardly, we avoided acknowledging that the past was all that remained of the dead. Each consoled the other regarding the future, with a sincere "she's in a better place" as the catch all to ease the pain.

Our tradition demanded that someone stay with the body all night; it was unthinkable to leave the body alone. Surely the body wasn't going to sneak off in the night, and it is quite doubtful that anyone would have stolen the body. So, more than likely, guilt was the underlying culprit for staying with the deceased. Did I do enough for them while they were alive? Or, since it is too late to change the past, perhaps if I stay with them now, they will somehow know how much I cared, though I doubt the deceased cared at this point.

Neighbors crowded into Grandma Brewer's house. I never felt so alone in such a crowd. Dad walked over to me and laid a tough but tender hand on my shoulder. He said nothing; he just lingered there beside me.

With eyes staring straight ahead, I asked, "Why'd she have ta die?" What's it like, Daddy?

Dad hesitated a long moment, I suppose collecting his thoughts, before he spoke. "Death is like a journey. The journey ain't exactly the same fer all, but I kin tell you what it's like fer yur Grandma Brewer."

"I don't like death, Daddy," I said.

Dad studied his fingernails for a moment before he continued.

"Yur Grandma, she wuz a Christian, baptized by yur Grandpa Charlie. Bible says we ar' buried with Christ by baptism and if'n we ar' buried with Christ we're gonna live with'im someday."

Dad knelt beside me and looked me straight in the eyes a good while before he continued, I think concerned that his theological explanation was a bit over my head. Perhaps he needed another approach.

"Do ya remember the time I took ya ta town on the passenger train?" he queried.

I remembered well, but what does a train ride have to do with death, I thought. It was the most exciting thing I had ever done up until then. We got on the train at the Copeland station, which was named after my Aunt Judy's family (the Judy married to my Uncle Fred). Her maiden name was Cope. Her relatives—three brothers—Levi, Wiley, and her Grandpa Sherman were the first white folks to settle our community. When the L&N abandoned the depot at Copeland, the name still stuck for us, though the mailing address was Saldee. Seems the first postmistress, Sally Deaton, wanted to name it after herself. But there already existed Sally and Deaton post offices, so, she combined the two names, Sally and Deaton, and came up with Saldee. The name never took with the local population. We still told folks we lived at Copeland. That's what the railroad sign said. We never bothered to change it; the United States Postal Service never knew—or else just didn't care. And mail addressed to Copeland, somehow, still made it to us.

So, on my first train ride we boarded at the Copeland Station for a trip to Jackson. Yes, I remembered that trip well, and I told Dad such.

Dad continued, "Do ya remember goin' through the Dumont Tunnel and the train becomin' suddenly dark?"

"Yes," I said.

"And do ya remember we soon escaped the darkness uf the tunnel, inta light—a glow that seemed suddenly bright'r than the mornin' sunrise?" he asked.

I can relive the entire trip in my mind: the anticipation the night before, the anxiousness of the morning wait (questioning if we might have missed the train), the exhilaration when I heard the train whistle, and the delight of being helped aboard by the conductor. And I definitely remembered the sudden darkness when we entered the tunnel.

"And in a moment, we exited on the other side uf the mount'n," Dad continued, his voice soft but certain.

"Yes, Daddy," I replied, sensing I was about to receive the answer to a great mystery.

"That ther' is what death is like," Dad concluded. "It's a journey through momentary darkness ta exit into bright light on the other side uf the mount'n."

That was a long explanation from my daddy who was usually a man of few words. I didn't quite understand what he meant, but I thanked him.

The singing and the preaching lasted a long time, but surely Grandma's life was worth us taking the time to do all the things that need to be done at a funeral. Grandpa Charlie ended the service with a reminder that she was with the Lord, and then he prayed.

The box was loaded onto a sled pulled by old Jack, and we trailed behind. The procession entered the cemetery atop the hill, a clearing surrounded by tall pines that swayed against the cold winter breeze. The stately pines kept watch over this sacred ground, pointing heavenward, as if to remind us of the endless hope of the believer. Still, a gnarled and knotted pine, lightning struck, and wind whipped, gave witness to a reality of life: eventually, death to all.

"Whoa," Dad called to Jack, who pulled up at a mound

of freshly shoveled dirt.

The men lifted the pine box from the sled and placed it on boards laid across the open grave that had been dug by caring neighbors wielding picks and shovels against the frozen ground.

All were allowed a final viewing, and I hid my face as Fulton Noble sealed the wooden lid with horseshoe nails he took from his coat pocket. Preacher Charlie prayed again: family and friends stared longingly. With three ropes supporting the box, twelve calloused hands lowered it into the hole. Shovels of yellow, clay dirt followed.

Dad's explanation about death helped some. I was glad Grandma Brewer's future was not one of eternal darkness inside the pine box.

The Monday we buried Grandma, more tragic news stunned the community. Alex Wadkins experienced a fatal car wreck crossing the steep and winding Jackson hill on his way to work at the Potter Mine in Elkatawa. Floyd Haddix and Alex's brother escaped by leaping out of the vehicle as it plunged into a deep ravine. So, the church lost a "sister and a brother in the Lord" in a couple days. That must have been emotionally rough on Grandpa Charlie, to lose two parishioners back-to-back.

I visited often where they buried Grandma in the yellow clay high on the hilltop overlooking the Noble Farm. I stood at the grave, longing to see her, wondering what mountain her tunnel exited, and how long the journey would take. Maybe someday I could take the train and visit her there.

Chapter Twenty

The Revival

A year seemed too terribly long to judge time; so, we judged time by events. If no major events played out, we judged time by the seasons. This gave us a safety net from the mundane; still, time crept by sluggishly at best. The farthest we planned was the season facing us, each with an annual event: Easter, Decoration Day, Labor Day, Halloween, Thanksgiving, and Christmas. Most anyone can endure a season. And per the wisest of kings, that seemed biblical: "… to every thing there is a season, and a time to every purpose under the heaven…." Seasons definitely worked well for us.

Like the seasons—with uniqueness and variation—we anticipated and welcomed the annual revival meeting. But unlike the seasons, the revival was less predictable for its timeliness and consistency. Revival seemed to never make it on the calendar; rather, it just happened. We always missed the cut on the evangelists' "list of preferred churches." Instead, we made the "when-you-absolutely-have-no-other-place-to-preach" list. That made us more vulnerable to the upstarts and the has-beens, not to mention the charlatans. And they somehow managed to find us.

Our community epitomized the story of a stranger asking directions to a destination inconspicuously designated on a hand-drawn map. "Ya kain't git thar from hur!" was often the conclusion. Though difficult to get to, once you arrived at our community, getting out was a breeze. You simply did a u-turn: there were no options to confuse you. We were the end-of-the-road. The road got narrower the farther you went, except for when it ended in a cow pasture. The farther you went, the closer you got to the turn-around or the "bridge-out" sign—and sometimes a warning sign: "Kep Out ur Prepar 2 Di." The usual conversation of strangers consisted of "You think we're on the right road?" or, "I think we should've turned back there!" Anyhow, one of the above may have been the fault for one very memorable revival, or more appropriately for us, survival.

Nancy York had left, and Grandma Brewer had died. Mr. Deaton had moved to Indiana, and his replacement, Miss Terry, vanished into thin air. With too many loses, the gray of life faded the colors of our soul. We needed revived.

News spread by word of mouth: "Revival this comin' week!" Just the thought brought solace to the weary soul.

The revival started rather normal: the opening night was hot and sticky, the dead-end road was dry and dusty, and the mosquitoes were thick and hungry. Preacher Charlie introduced the evangelistic team as "… a nice fam'ly I jist recently met…," or "…give'd directions to…," or something to that introduction. Perhaps they expected us to clap; we did not. We just stared, for they had not yet won our applause.

The service began like most: a handful of the saved formed a semi-circle around the pulpit—we call them a "praise team" today—to get the service going with some selected hymns. Wise Solomon was so true: "Nothing new under the sun." But I'm rather glad some of the old stuff of my childhood has improved a bit.

Congregants requested favorite songs that burned in their hearts. Each praise leader carried his own soft back version of *Don and Earl's The Heavenly Call Favorite Gospel Songs and Hymns*, but not necessarily of the same edition. This often created some confusion as to the page number from which they were singing. The men carried their paperbacks rolled up in one of their hip pockets, with the corner of a handkerchief protruding from the other. The women carried their songbooks in large purses. As for hankies, the women carried two: one tucked in the belt and the other carried in the hand. The hankies served multipurposes: an instrument of worship, a fan, and a swat to chase away mosquitoes. And the purpose for two hankies? One for "show" and one for "blow."

"It's 'bout time ta start the service," Grandpa Charlie began. "We're askin' the singers ta take ther' places and git us started. We wanna thank ever'body fer comin' out tonight." A few "amens" affirmed his welcome.

The pickers did a last-minute tuning. A tambourine jingled. "Praise be ta the Lord" and "Halleluar" ricocheted from the unpainted, hardboard ceiling. A sleeping baby, startled, joined the ruckus.

The "singers" gathered around the pulpit and sang a medley of *My Mother's Bible*, *Hide Me Rock of Ages*, and *Where the Soul Never Dies*: all in the same key. The unsaved vacillated between remaining a sinner or getting saved, but whatever the decision, all enjoyed the bluegrass gospel. The electrifying atmosphere was contagious.

Hill folks love music, secular and religious. So, some of the musicians around our community were using their talents for the devil on Saturday nights but experiencing rather quick conversions come Sunday. It was a common occurrence to hear Elbert Haddix (we called him peg-leg Elb) walking up the railroad track on Saturday night on his way home from drinking, quite spiffed, but singing *Amazing Grace* at the top of his lungs. You could tell Elb from all the others by the uncommon rhythm of his walk. His peg leg made a rather peculiar thump as it struck the crossties, and it made a scraping sound as it kicked up the gravel in between the ties. Thump, scrape. Thump, scrape. Still, in the quietness of a black, humid night, chasing sleep and fighting off apparitions conjured by the darkness, I sometimes succumbed to my imagination. Wide eyed and frightened, I envisioned a chain gang, dragging crossties and pounding gravel, sneaking closer and closer. Mean and revengeful, they demanded cornpone and a file. It didn't help that Joyce had read Great Expectations to me some time back. I saw the gnarled hands, with cracked and dirty fingernails, tightly griping the handle of a knife, a grip that, around my throat, could squeeze out life quicker than I could blow out a lantern or end a prayer. I strained to make out the sounds coming through my open, bedroom window. A smile chased away the darkness as I recognized the slurred singing of peg-leg Elb. It was not a *Hang Down Your Head Tom Dooley* song, to add to my already terrified state of mind, but a calming and reassuring hymn of *Amazing Grace*. I mouthed the refrain as he sang, "how sweet the sound, that saved a wretch like me" and laughed silently at myself for being so scared.

Elb caused us a blend of comedy and fright as he sometimes got his peg leg caught on the tracks. You would think one time would have cured him, but it didn't. More than once a caring soul rescued him out of the way of an approaching locomotive. They dragged him off the track—minus his peg leg but drunk as a skunk. But then again, was he really stuck? Or drunk? Perhaps he reveled in creating excitement on an otherwise monotonous day, payback to those who joked about his peg leg. Opinions varied from pity to scorn. "Poor ole Elb" expressed the sympathies of some, while others were not so empathetic. "If'n ya make yur bed hard, ya still gotta sleep in it," some judged.

Anyhow, this revival, with lots of singing, would be a real treat from peg-leg Elb episodes. We did not quite anticipate how big a treat. What we assumed to be containers for small musical instruments (tambourines, Jews'-harps, and spoons) that the evangelistic team played, turned out to be the cages for their pets—that is, pet snakes.

News spread like wildfire in a forest carpeted with dry, pine needles. The fiery arguments, with varying opinions as to the sanctity of such in church, created intense heat among us. Folks quoted Scriptures I'd never heard before.

Some argued "fer," since the Bible says something about the faithful "taking up serpents" and Moses putting up a statue of a serpent in the wilderness. "Such external signs are evidence uf yur inward faith and spiritual renewal from Adam and Eve's failure," they explained. Those "aginst" talked about "the evil uf temptin' the Lord." Both sides quoted so many Scriptures it got some of us plain confused as to what we believed. No animal activists spoke up for the caged serpents. Neighbors took sides; strangely, saints and sinners joined on the same teams. But no matter if you were "fer" or "aginst," folks packed out the church house the next service.

You must understand that rattlesnakes, coiled in wire-mesh containers setting in the back of a beat-up station wagon parked by the side of an unpainted clapboard church all day long, in the middle of summer, stirs curiosity. And especially when there is little to do all day except lying on your back on a grassy knoll, swatting flies and counting cotton-candy clouds drifting across the wide-open sky. Such boredom stirs the curiosity of boys and amplifies their mischievousness. Furthermore, we had a difficult time figuring out if we were "fer" or "aginst" the evangelistic team handling snakes to show us they had the "pow'r uf the Lord," cause we weren't sure if the snakes themselves were "fer real" or "fake rubber snakes" won at some carnival. So, it was no surprise when a couple of young, truth seekers decided to have a closer look.

The crowd gathered long before the service started, "talkin' a'plenty." Children played tag, hide-and-seek, and kick the can. Teenagers played drop the hanky—a game the ladies' gossip society eventually branded as carnal, thus banned. A couple of innocent-looking seven-year-olds hanging around the station wagon provoked no undo suspicion. They climbed onto the back bumper of the vehicle and had a look. The snakes seemed real enough, but they weren't moving. The litmus test came when they poked sticks through the wire mesh. Sure enough, they were real. And they didn't cotton to such abrupt awakening by strangers—especially strangers with mischief instead of mice.

The snakes struck out to beat the dickens. They coiled and hissed and postured for dominance for a good fifteen minutes. They were pretty riled up before curiosity was satisfied. The culprits slipped leisurely away and settled onto the slatted pew farthest back in the church house, nearest the door, with a window view of the station wagon. They anticipated the service might be a tad more exciting than the night before.

The women were fanning, the youth were flirting, and the children were climbing over and under the benches. While the men wiped sweat with their plaid handkerchiefs, the teenagers passed notes and shy glances, and the two, mischievous culprits sat on the back-pew grinning. The praise leaders got things started a little late: there was a slight dispute over the key the guitar player chose. They finally turned the pulpit over to Preacher Charlie. He exhorted for a few minutes and took up a love offering for the evangelistic team, whose absence, by this time, created a noticeable concern. We could see the evangelistic team through the open windows, huddling at the back of the station wagon like parsons in prayer, or generals deciding a war strategy. They eventually entered the door next to the platform, absent their snakes, but carrying a guitar, bass fiddle, and a couple of tambourines. Preacher Charlie turned the service over to them, but the ting, ting, ting of the guitar had to be in harmony with the thump, thump, thump of the bass before they began to sing *He Set Me Free*.

The sermon was shorter than anticipated, and the service broke up with no mention of the snakes, though there was a lot of talk about hell, sin, the devil, and some insinuating comments about the judgment to come for the devil's helpers. No one got saved that night. The audience seemed more than a little disappointed—not that no one got saved.

We came back the next night with anticipation. The evangelistic team offered an explanation for why they were compelled to handle the snakes. They professed that God called them to preach and to "take up serpents." S.B. (He went by initials instead of a name, but no one seemed to know what those initials stood for.) and James Thomas were in charge of the team. Local folks called them the Thomas brothers. Mom said they were my cousins, but she also said that James was always fanatical, a more euphemistical term I chose for the adjective she really used. Aunt Judy said S.B. and James once persuaded her brother to join them for a service to help with the music, but when they fetched the snakes from their cages, he crawled out on all fours, with his guitar strapped to his back.

The Thomas brothers raised quite a ruckus that summer, but I doubt that you could call it revival. Dad came home that weekend and assumed a role some children take in the latter years of their passive parents. Grandpa Charlie couldn't find it in his heart to confront the snake handlers. Since the Thomas brothers were our blood cousins from the Clemons' side of Dad's family, Dad decided he best have a talk with them.

Dad's talk worked, somewhat. By Saturday night the evangelistic team had abandoned snake handling. In fact, they traded their snake handling for fire handling. And proving their faith by fire seemed more important than saving souls from the lake of fire. From under the platform benches, they retrieved pop bottles half full of coal oil, with homemade wicks protruding, which, when lit by a cigarette lighter, produced pretty-impressive flames, not to mention a potential fire-bomb. They ran the flames up and down their arms, which singed the hairs but otherwise did no harm. The meeting room looked like a combination of Moses' cloud by day and fire by night, for flames were shooting from the wicks and black smoke hovered like clouds near the ceiling.

"Jist like the miracles in the wilderness, it's a showin' uf the pow'r uf the Lord," S.B. explained.

"Ain't no fire uf the devil kin harm the believ'r," Thomas screamed out. "Thomas in the Bible wuz a doubt'n Thomas, but this hur James Thomas ain't no doubt'n preacher." He thumped his chest with his thumb to make sure we knew who he was referring to. "I'm a voice from the Lord God A'mighty out uf the wilderness. Prepar' ye the way uf the Lord!" he exclaimed.

Some seemed like they were beginning to believe, with shouts of "halleluyar" and "amen" rattling the rafters, but Dad just sat there doubting, getting redder behind the collar the longer the situation continued, no matter how sincere they were. I reckon even sincerity has a moment in time when it needs to be challenged.

Dad finally stood. "I'm a wantin' to believe," he began slowly, "but I'm a doubtin'. Maybe if'n I could see more proof, say like some real coals uf far' like is in ar' coal stove 'stead of them flickerin' flames yur'r handlin'. Why don't I make us a live far' in that pot belly stove back yonder, like they done fur them Hebrew child'ern, and give ya a chance to really prove yur faith?"

A sudden silence blanketed the room. All eyes turned toward Dad, some accusingly and others approvingly. Stunned, the fire handlers, one by one, found occasion to extinguish their flames; however, the fury in their eyes burned like the fiery furnace Dad had suggested.

The revival meeting ended abruptly. Dad helped the team to their station wagon and gave them a hardy sendoff. A friend and I watched through the window from our back-row seat. The old station wagon, loaded to the gills and dragging in the rear, sped hastily down the dirt road, and it disappeared in a cloud of dust, the bouncing snakes sounding like a nursery full of babies with toy rattlers.

They too, had come to save us, to charm us with their works of great faith, to use us as a statistic on their stairway to stardom. We didn't want to be inhospitable, but we had long ago learned what to do with fire and snakes. It certainly wasn't to handle them; rather, you fetch up the snake with a stick and toss it into the fire, after you've chopped off its head with a hoe. Sometimes you've got to save yourself.

Chapter Twenty-one

Captured

The sleuth within lured me back to Coffin Rock. No amount of personal persuasion convinced me otherwise, though I tried to reason with myself about not sticking my nose in other peoples' business. I climbed the same path taken before, cautious not to interrupt another secret meeting.

The rock stood deserted. The blood was gone, washed away by the rain. Still, it showed signs of recent activity. I laid down upon a mossy cushion that carpeted part of the rock, closed my eyes, and daydreamed of the distant past. Was this a sacred place of the native Cherokee? Perhaps a burial ground. Did an Indian carve the head on the corner of the rock? Was the chin of the carving a landmark for distant travelers, pointing the way? Then again, what about the present? Whose blood had I seen covering the rock? Who were the masked boys? My thoughts drifted. Sleep overtook me.

They were on me before I had a chance to get up. The leader stood over me while four others held me down, spread eagle. I wanted so very much to know their identity; I wanted much more to be home.

"So what cha doin' snoopin' round ar meetin' place?" the leader asked.

"Wusn't snoopin', just a restin." I feigned boldness, but my voice cracked with fear.

"What're we gonna do with'em? another asked.

"Kain't just let'em be," another chimed in.

"Le'me thank a minute," the leader shouted, as he paced on the rock's edge.

The sky above revealed a flawless blue, augmenting the baby-blue eyes that stared at me from behind the masks. I closed my eyes and gazed beyond them, beyond the visible, into the heavens mentioned by the writers of Scripture and preached about by Grandpa Charlie. I will be going there soon, I thought. Surely somewhere up there, God is looking down at me. I sneaked a peek and tried to distinguish their faces, but I could only see their eyes peering from the masks. I prayed silently. Lord forgive me was all I could think of to pray. I realized how much unlike Jesus I was, for I hadn't prayed for days on end, hadn't got baptized, and surely wasn't quite ready to forgive my enemies.

The leader spoke again, his tone less determined. "Confound ya, Larry. Ya done gone and messed up ar' secret club. Now we gotta take care uf ya."

I wiggled like a worm on a fishhook, trying to escape their grasp. "I ain't gonna die no coward," I said. My right hand slid loose. I grabbed for the mask of one of my assailants, but he jumped back, mask still in place. The leader tackled me, pulling my face close to his. I smelled his onion breath, but worse, saw the fiery eyes. I was angry and wanted to see behind that mask, but I was scared and alone in a world of mummy-faced ruffians.

"I'm gonna give ya one chance," the leader screamed. "Ya hear me, son? Just one chance. If'n ya take it, we'll let'cha go. If'n ya don't, nobody'll ever know what happen'd to ya. You ever see'd a dog runned over by a freight train? That'll be whatcha look like by the time we git finished with ya. Now listen ta me real good, son, 'cause it's yore one and only chance."

The others slowly loosened their grasps. What are my chances against all of them? I wondered. I'm smaller than the least of them and certainly outnumbered. Considering my lack of options, I decided I'd just play along and see what happened, kind of like Preacher Charlie said David in the Bible did when he was among his enemies and needed to convince them he was one of them.

"Whatta I hav' ta do?" I asked, feigning submission.

"You gotta swar', swar' you'll join us and never identify any uf us. And like the 'postle Peter, ta make it official, ya gotta cuss."

I wasn't totally innocent, but I was trying to obey Mom and not cuss anymore. But my options seemed slim. "What else do I have'ta do?" I asked.

"Whatever the club decides. We all gotta follar the same rules," the leader explained.

"What about the blood I see'd on the rock?"

"What blood?" the leader asked.

"You know what blood I'm talkin' 'bout. Kain't fool me with yore actin' innocent. See'd it with ma own eyes. Wuz hidin' over yonder in the bushes the whole time y'all had yur meetin'."

"Kain't tell ya afore ya join ar' secret club," the leader explained.

"Whatta 'bout the masks?" I asked. "Do I have ta wear a mask?"

"Yeah, 'cause we don't want no adults a'knowin' who we ar', ner what we ar' a'doin'," the leader said.

I studied the situation a long minute before I agreed. With everything in me screaming for me to fight back, to run, to tell my mom, I agreed to the oath. I became one of them; I became a cussing, secret meeting, mask wearer. I wanted to say no, but I said yes to all their demands. And I said yes to the very things Mom and Dad spent my lifetime teaching me against. The leader helped me up, patted me on the back, and gave me the secret handshake, kind of like Grandpa Charlie did for a repenting sinner, but I knew this was totally different. I managed a smile, but I could not see whether they smiled back behind their masks.

The trip home seemed the longest ever. I found a thousand reasons to stall along the way. Ironically, it felt good being a part of a secret club, accepted and all, but I felt ashamed. At the fork in the road that Dad told me I would someday face, having to choose for myself, without him there with a belt and all, I made the coward's choice.

I'd never before understood what the preacher meant by "lost in sin." But now, for the first time in my life, I felt like a sinner. And lost.

Chapter Twenty-two

When Snakes Had Legs

Another summer day dawned beautifully. With art-inspiring splendor, a blue-canvassed sky backdropped downy-white clouds that floated effortlessly upon a gentle breeze. The usually barking dogs napped in the sunshine, and the sometimes-annoying blue jays chirped a calming tune. Energized by the lovely weather and the need to escape the humdrum of monotony, we took to the task of hoeing the vegetable garden and picking potato bugs off the plants. The environment facilitated thought. It was a time for deep, daring, exercising of one's imagination: at least it was for me. I drifted from the Alamo to Pickett's charge, and I was just about to ride the first waves of the invasion of Okinawa when Aunt Fannie shattered my daydreaming with a blood-curdling war hoop.

We rushed to her rescue. She stood paralyzed, mouth agape, voice frozen into speechlessness, with a spastic finger pointing somewhere between the sky and the tomato patch. She resembled a modern rendition of Lot's wife turned to a statue of salt.

Some misinformed urbans think living in the mountains makes one accustomed to snakes, like a postman becomes accustomed to dogs. Every dog doesn't bite, nor does the postman kill every dog that does, but not true with my family and snakes. We assumed all snakes bite, and all snakes should therefore be killed. Maybe it was an over-developed case of ophidiophobia, for truly, if we got bit by a poisonous snake, we were too far from a doctor for help, and a hospital was out of the question. A knife and turpentine had to suffice. We held to a lot of superstitions, such as a copperhead can still bite before sundown even after you chop him up. The conclusion? Always crush his head. Perhaps that's why Grandpa Charlie came running with his shotgun instead of a hoe when a copperhead once blocked out path, though a shotgun seemed too formidable a weapon for a skinny snake. Anyhow, Grandpa blew its head to smithereens, so sunset didn't matter in this case.

Snakes weren't yet considered a candidate for the endangered species list in our neck of the woods, though we probably facilitated that list; conversely, we considered humans to be the ones in danger. I can't understand why God made copperheads and rattlesnakes, like I can't understand why He made poison ivy and poison oak. I guess it's a reminder we are the creation and not the Creator, and there was a tree from which we shouldn't have eaten.

We're told snakes walked on legs before the tragic decision in the garden. Adam blamed Eve for the explusion, while Eve blamed the snake, and the snake, well, after the curse, he didn't have a leg to stand on. Or at least that's what a preacher said in a sermon I recall. The serpent proudly walked into the garden but crawled out in disgrace. And he has been without legs ever since, that is before this discovery by Aunt Fannie.

I probably should tell you that Aunt Fannie lived on the frantic side, but snakes pushed her frantic button to frenzy: 0 to 60 in .001 seconds. Snakes terrified her. If her frenzy was measured like earthquakes are, there would be another scale that goes beyond mass destruction to total annihilation. There she stood, screaming, pointing, and shaking like a sheared lamb in an ice storm.

After a brief interrogation by my dad, Aunt Fannie stuttered hysterically, "Iiiiit hhhhhas llllegs!" She then engaged in a total body-shaking fit. She could have won a belly-dancing contest hands down.

Dad questioned, "What in the world's a matter with ya, Fannie?"

She didn't answer a word; rather, she continued her Lot's wife's routine of just standing there, except she was shaking like a statue in an earthquake. So, Dad did what seemed to work best on her: he held her by the shoulders and gave her a couple of firm shakes, demanding that she "snap out uf it." If that didn't work, a couple of light smacks across the face followed. Dad discovered, over a period of time and through trial and error, that these shakes and smacks generally snapped her from her occasional state of fits.

Aunt Fannie hadn't always been this way. In fact, in her teen years she was full of zest for life. When Grandma Brewer died, she left Aunt Fannie with two younger brothers to raise, my uncles Billy and Fred, even though she was almost a young'un herself. She was a favorite aunt and made a hard life not just bearable, she made it fun. With brooms for rifles, we marched to her commands of hup, two, three, four. During Halloween she was an instigator of parties, overturning outhouses, and such. But something happened that changed all of that. A more seasoned man robbed her of that youthful side of life, and I was robbed of the merriment exuded by Aunt Fannie. Her brothers were robbed of her inspiring survival spirit. Mom and Dad had to step up to the plate and raise the boys and care for Aunt Fannie.

It had happened some time back. Her joy left, and seizures moved in the night she came home from a date with a schoolteacher from the county next to ours. Today we call it date rape. Her attacker held out that it was a consensual romance. Whatever, she came home broken and babbling and bleeding. She gave birth nine months later. The community took sides. Dad and Mom took her in. The court in Perry County determined the teacher to be the father and that he should pay child support. Since he predated deadbeat dads, Aunt Fannie had to garnishee his wages. Did that ever get embarrassing for a schoolteacher! He vanished for a while. She determined it was not worth the trouble trying to collect support, though I always thought she should have done it for her son's sake. With time, she overcame the anxiety attacks, made it without child support or government welfare, worked a job, and raised her son as a single parent. In retrospect, Aunt Fannie made me proud.

I'm not quite sure how the rapist escaped the wrath of her brothers; maybe he didn't escape altogether. Still, it's hard to imagine how he, or any man with an ounce of character, can neglect a child he fathers. I heard some time back that he had a heart attack. I can't imagine that either; I figured he didn't have a heart. It may sound a bit like I might have some suppressed vengeance towards my should-have-been uncle. After all these years, I think not. Maybe some pity, for he missed an opportunity of life with a wonderful person.

I visited Aunt Fannie a few weeks before she passed. She lived to be in her nineties, so I shouldn't have been surprised that she didn't recognize me, but I was. "I'm your older sister's son," I said. She wasn't buying it. When I pressed on, she stared at me for a long time before finally acknowledging I was her nephew by asking, "Have you put on some weight." So, I go down in history not as Aunt Fannie's favorite nephew; rather, I am the fat son of her older sister.

We best get back to our snake story. Where was I? Oh yes! After a couple of light smacks, since the shakes weren't working, Aunt Fannie settled down. The sting of the insulting slap proved stronger than the hold of her hysteria: post-slap sensibility may be the professional name. Perhaps the remedy sounds a might cruel (or mighty cruel, depending on whether you're Freudian or of a more confrontational school of Psychology), but we had no professionals to advise us; we learned by trial and error, mostly by error and sometimes accidentally—not too unlike some professionals today. We now call the process of discovery scientific research—though we still begin it with an uncertain hypothesis, kind of like we did back then. In dealing with Aunt Fannie, the term—hypothesis—was actually an acronym: HYPOTHESIS. It stood for: Hit-your-patient-on-the-head; either-side-is-satisfactory. Anyway, that day in the garden, we finally realized Aunt Fannie's consternation. Stretched out on the freshly, fallowed ground, between the rows of tomatoes, soaking up the warm, summer sun and momentarily immobilized by food consumption, was a huge and scary black snake. And sure enough, it had front legs. Perhaps Darwin was right after all. The evolutionary process was taking place in our garden patch and right before our eyes. Legs now, arms later, and who knows, in a million years, wings. What a spectacular discovery! Perhaps we should be more scientific and spare this species from the normal manner of dealing with snakes.

Now, we hadn't invited the snake into our garden. And we didn't know its intentions. So, without a second thought, we dispensed with being scientific about our discovery. While the rest of us cornered the snake with our hoes, Dad retrieved his shotgun. It looked like Little Big Horn reenacted: the snake was outnumbered and surrounded. I'm not sure why Dad hesitated, but on closer investigation, he exclaimed, "This snake ain't growed no legs; it's just choking down a frog fur' lunch."

Sure enough, the legs of a frightened frog protruded from the snake's mouth, its little feet clawing for dear life. So much for our hasty conversion to evolutionism! Instead of saving the snake, we rescued the frog: in our usual manner of dealing with snakes.

We continued our work in the garden as the lazy, summer day snaked by. The start of another school year looked promising. Boy, did I ever have a story for "What I Done Over The Summer Break!"

Chapter Twenty-three
Preparing For Winter

Spring. Summer. Fall. Winter. Each season contrasted the other; each had definitive qualities. While summers in Appalachia can be terribly hot, winters can be extremely cold. Keeping houses cool in the summer was impossible, for we didn't have any type of cooling system; we just opened the windows that had screens and sometimes those that didn't. That was a tough call, for the mosquitoes were a close match to the heat for discomfort. In contrast, keeping the house warm in winter proved challenging, for most houses lacked insulation and central heating, ours included. A coal-burning stove in the middle of the living room had to suffice in heating the entire house. It proved insufficient, for the living room became hot while the bedrooms could freeze a glass of water left on a nightstand. The kitchen had a wood stove for cooking, but it didn't put off much heat, and its heat certainly never made it to the frigid bedrooms. We slept under a thick stack of handstitched, feather quilts.

Our house consisted of four rooms and a small add-on created by boarding up part of the back porch. That room belonged to me, being the eldest son, or else because it was the farthest from the stove and no one else wanted it—I'm not sure which.

During the summer and fall, we worked diligently storing up coal for winter. Like the Bible Proverb's busy ants, we prepared for winter, for once the cold set in, slothfulness proved costly. However, my uncles, Billy and Fred, stretched the context of this Bible verse a mite farthur than they should have. They prepared for the winter but with a Robin Hood mentality.

I'd want to justify their thievery by explaining that they

were teen orphans fending for themselves before there was such a concept as latchkey kids. After all, they weren't taking from the local folks; conversely, they were simply making a few chunks of cannel coal disappear from the tops of passing open-top hoppers. Their philosophy? What does a few pieces from a million amount to in an empirical corporation like the Vanderbilt's? And the coal laying on the top edges of the train cars could fall off on its own and might hurt someone in the process, creating a lawsuit. They could very well be doing the coal company a favor by removing the risk of this liability. A few chunks of coal seemed a molehill to the giant company shipping it, but the coal represented a warmth instead of freezing cold to a couple of orphaned teenagers. The Vanderbilt family should be thankful instead of greedy.

The distant whistle of an approaching train signaled it was time for Billy and Fred to get to work. Feigning innocence, they waved at the train engineer, but soon after the engine passed, they grabbed up long, willow poles hidden in the brush alongside the railroad tracks. As the train rumbled by, gusting their hair and driving dust into their squinted eyes, they lowered their poles against the top of the coal gons, careful to prevent them from slipping between the coupled train cars and jerking them to their death underneath the train. It seemed somewhat biblical, like young David of Scripture facing Goliath, as they stood their ground against the rumbling giant of steel. Any coal laying on the edge of the coal gons became fair game per their rules of warfare.

As the caboose approached, they tossed their poles back into the brush and gave a friendly wave to the conductor— as if he didn't know their scheme. Once the train passed, they gathered their bounty and carried it to the storage bin, preparing for the coming winter. Yes, they were expeditious, like the ant, about storing up for the winter—and they looked like ants silhouetted against the huge freight train roaring by.

With the passing of time, they didn't bother to wait until

the engineer passed out of sight before they gathered their poles out of hiding; instead, they waved to both the engineer and the conductor with poles in hand. It became more like hunting for sport than scraping for survival.

Poor decisions that produce a measure of success can create habits of monstrous proportions, at least that seemed to be the case for Uncle Fred. He'd purchased his first car—a big yellow '55 Buick that was straight from the lemon-line in Detroit, but not long afterward, the engine went kapooey. Now if the truth be told, Fred probably blew the engine while racing on the Cragin stretch between Haddix and Jackson. Some say it was the only straight stretch of road in our county that was long enough to drag race—being about a quarter of a mile long. Anyhow, Billy and Fred, along with a friend, Pete Sizemore, tried unsuccessfully to repair the car's engine, but they concluded it was not worth the time and the expense to fix it. Perplexed about this unfortunate investment, Uncle Fred reflected upon his successful, entrepreneurship days as a teenager in the coal business, and so he concocted a plan.

"That insurance salesman pressured me purty hard ta take out full cov'rage on the car," Fred commented to Billy and Pete.

"Shore did," Pete said.

"Then why not wreck this hunk of junk and collect?" Fred asked.

"Sounds like the best thang you've thought uf all day," Billy responded.

"And I know just the place," Fred said, flashing a grin that smacked of mischief.

Fred maneuvered the car to the edge of a steep ravine where he accelerated the knocking engine and leaped from the driver's side. The car crashed through the brush towards the North Fork at the bottom of the hill. Fred's miscalculation sent him tumbling end over end along the gravel—a bit harder than the soft upright landing he'd anticipated. The fake accident turned out a mite more realistic than planned; Fred's cuts and bruises gave proof.

Mom and Dad seldom argued, but this event brought on a never-resolved standoff. Mom defended her young brothers' honor, while Dad concluded Fred and Billy had faked the accident to collect insurance money.

"Them young'ns wouldn't do a thang like that, Delmar," Mom protested.

"Them young'ns ar' growin' up, Fairlean. They ain't the angels they played in the Christmas program," he said.

Mom went into her silent routine for a couple weeks. Dad laughed himself silly over the boys' explanation of how Fred escaped a near-death wreck. After a while, Dad thought it best to stop teasing about the incident.

The insurance company reluctantly paid up. Uncle Fred eventually healed up. His yellow Buick, upside down at the bottom of the hill, leaked enough oil into the river to attract prospectors from the Sinclair Corporation.

Chapter Twenty-four
Kentucky Whiskey

Billy and Fred were on a roll; one mistake led to another. If the saying "give a person an inch and he'll take a mile" is true, then they were on their second mile. Maybe it was the independent spirit of the Appalancian region, or the antics of claiming Vanderbilt coal, or being orphaned at a young age, whatever, they deviated further from the straight and narrow toward more deviate behavior.

We had no idea how far they had strayed until the news blindsided us like a flood in February. A caring and noble soul, bordering on nosey and self-righteous, stopped by to deliver the news.

"Mornin', Delmar."

"Mornin', Sam. How's the family?" Dad asked.

"They're alright. Yur's?" Sam asked.

"Good," Dad said.

"Hav' ya' heard yet?" Sam asked.

"Heard what, Sam?"

"Bout them boys, Delmar."

"What boys, Sam?"

Sam looked compassionately toward Dad, surprised by his naïveté. "Sorry ta hav' ta be the one ta tell ya, Delmar, 'bout Billy and Fred." He paused.

"What about themn boys?" Dad asked.

"Well, um, I just saw'um down under the swinging bridge, drunk. Pains me ta tell ya, but I know'd ya'd wanna be told. Them boys still needs a daddy, Delmar."

"Yeah, they do need a daddy, Sam."

"Well, I told ya, so I'll be going now. Guess you'll wanna be gittin' down ther." Sam bowed his head in humility for being the bearer of bad tidings, kind of like the preacher does after he deliveres a message of doom if we don't repent. And it helped us a mite when he showed he didn't necessarily enjoy doing so and that he actually cared, unlike a card shark or bounty hunter or Mr. Deaton with his hickory switch.

Dad donned his fedora and went to check on them. He found the once "young and innocent" in route to manhood, acting "wild and restless." They were wallowing in the mud like pigs in a pen, and they were drunk as skunks (whatever that means)—so much for manhood. They had gotten hold of a fifth of Four Roses Kentucky bourbon straight from Cox's Creek by way of some pile of driftwood or some local scoundrel. They had passed it around a few times and eventually passed out. Dad marched them home, like errant schoolboys on their way to the principal's office. They were a sorry mess: caked with mud from their heads to their shoes. I wondered, maybe that's why pigs wallow so in mud— there couldn't be much difference in corn whiskey and the soured slop we fed them daily. Maybe the pigs were simply drunk. I wondered too, how do distilleries get away with contributing to such animalistic behavior in humans, when a food processor would get into big-time trouble peddling food for human consumption that made them crazy? I was ignorant of the power of money and the degradation of humankind.

Booze was not new to our community. It had already wrecked the lives of many, some of them my relatives. A freight train ran over and killed my great-grandpa Arrowood as he laid on the tracks passed out from liquor. Liquor contributed to the early death of Grandpa Brewer, who died before I was born. My great-great uncle, Captain William Strong, was a demon on horseback, partly contributed to self-ambition, partially to the devil, and partially to liquor. A captain in the Union Army during the Civil War, he failed to relinquish his duties after the war. Along with a following of ruffians, he wrestled control over Breathitt County, once commandeering the courthouse in Jackson with a list of complaints. Riding the theme of the "protector of the freed Negroes," he assumed powers not allotted to laity, controlled politics by ambush, and acted as judge, jury, and executioner on more than one occasion—some suggest maybe a hundred or so. But what goes around comes around, for Ed Callahan finally bested Captain Strong for control of Breathitt County. Uncle Bill, as some called him, decided to call it quits, but the younger Callahan, motivated by the hostility from the past, refused Captain Strong a peaceful retirement.

"To live by the sword is to die by the same," the wisest of all once said. It certainly was true for Uncle Bill. With his young grandson, Carl, riding double behind him on a mule, Captain Strong, though short of stature, sat tall and adroit in the saddle as he rode down Lick Branch to the local store. He never made it home. The feuds he fed in the past, fueled an enmity that remained relentless until Captain Strong was laid to rest in a family cemetery at Whick. A volley of bullets riddled his aged body. In horror, his grandson witnessed the violent fate. What a horrible price! Both outlawed moonshine and legal Kentucky whiskey were strong factors.

The dirt path onto which Great-great Uncle Strong fell ran through Grandpa Charlie's farm. Hid away in the surrounding hills, distilled moonshine dripped into jugs, then into the bloodstream of individuals, and bloodlines of generations. Grandpa Charlie broke the curse: he became a preacher and teetotaler. But local tombstones in various cemeteries in the county were witness to the premature destruction of many from alcohol.

I played on the hill where the ambushers hid who killed my great-great uncle, Captain Strong. I walked a hundred times over the soil that lapped up the blood spilt a half century prior. I, along with a few dozen relatives, inherited the land over a hundred years after the murder of Captain

Strong. And now my uncles, Billy and Fred, were treading the same downward path just like our relative on their mom's side. But one person stood in their way: my daddy. And he was as tenacious for virtue as Captain Strong was for vice.

As Dad marched the staggering and babbling brothers into our yard, I found the sight hilariously amusing. Dad's restrained demeanor demanded that this was no laughing matter. Still, his harshest reaction was the tone he used as he told the boys to "clean yurselves up fer supper."

Uncle Fred, whimpering about "how sorry he wuz," stumbled to the fifty-five-gallon barrel that caught the rainwater from off our roof, leaned over the side to wash, but instead, fell in headfirst. His feet and legs stuck out of the barrel sort of like the frog legs stuck out of the mouth of Aunt Fannie's snake discovery. Dad let him stay in that position a little longer than I thought he should have before he rescued him.

Uncle Fred hugged my dad, and with slurred speech he slobbered something like "Delmar, I love ya just like ya wuz ma' pa." Sober men usually don't say things like that. Too bad! Dad showed an ever-so-slight smile.

While Uncle Billy laid passed out on the front porch, Uncle Fred babbled incoherently. I thought it might be a good time to ask him how he really got those scars on his arms. But I thought otherwise when I noticed Mom viewing the scene through the sheer curtains of the living room window. Crying.

Chapter Twenty-five

The Boat Ride

D ad kept them stored under the house, hanging from nails a couple feet off the ground. Though it seemed like years, it was more like a couple months, but since I lacked experience in tracking time, a couple years and a couple months were all about the same. Both were extremely too long.

I recall the excitement the day Dad hauled them home from the sawmill, in the sled pulled by ole Jack, Grandpa Charlie's mule. We unloaded and dragged them underneath our house where Dad nailed them onto the supporting stilts. They were two, twelve feet long, poplar boards, designed especially for gunnels of a boat Dad was going to build us someday: the emphasis being on "going to." With my misperception of time, it seemed Dad would never get around to the project, since making a living for the family consumed most all his time, and the rest was taken up by gardening, taking Mom into town to do the grocery shopping, and going to church. Pondering this dilemma, a brilliant idea popped into my brain. Why not surprise Dad by building the boat for him. I knew he would be proud. Impatiently, I awaited the right opportunity, which seemed terribly long in coming but finally came.

The break came one beautiful, summer Saturday— one of those Saturdays that tempts you into adventure. I awakened to a quiet house, found my siblings still asleep, and then remembered Mom and Dad had planned an all-day-shopping trip to Jackson. "Time ta build ar' boat," I said to myself as I tugged on my brogans.

I lugged Dad's toolbox underneath the house and locked the door from the inside. With the claws of a hammer, I removed the nails holding the boards. They tumbled to the ground, and the project began. The handsaw stuck often on the forward motion and the backward. I lacked knowledge in the finer arts of the wooden ruler, but perseverance paid off, for a resemblance of a boat slowly emerged from the sawdust. All the while I had to calm the shouts coming from my siblings: shouts like, "What in tarnation are ya doing under the house, Larry?" My most consoling answer seemed to be, "Nothin' much."

Some relief came when Joyce yelled to me, "We're goin' down to the store. You need anythang, Larry?"

"Not now," I said. "Take yur' time and don't worry 'bout me none."

The finished project looked more like a sandbox with a bottom than it did a boat. A new dilemma surfaced from the many cracks between the floorboards: some were as wide as the cracks in our woodshed and would certainly leak. After much consternation, I eventually remedied the problem by stuffing the cracks with rags and sealed them with roofing tar Dad planned to someday get around to using on our roof. I thought, maybe that can be my next project.

With a sticky mess smeared all over the floor of the boat, and my leather brogans looking like they'd waded through a tar pit, I decided the tar itself needed sealed. I studied the situation and concluded the most economical and convenient remedy was to sprinkle sand over the tar. Once completed, I dragged the monstrous four-foot boat from under the house—barely exiting the small doorway—and into the backyard. I was fortunate that my sisters had gone down to the store, and I hoped they'd stay away a mite longer. With grunts, grit, and lots of breaks, I tugged the project down the embankment behind our house, forging a pathway through the field of horse weeds to the water's edge. With a salute, I christened her "*Success*" as I shoved her into the river.

She sank almost immediately! It was not a "she sprang

a leak and after much effort to save her, she listed to the right and sank." She just sank—right there before my very eyes, water rushed in from every direction, and she quickly filled to the brim and sank to the bottom of the two feet of water. I imagined it resembled the walls of Jericho: suddenly crashing down flat. She sunk down into the water and laid there flat beneath the surface. How awful!

By now, awareness dawned of the consequences awaiting me because of my failure. But then again, since Dad would probably never get around to building the boat, I'd be off to the army before anyone noticed the missing lumber. They'd be too proud of me by then to say anything. Then again, maybe they'd think someone stole the lumber. And some years in the distant future an archeologist might discover *Success*, and instead of Dad being upset, he'd boast that a prehistoric boat was found on his property. They might think it to be an Indian canoe sealed with pitch from a special tree that once grew here, or maybe that Daniel Boone used it like a raft to discover this Kentucky wilderness. Of course, the boat was too dadburn small for Noah's Ark, though I pitched it within and without with tar, and it was probably too far from Mount Ararat to be mistaken for such. To assure the archeological find would be on our property, I double knotted the rope to a willow tree and drudged on home before Mom and Dad got back, fully persuaded it best to hide the evidence and say nothing.

As soon as Dad and Mom arrived home, Joyce blurted out, "Larry's been doin' somethin' all mornin' under the house."

"Gotta do somethin' afore I die of boredom," I said.

I might have pulled the whole charade off except for my black boot-prints all over the place. Mom demanded to know the truth and "right this minute!" I feigned ignorance for a while, but I did so short of telling a lie. Now, I had my reasons for stalling the truth. Like I already said, at the rate

Dad was going, by the time he discovered the missing lumber, I could be off in the army or maybe college if there wasn't a war going on. Further, he might think Harlen Chaney had stolen the lumber, for after all, Harlen was up for parole, and this could be enough to send him back to prison. And since Harlen Chaney deserved being behind bars for all the crimes he'd committed in our community, I felt justified in saying nothing. My stonewalling proved effective until Mom, point blank, asked, "Larry, have you been in yur Daddy's tar he got ta fix the roof?" What a leading jab! She followed with, "Wher' are yur boots?" How do mom's do that? That's all it took. Like a gully washer on a steamy, July afternoon, my confession poured forth—even to the trifling details of tearing up my bed sheet to stuff between the cracks of the boards. But I told her, "I wuz only tryin' ta help Daddy out, him being so busy and all."

I guess it was all the tears and repenting that prevented the worst whooping of my life. I certainly took note of that—the tears and repenting results—just in case I got into some more trouble in the future.

Weeks passed before I ventured to check on *Success*—not for any particular reason other than to pass away a long summer day. I looked into the water and there she was, still laying on the floor of the river. I said, "She shore is a purty thang a'layin' at the bottom uf the North Fork. What a shame ta let such a good boat just lay ther' and waste away like a snowman in March." So, I tugged her onto the bank, flipped her upside down to empty the water, inspected the damage, and wishing her seaworthy, pushed her back out into the water. To my amazement, she floated. Like Noah's ark, it was another miracle! I wanted to shout "hallelujah," but that seemed sacrilegious. I couldn't wait to tell the family. I hoped it would venerate my previous failure.

The supposed miracle had its explanation. The water had caused the boards to swell and seal the cracks. Elated and wanting to show off my ingenuity, I hit on an idea. "Why not give tours uf the North Fork," I said to no one in particular, especially since no one was there. But right away, Joyce and Sue showed up, and turned out to be my first prospects.

"Wanna ride in ma boat?" I asked.

"Ain't gittin' me inta that contraption you call a boat." Joyce refused.

"Ah, come on and take just one ride fer free," I begged.

I found a stout stick for a paddle, climbed into *Success*, pushed her out from the shore, and made a couple passes by the shoreline where they sat with their feet in the water, their wiggly toes attracting minnows. With my cap turned sideways to look like a sea captain, I bellowed out a few orders. "Avast ye mates. Up the mast ye tars. Lean to the starboard thar scurvy sailors." Since Joyce had just finished reading Treasure Island to me, I had picked up on some sailor lingo. She thought me hilariously funny, and that egged me on. "Git below deck ye bilge rats. Trim them thar' sails ye salts." Running out of sailing jargon, I continued, "Shuck that corn ye huskers. Slop them swine ye maidens."

Sue rolled on the bank laughing from my cornball antics. "Stop it, Larry. Yur're crazier than a bed bug." She begged me, between bouts of laughter, to shut up.

"Then how 'bout a ride, Brenda Sue?" I asked.

"Only if'n ya promise ta shut yur trap," she said.

"Cross ma heart," I said.

"Come on, Joyce. Let's take a ride in Larry's old tub," Sue begged.

I sculled to shore, and they climbed in. The boat wasn't big enough for the three of us, so I swam behind, clinging to the back of the boat as I steered the entourage downstream. We drifted through the deeper part of the river which was over our heads. I knew how deep it was, for Uncle Billy once tried to teach me to swim there. The old wives' tale about "learnin' a person to swim by throwin' em into the water" did not work for me.   But there I was, now a nine-year old, clinging to the back of an overcrowded (two sisters and one angel) disaster-waiting-to-happen dinghy.

We drifted past Laney and Tari Peters' property and Tommy Lee's fishing poles. Like a thirsty drunk downing a mug, the boat took on water faster than I anticipated. Concerned, I guided her onto a sandbar for inspection. Joyce and Sue stepped out and helped me upend her to empty the water. Since Dad was away working and wouldn't be home till the weekend, and Mom would eventually miss us and come frantically searching, we decided to hurry back home and therefore dispensed of the ritual of "claimin' and namin'" the sandbar.

Going upstream required much more effort and time. Gripping the back of the boat, I paddled with my feet in the deep parts of the water and waded in the shallow, slowly forcing *Success* upstream. Joyce and Sue just sat there on the little built-in crossbench—after all, they were passengers, not mariners. By the time we cleared the deep part of the river, *Success* had drunk a dangerously amount of water. In fact, she looked more like a submarine than a ship. Joyce and Sue, their glee turned to grousing, reluctantly turned to salvaging the ship. Sandwiched somewhere between hysterical laughter and laconic hyperboles, not to mention fear, and a smidgen of self-effacing stupidity for getting into this situation in the first place, they bailed water with their cupped hands, but they couldn't keep up with the leaks.

Mom overheard the commotion and came running. She stood on the bank yelling her overused phrase, "Y'all just wait 'till yur daddy gits home and hurs 'bout this! He'll skin yur hides." Skin your hides was her most threatening line! I hated that line.

"We're funnin', Momma. No need ta worry none," I assured her.

Joyce and Sue, hiking their skirts from the water, waded to shore. We had survived again, without disaster. Some folks don't believe in angels and miracles, and such. They call it luck. I have reason to believe in divine intervention, for no one could be that lucky.

By the time Dad got home, Mom had settled down and was so glad to see him that she never got around to telling him about the boat incident. Plus, I made a lot of promises, and she didn't have to remind me about chores the rest of the week.

I contemplated taking *Success* on a longer run down the North Fork to the Kentucky River, then north to Carrollton, where the Kentucky River emptied into the Ohio River. I did some research and became excited about sharing this important trivia of the North Fork.

"Do ya know ar' river runs inta the Ohio River?" I asked Mom and Dad one evening.

"Of course," they answered nonchalantly.

That answer almost made me mad, especially the way they said it, like maybe only dumb hillbillies didn't know that. All these years I thought our river was just another unimportant creek, like Lick Branch or Big Branch. But all the while, our river made its way northwest across Kentucky and fed into the Ohio River. A long way from there, sandwiched between Ohio, and then Illinois, it ran into the Mississippi River, and down to New Orleans and into the Gulf of Mexico. I could've boarded *Success* from our riverbank and traveled all the way to Europe without stepping on shore. Had I known that earlier, I might have been tempted to make the journey. If born in another time, I could have joined up with Colonel Jackson and fought the British at New Orleans, or gone up the Mississippi with Lewis and Clark to explore the Northwest Territory, and maybe have been one of their interpreters—considering my ancestry had some Indian blood. I might have met up with Tom and Huck and caused their book to be completely revised—*The Adventures of Tom, Huck, and Larry*. But I knew I would have to go alone, for Joyce and Sue no longer trusted me or my boat.

Chapter Twenty-six

Rebel

Like one of the mamy miracles in the wilderness, I escaped, unscathed, Dad's wrath for cutting up his lumber. Evidently, he reasoned I was only trying to help, and therefore I wasn't guilty of any wrongdoing, especially since he hadn't gotten around to building our boat. What I didn't know, but learned much later, he was simply waiting for the lumber to cure. I remember nothing Dad said about that incident; I guess he viewed it as water under the bridge. To this day, I can't recall his reactions, as if there weren't any. Now, I can only speculate as to why he didn't whip me? In fact, I can only remember him whipping me once, not for something I did, but for something I refused to do.

I was growing up and hinted of more freedom, like spending as much time as I wanted playing marbles with the fellows. But Dad said growing up meant more responsibilities to go along with more freedom, so he gave me a few extra chores. One such chore consisted of walking a half-mile to Grandma Emily's house to fetch a gallon jar of warm, fresh milk, squeezed by Grandma's strong and calloused fingers, from a docile Maude. We did not call it Grandpa Charlie's house, though it was his, too, but we called it Grandma's house, for she ruled the roost and did the milking. After Grandpa's heart attack, Grandma became protective of him stirring around too much. Grandpa mostly sat in his rocker thinking up sermons to preach at the Sunday meeting, while Grandma busied herself with all the chores of their small farm.

Some of the other grandkids affectionately called my grandma "Big Mommy," while they called their own mothers "Little Mommy." This came about because my cousin, Barbara, as a child, called our grandma Mommy, and she called her own mother by her first name: Georgie. But Aunt Georgie didn't like her daughter calling her by her first name, so Grandma Arrowood came up with a solution.

"Call yur real mommy, 'Little Mommy,' and call me 'Big Mommy,'" Grandma instructed. The name stuck. But my family always called her grandma. I think because Mom refused the title of Little Mommy. She was particular about some things, and that, evidently, was one of those things.

The name, Big Mommy, seemed appropriate, for Grandma was strong both physically and emotionally. She raised twelve children of her own, buried one baby, and raised a few of her grandchildren. She cooked three full meals a day, a truly *Cracker Barrel* spread before there was ever a *Cracker Barrel* franchise. I suppose that's why I enjoy *Cracker Barrel* so much. Along with raising kids, Grandma raised a garden, quilted, read her Bible daily, and wrote poetry. Though her formal schooling ended after the third grade, still, she expressed herself quite well. Here's one example, copied as she wrote it, misspelled words and all.

I've left at last the downward way
For night has changed to smilin day.
I've heard the call of love devine
And now true peace and joy are mine.

I'm facin home and lif is brite
For on my sol shines loves true lite.
I'm safe at lass I've ceased to roam.
Christ holds my hand I'm facin home.

What precous years I lost in sin.
How sad I was, how staned within.
But, prase the Lord, I'm his today.
And singin on the homeward way.

I know He will keep what's his own
How saf am I with God's great son.
He'll kep me true by saving grace.
Until I meet him face to face.

Grandma seldom missed a Sunday meeting and always had "a testimony fur ma good Lord." She braided the girls' hair and did laundry on a scrub-board. She slopped the hogs and milked the cow—twice daily. Still, she ended each day in prayer with Grandpa. Theirs weren't now-I-lay-me-down-to-sleep token prayers; rather, they were full-fledged hallelujah prayers that rocked the gates of heaven with names and needs. The prayers she and Grandpa prayed nightly, kneeling by their bedside, brought a holy hush to an otherwise bustling household.

After his sickness, Grandpa mostly sat and rocked, reading his worn Bible, asking if the next meal was about ready, inviting any neighbor that might just happen along at mealtime to "come set and have a bite ta eat," and waiting on the evening prayer meeting. Grandma wanted it this way, cause Grandpa needed his strength for preaching, and boy, could he ever preach.

We'd best get back to the one whipping Dad gave me. It had to do with my refusal to go to Grandma's house and get our daily ration of milk. For reasons that Dad rejected, I still refused to go.

"Late in the evenin' the shadows uf the settin' sun and hund'erds uf noises I kain't see scare me half to death," I pleaded. "So, I ain't goin' by myself ta git milk," I protested.

It was that simple: I flat out refused to go. Period. But it wasn't that simple to Dad, and all statements in our house didn't end with a period. Dad followed me as I retreated to my bedroom, and he told me one last time, "I need ya ta go git the milk." Or at least I thought it was the last time. I also thought he was asking—wrong again.

I stuck to my emphatic "No! Ain't goin' a'tall."

He whipped out his belt like it was a six-shooter and unloaded the entire cylinder across my backside. Then he said again, "I need ya ta go git the milk?"

I went.

After Doctor Spock, there are modern questions to consider about such obsolete parenting. Did it leave me with a subliminal bitterness? Did his raw-parenting ways bring lasting emotional harm? I've formed my own opinions, like, the fresh warm milk we had for supper that night diluted my venom somewhat, and the sense of accomplishment in completing my chore eased some stubbornness. The whipping might have left a wee tiny emotional scar for a few hours (which served as a deterrent the next time I considered doing things my way), but that was miniscule compared to the ruined life my unchecked rebellion could have brought. In retrospect, I could have become a redneck rebel had not Dad beat the tar out of me. Even today, when I see a couple of long-haired, muscle shirted, chain smoking, unshaven, drug-induced psychos in a pick-up truck sporting two Rebel flags, I give them a thumbs up. Not that I believe in their cause; rather, it's a thumbs up to my daddy for thumpin' my back side 'til the lights came on in my head.

I struggled trying to figure out why he didn't whip me for wasting his lumber, yet he beat me to kingdom come for refusing to go fetch a jar of milk. I guess it had to do with the crime: the former was ignorant wrongdoing with good intentions, while the latter was insubordination.

Oh, by the way, Dad finally got around to building us a boat, so we didn't need my skiff anymore. The flooded North Fork probably carried it away to who knows where. I still have an affinity for boats. I've owned a couple in my lifetime besides the one I built, but I never quite acquired the skills to make it safe for me to be on the water. I kept forgetting to put the drain-plug into my motorboat. And my sailboat?

I purchased it for fifty dollars from a Boy Scouts troop. I suppose that explains why it didn't work out well. And of all people to be in the boat with me on a major mishap? It was my dad. He should have whooped me back yonder when he had the chance.

Chapter Twenty-seven

Change

The fifties brought their share of change, not only around the world, but in our small community as well. Still, a couple things in our community seldom changed: the serenity of the landscape and the meandering North Fork. These reserved their tranquility in our Cumberland Plateau.

Our world remained uncluttered. As the census revealed United States cities bursting at the seams with a population of 150 million people, our population shrank. That ought not to have happened since feuding was in decline with the death of my great-great uncle, Captain Bill. And with folks moving away to the north and causing our population shrinkage, we were certainly glad the feuding stopped, else we'd hardly have anyone left. I wonder why the feuding stopped when it did. Perhaps folks quit passing along the vengeance, or maybe they just got tired of the killing. And maybe Grandpa's sermons helped change the tide. Sometimes it takes a generation that is willing to turn the other cheek, that says, "At any cost within reason, this killing must stop." Anyhow, with Captain Strong dead and Harlan Chaney settled down from his need of vengeance, our community appreciated the calm, however short-lived.

Wars still raged in the rest of the world. The Great Wars had not ended conflicts; *in statu quo ante bellum* (in the same state as before the war) described the world scene. Though the landscape of Europe was forever changed—with crosses inhabiting fields where once only poppies grew, and common landmarks, felled by the madness of mankind, would never rise from the ashes—the political power brokers of the world still reflected the same struggles as before the war. Only the powers had shifted. The strife continued. The primary difference, the victims of the last half of the century would be of another race, for bigotry is a heart problem that is not cured by bombs or Bastilles or even treaties: maybe temporarily curtailed or briefly contained, but not cured.

The Soviets, arising as one of the superpowers, downed a United States bomber near their western border over the country of Latvia, escalating the cold war. The Reds invaded South Korea, but the United States forces retook Seoul and pushed them north. Sixteen United Nations countries joined in the fighting, and by September they had pushed the communists north of the 38th parallel. The conflict raged until the armistice in '53 but not until 54,000 American soldiers died in combat.

China, that enigmatic land for millenniums, continued a well-worn political path. Maoism masqueraded as the peoples' choice. Still, London established political relationships. The caldron of the cold war boiled to the point of overflowing.

President Truman, with a philosophy of peace by deterrence, ordered the development of the hydrogen bomb, heading the world in the direction of biblical warnings: mass destruction. Other nations followed, creating a *force de frappe*, hoping to deter agression by the ability to destroy all, but alas, even though everyone could die if this path continued, nuclear stockpiles grew. Russia reigned in the tug-of-war space race. McCarthy launched his campaign against communism, convinced it posed a threat to world freedom, and many were eavesdropping on their neighbors, just in case they might be a communist. Einstein's knowledge had paved the way for the production of the A-bomb, even though he had voiced his concern: "...annihilation of all life on earth is now possible...." Other countries were following suite of the Manhattan Project. Armageddon loomed ominously.

Another intimidating storm lingered, hovering low with the commencement of the mid-century decade—polio. It poised, like a coiled Cobra, ready to unleash its dreadful and debilitating consequences without discrimination. President Franklin D. Roosevelt became a victim—at least they assumed polio at the time. Doctor Jonas Salk brought a welcomed reprieve in '54 with the introduction of his vaccine, caging this monster by decade's end and calming the apprehension of every young bride whose dream included a two-bedroom bungalow and a healthy baby. The discovery offered a calm for us but not for the entire world; their storm continued to rage. Many nations would enter the next millennium still plagued by this debilitating disease—a billion children still needing to be vaccinated.

Our neighborhood experienced some changes: good and bad. We finally got a road. But the road was on the opposite side of the North Fork, snaking its way past us. And the passenger train closed our depot, since the convenience of automobiles cut into its profit. Dad bought his first car in '55—a black '48 Ford. He still couldn't get the car to our house. We would park alongside the road, cross the swinging bridge, and walk the railroad tracks to our house. He finally got around to building boat that would actually float, so we paddled the boat straight across the North Fork at our house. Those were our two options: neither were convenient.

Dad eventually built us a garage on the other side of the river. If Mom wanted something from the garage, she requested, "Delmar, would ya mind takin' the boat and gittin' me a box uf jars from the g'rage? It's 'bout time ta do some cannin'." Thirty minutes later, Dad would return from the garage with the jars, and with a little luck, a mess of fish from the wire baskets and trotlines he kept baited with chicken gut.

Indeed, these were changing times. The school system transferred us again, this time from Quicksand to the newly built school, Marie Roberts, located over by Lost Creek and a stones throw from where it run into Troublesome Creek.

The blue skin Fugate descendants lived up on Troublesome Creek. The abnormality had been going on since somewhere in the early 1800's, but the cure for their blue-tinted skin would not come until the sixties. I never saw one, but they had populated all up and down the Troublesome and Ball Creek before a Doctor Cawain from Lexington would figure out a remedy.

Mr. Deaton and Ida Mae sold the store to Saul and Mary Emily Clay. She became postmaster, or more correctly, postmistress. We never got entangled with the women's lib movement; our women were too preoccupied helping make a living for their families. The passenger train continued to deliver the mail, but the train didn't stop. It tossed out a mail pouch as it passed. A mail truck finally took over delivery, but the mail still had to be carried across the swing bridge.

Uncle Billy became less and less inclined to play games with me and more prone to hang out with the older fellas. Fred developed an interest in girls. The elderly died. Some folks moved away. I still belonged to the secret club, though Mom and Dad didn't know.

Electricity finally arrived. Dad bought Mom an electric stove and a square, aluminum, Maytag washer. He built an addition onto our house. I spent a whole summer painting the clapboard siding. We still lacked a telephone, and television reception remained near zero, which didn't matter to us, for we never acquired a TV. Our outdoor toilet continued to work just fine, so long as we moved it to another location once-in-a-while.

Other things continued pretty much the same. Sidgel Diddle remained a fixture on the front porch of the store. We never did get a bridge for cars to cross the North Fork; instead, we kept on parking on the opposite side of the river and walking across the swinging bridge or paddling a boat across to get to our homes. However, in the summertime, at low tide, we forded the river at Copeland and drove the rutted, dirt road made by mules pulling sleds. Work remained hard to come by, so Dad continued to work way up north. We occasionally collected commodities: cheese, peanut butter, canned meat, and powdered milk. Even today, my senses are stimulated by such memories of those pleasant times of a full stomach and satisfied taste buds. I still crave the taste of the government cheese, and I do on occasion get blessed by a kind soul who knows my secret, but I never acquired a taste for the powdered milk. We were too accustomed to drinking freshly-squeezed milk from Grandma's Jersey cow, Maud (the cow's name, not Grandma's), so powdered milk tasted more like something you took for an upset stomach, especially if your well-water was of a sulfur nature. Ours was, and yet it wasn't. I should explain.

We boasted two wells. The first—no sulfur taste at all—was hand-dug, about four feet across, lined with stone and covered with a weathered, wooden box. A bucket attached to a rope dangling from a rusty pulley, somewhat resembling a hanging scaffold, offered us cool water most of the time. However, the water level got low during hot, rainless summers, so Dad contracted for a modern, machine dug well, with a six-inch metal encasement sunk deep into the ground. The well diggers forded the river at Copeland and came with their machinery and witching wands. They found a vein of water and bored into it. We watched with excitement as the machine rumbled all day snaking out, first dry dirt, but eventually mud—the kind that made fantastic mud pies. Finally, they struck water.

The company owner expressed to Dad, "I wanna go down a few more feet, and I guar'tee we'll hit a vein that'll last till kingdom come. Fer just a few extry dollars," he added. Dad agreed. The machine roared to life again and found a reservoir all right, but it tasted like over-salted, rotten eggs. This water, even when mixed with powered-milk, tasted horrible. Still, even powdered milk mixed in sulfur water tasted better than cow's milk after Maud got carried away in a patch of wild onions. So, the powered milk had to suffice during those times.

It never dawned on us that our lifestyle was destined for change. And it certainly didn't enter our minds that we would ever leave the plateau. How do you leave graves of loved ones to be overrun by briers and brambles? How do you say goodbye to neighbors that have seen you through the toughest times imaginable? How do you give up favorite apple trees and wild-strawberry patches that have sustained your connoisseur tastes for years? But more so, how do you pull up roots that are deeper than wisdom teeth? Such extraction is extremely painful, but sad to say, sometimes necessary. Still, we postponed brooding over the future and kept right on making memories.

Chapter Twenty-eight

The Mail Order

Summer loomed on. News surfaced about the secret club. For some reason the club suspected my allegiance. Perhaps my objection to wearing the mask produced the suspicion. My reasoning? They already knew my identity, so why should I put on the mask? I wondered what names were associated to those hidden faces. I had an idea of their identities but no proof.

A combination of boredom and fear brought my entrepreneurship to the surface. I needed some money in case I had to skip county to escape the club. And I needed a project to endure the timeless summer. Dad warned me not to touch his replacement boards for the boat he was "gonna build someday," and after the licking for my rebellion over the milk incident, I was inclined to obey.

Mom spent her days putting up canned goods for the winter and planning our school outfits. Our *Aldens* and *Sears and Roebuck* catalogs bore marks of frequent use, though more from perusing than ordering. But Mom made out an annual order, especially since we were going to the new school, Marie Roberts. Everything there was new, and Mom wanted to help us fit in.

She sealed the envelope with satisfaction, fussed because we left dirty fingerprints on it (as if those prints might identify her as an untidy mother), and marked the Norman Rockwell illustrated calendar hanging on the living room wall to keep track of the order. The next day she made her way to the post office where she and Mary Emily discussed the order at length.

We eagerly anticipated the arrival of our mail ordered clothing. Seldom did my new Levi's fit; however, that was more purposeful than in error—Mom hemmed the pant legs about three inches and let them back out as I grew. But my growth scaled on the slow side, so the jeans sometimes wore out before I grew out of them. I still have my silver-studded, western jacket with rhinestones, made by Farah of Texas. The company, started by a Lebanese immigrant family in the '30's, exists still. The jacket must be nearly seventy years old. Mom bought it second hand in '55. Counting myself, and the stranger who first purchased it, the jacket survived eight owners. I'm waiting on my great-grandson to grow into it. I'll probably need to shine up the rhinestones.

In the '50's in our neck of the woods we got embarrassed when our denims faded, but now real styling requires the faded look. A tear was mended; a hole was patched. Dressing us well remained high on Mom's priority list. So, ordering school outfits was a big ordeal to her—and us. She seldom expressed affection, but we sensed it in the sacrifice she made for us; conversely, she rarely bought for herself.

Mom didn't know about it, but that same summer I filled out my own order for twelve cases of White Cloverine Salve advertised in *The Grit*, or some other such magazine. It was a tough choice between Charles Atlas' "twelve easy steps to a masculine figure" or twelve cases of miracle salve. But since Mr. Atlas' program promoted self-esteem—a word a nine-year-old wasn't motivated by in the fifties, though the picture elicited a sneak second peek—I opted for the miracle salve, for it would make me money, perhaps even exceed the dollar-an-hour minimum wage law the government had passed but didn't necessarily make its way into our community. As a case in point, Dad hired Greenberry Turner, after Greenberry had retired as mail carrier, to help remodel our house for three dollars a day.

I set my sights on money more than muscle for some reason I have long since forgotten, though I still owed Dad for the sawn up boat gunnels. In fact, I had already sold my new $39.95 Schwinn Tornado Christmas bike to Lloyd King for fifteen dollars and a box of marbles, but that still wasn't enough money for my plans. To my consternation, Mom and Dad got awfully upset with me for selling my bike. They thought for sure Lloyd had used some power ploy, even though I told them he hadn't.

"Lloyd hain't threatened ya, has he?" Mom asked.

"Nope."

"Ya don't hav' ta be afraid uf Lloyd," Dad said.

"I ain't afraid uf him, and besides, he's ma friend," I assured them.

I sold the bike because I wanted money, and I waited anxiously on my salve, so I could make more money. I visited the post office daily. When a huge box addressed to me finally came, Mary Emily questioned me in front of the whole store.

"What ya got ther', Larry?"

"Nothin' much," I said.

"Shore is a big box uf nothin' much." She grinned.

I think she had an idea to jump-start my business. A few folks gathered around, ever so curious. I wanted to hop onto a wooden pop crate and give my first sales pitch for my miracle salve, but a case of the shies prevented me. I hastily retreated home instead, barely able to manage the heavy package but eager to inspect its contents.

The miracle salve arrived before I had gotten up enough nerve to tell Mom and Dad or had saved enough money to pay for it. Boy, were they upset when they found out—even more so than me selling my bicycle. To make matters worse, I had failed to read the fine print from the magazine advertisment. Each case contained twenty-four tins of salve. With twelve cases, that was two hundred eighty-eight tins to sell. Considering the neighborhood households (excluding my family and maybe Sidgel Diddle, whom I assumed wouldn't purchase one) in easy walking distance for a traveling nine-year-old salesman, my potential sells numbered about ten. My calculation had been right for twelve tins, with ten neighbors buying one each, Mom buying one, and giving one to Sidgel. But selling two hundred eighty-eight tins presented a major problem. The magazine advertisement suggested one tin of salve, with normal use, would last a year. So, if each family bought one every year, and I gave one away each year to Sidgel, it would take twenty-four years to sell them all.

After a few days of door knocking and giving my sales pitch, I realized most everyone already had salve I got more than a little discouraged, especially since Mom refused to buy more than one tin, with no promise for the next year. I was beginning to think I should send the whole lot back but held out in hopes a lot of neighbors got into some chiggers, or a patch of poison ivy, or a beehive. If so, surely, they would need a few extra tins of my miracle salve. But there were few casualties that year, and the hot summer days proved rough on my salve—the contents tended to liquefy in the hot sun as I hauled the boxes of tins around the community. I concluded the company wouldn't take them back in that condition, sells tapered off drastically, and worst of all, I didn't make enough money to pay for them.

Bankruptcy wasn't an acceptable option in our part of the country, and lawyers didn't advertize on giant billboards like it was the Christian thing to do, so I just kept receiving threatening letters from the salve company. I knew any day they would show up to confiscate the unsold salve and haul me in handcuffs off to jail. Mom warned, "It serves ya right, orderin' them salves without tellin' me." I stashed the remaining evidence underneath the house. I'm not sure why my parents didn't insist I send back the unsold containers. Dad muttered something about, "Them people aught'a know'd better'n ta send twelve cases uf salve to a kid without his parents' permission."

I haven't heard from the salve company for over sixty years, though I do find a Cloverine tin occasionally at some antique store. I get a mixed sense of nostalgia, guilt, and fear. An approaching clerk causes panic to momentarily overtake me, like I might be trying to steal the tin. The salve company eventually stopped corresponding with me. Maybe the last letter I sent them, with a self-portrait and plea for leniency enclosed, did the job. The letter said something about "cryin' myself to sleep at night." Occasionally, when my melancholic nature sets in, I wonder if my failure to pay what I owed the miracle salve company has contributed to some kind of unconscious character flaw, though I haven't used that as an excuse for any other unpaid debts—at least not yet.

With penalties and interest, if it's like the IRS, my bill could be somewhere near a million dollars by now. I sure hope they never catch up with me, but I sometimes wish, even more so, that I had sold all those tins. Had I sold all two hundred eighty-eight tins and invested the profit in 3M stock these sixty-plus years, who knows, maybe I would be a millionaire by now. And my story could help other nine-year-old kids with an entrepreneur spirit get a wonderful jumpstart in life.

Chapter Twenty-nine
The Fight

The love of money is the root of all evil, so says the wise man of Scripture; further, the lack of money erodes self-esteem—at least that's the way I see it. Both conditions impede emotional maturity. Some rich folks, because they have money, frolic their way through life as if it were a game; while some poor folks, because they lack money, fight their way through life, nursing a grudge. This doesn't mean all who are wealthy are evil; rather, all evil can be traced to a root of greed. Likewise, all poor folks do not lack self-esteem; rather, low self-esteem can be traced to an inordinate sense of lacking—be it money, friendships, good looks, or smarts.

Exceptions exist. Take for example Saul and Mary Emily Clay. They had money, but they hobnobbed with the poorest among us. They were some of the most selfless and caring people in the world—I know this because I spent many a day in their home. Their only child, Gary, and me were good friends. His one lavish perk for being an only child was to have almost every comic book in print—still in mint condition. Books were scanty in my household of seven kids, and they were considerably worn at best. Gary's collection seemed endless and remained flawless. Yep, the Clay's possessed money, but they remained ordinary folks and blended well in our community.

My Uncle Verdie was an exception on the other side of the fence. In contrast to Saul and Mary Emily, Uncle Verdie was raised on fatback and pinto beans. Still, he never met a stranger. Poorer than dirt himself, he could talk to a hobo on the L&N and make him feel good about himself; still, he could talk to the governor and convince him he needed his vote to carry our county. Both the Clay's and Uncle Verdie were exceptions to the rule.

Conversely, Sidgel Diddle exemplified the rule. He was poor, and he was a mite touchy. He sometimes looked like he had just crawled out of a dirty laundry basket and mostly appeared on the defensive, like someone might suggest he should once in a while take his clothes down to the river and wash them. Though his poverty aroused pity in most that knew him, his anger built walls that kept others out and imprisoned him; few people neither dared, nor took the time, to scale those walls. They simply tolerated Sidgel. Further, his misfit mannerisms made him the patsy for a few narrow-minded folks. If a chicken turned up missing, or eggs got sucked dry by a dog, some folks blamed it on "that ornery Sidgel Diddle," whom they viewed as being as much a nuscience as they did an egg-sucking dog.

Sidgel was his real name. Diddle was a nickname made up by hard teasing schoolboys who enjoyed seeing him get mad. Plus, Sidgel and Diddle had a rhyme to it. Though teased by some, Sidgel mostly received our community's goodwill. Preacher Charlie included him in the church membership. But his genealogy carried a Melchizedek enigma to the younger folks—none of us seemed to know his roots.

A more benevolent family gave him a place to sleep. They lived along a bend of the river, a couple miles downstream from us. If you followed the train tracks north, you eventually came upon their place. Mary Emily gave him pickled bologna and crackers sometimes. Others saw to it that Sidgel had clothing. But the one thing the community couldn't quite help him with was his anger—he could get angry quicker than a mosquito bites.

My Uncle Billy epitomized the contrast to Sidgel. He always dressed in crease-pressed pants, his wavy hair freshly combed, and smelling like he had just crawled out of an Old

Spice bottle. Billy was a fun-loving uncle to hang out with, whether killing frogs with homemade spears, or laughing it up with his peers. So, the warm summer day found him in a jovial mood, laughing and carrying on with the fellows, but Sidgel Diddle singled out Uncle Billy as the object of his embittered scorn. Sidgel sat there on the front porch of the store eating his pickled bologna sandwiched between crackers, imagining more and more that Billy was making fun of him. Sidgel got madder by the moment.

Maybe there was a time this group had made fun of Sidgel, but this time they were innocent, and as Sidgel walked past them to go into the store, grunting something that sounded more like *et tu Brute* than it did English, young Bernie Haddix yanked on Sidgel's moth-eaten sweater. Sidgel whirled around, and seeing Billy closest to him, assumed a lot, and punched him in the mouth with a wallop like that of a mule-kick. Uncle Billy, caught off guard, and momentarily stunned, was no match for an angry Sidgel. By the time the buzz in his head cleared, Sidgel had retreated into the store for asylum. Mary Emily kept a resemblance of civility inside her store, so Sidgel felt safe, kind of like the cities of refuge that Grandpa Charlie preached about from the Old Testament. The only downside to the cities, you could not leave the city until your name was cleared. Uncle Billy sat on a wooden pop crate, wiping blood oozing from his busted lips, straight as George Washington sitting on his war horse, waiting and thinking: *al-ki*, he thought, *al-ki*—by and by; by and by. Of course, Uncle Billy never knew any of those foreign words, but he definitely thought those thoughts.

Now, I should mention that Uncle Billy had at least one flagrant fault; he was a grudge-bearing sort of fellow. So, he sat there on that crate for what seemed like hours, saying nothing, just thinking hard, until it was time for the store to close. When Sidgel, hoping the way was clear, stuck his head out the door, Uncle Billy didn't say a lot, but the punch of his fist was a facsimile of what he was thinking about saying. The blow caught Sidgel on the cheekbone just under the left eye—making half an inch cut that bled like a stuck hog. Sidgel squealed about the same. The blow knocked him backwards about ten feet into the store, where he bounced off the potbelly stove and slumped to the floor.

Uncle Billy looked down at Sidgel lying there, and with clenched fists and trembling voice, simply said, "Sidgel Diddle, you aught not to have hit me that-a-way. Don't ya ever hit me agin."

Sidgel never did.

Chapter Thirty
The Baptism

We met down by the Copeland ford of the North Fork, instead of the church house, for the annual baptism. The congregation stood on the shore singing Robert Lowry's picturesque hymn:

> Shall we gather at the river?
> The beautiful, beautiful river,
> Gather with the saints at the river,
> That flows by the throne of God

Back then, I couldn't always make sense out of some of the songs. I wondered how far the river had to flow to reach the throne of God. And if at the baptism, should Grandpa Charlie accidentally drop one of the candidates, would they float all the way to God's throne? Maybe this is what caused me to put off baptism as a child, though I must confess I always had a tender place in my heart when it came to church, especially during solemn times such as altar calls and baptisms. Still today, the old hymn by Charlotte Elliott, *Just As I Am*, always grabs my heart, so as a child, my heart was like Play-Doh in the hands of a Leonardo— and that true listening to most all preachers, excluding the snake handling kind. To think that God would accept me as "I was" gave me hope, even though I was a member of a secret society. Then again, maybe membership in the secret society was why I was able to say no to the songs, songs that, like a magnet, tugged at my heart, but somehow, I managed to fight off the urge to go forward during altar invitation. I mentally bargained with God with thoughts like if they sing the verse one more time, I'll go to the altar. And they always did sing the song again, but I reasoned myself through altar call verse after verse. I needed to know His Spirit called me and not just my emotions tricking me. Gripping the slatted, wooden bench with both hands, my knuckles turned white, then blue, I assumed kind of like the blue skinned people up on Troublesome Creek. I knew they couldn't go on singing the song forever, so I fought off the preacher's invitation, and the singing eventually stopped, and the urge subsided, and I felt a bitter-sweet sensation in my chest. I had escaped the moment; in a lifetime, I have never escaped the memory.

Coy Wells was of a different sort: he seemed to get saved every revival. I suppose some folks are more tender to the Spirit's call. Sometime during the meeting, he made it to the altar where he poured out his heart for a good ten minutes as he repented "fer being a child uf the devil." And then he thanked God profusely "fer takin' me back this one more time." He then rushed to the back door of the church and flung his tin of Prince Albert as far as he could. Suspicion abounded that teenage boys waited to retrieve the tobacco— not to suggest that Coy staged the moment—for his sincerity lacked nothing, but that tobacco sure had a hold on Coy. It wasn't long until he sneaked into the Copeland store and bought another tin. The revival always gave him a brief window of freedom from his addictive sin, but it always cost him a tin of tobacco.

Coy was unique, to say the least. He once sent a song he had written about himself and his dog to a recording studio down in Nashville. He affectionately called the song, "Blackie and I," though I doubt he ran it by a proofreader. The company probably lacked a bit in integrity with their promo department, but it sent him back a recording. Since we were one of the few houses that boasted a record player, Coy stopped by to listen to his recording. We excitedly gathered around the player and listened as a piano twanged out the melody to Coy's song. Ours wasn't an expensive record player, so the recording sounded like an irritated cricket caught in the bottom of a tin can, squeaking out the words.

"That's a right good song ther' Coy," somebody assured him.

"Shore is," resounded the rest of us.

Coy nodded his appreciation. "It'll sound a whole lot bet'ern this when they add the fill-in music. Gotta send'em a little more money ta git that done though," Coy explained. Yes, Coy was unique, whether he was writing songs, confessing sins, or getting baptized for the umpteenth time.

I wanted salvation, but I sometimes looked at the wrong person to evaluate salvation's effectiveness. Then again, I belonged to the secret club and the club controlled me like Coy's tobacco obsessed him. The club had its agenda; the agenda certainly conflicted with the teachings of the church—and my parents. I continued to put off baptism "til I wuz worthy," I told myself.

So, once a year, I remained a spectator as converts came for baptism. Like school children lined up at the drinking bucket, or coming in from recess, the converts lined up, hand-in-hand, and waded into the water, singing a song attributed to George H. Allan:

> Oh sinner let's go down,
> Let's go down come on down,
> Oh sinner let's go down,
> Down in the river to pray.

One at a time, Preacher Charlie baptized them. He wasn't a sprinkling preacher; it was all the way under, and some suggested he held some converts a little bit longer if they hailed from a more sinful background. That went against his usual docile nature—you can tell that by the way he hesitated in telling the Thomas brothers to pack up their snakes and skedaddle. But when it came to baptism, Preacher Charlie resembled John the Baptist more than John the beloved. It was a whole lot about repenting and less about how much God loved you.

Customarily, just before he exited the water, Preacher Charlie called out to all of us lining the bank. "Does anyone uf ya out ther' feel yur need fur baptism? Don't let this op'tunity pass ya by," he entreated us.

Silence dominated the riverbank. This was a sincere moment in time, like the star over the stable or the angel lingering at the empty tomb.

"Ya know ya kain't git ta heav'n shy uf baptism, cause the good Lord told Nic'demus that ya gotta be borned agin uf the water and uf the Spirit. We got plenty uf water hur, and the Spirit's a'lingering," Preacher Charlie pleaded to the sinners, me included. I wondered if Grandpa Charlie might be speaking just to me, being his grandson but not yet baptized. All heads bowed in soul-searching silence as he waited.

I knew I needed baptism, especially for my involvement in the secret club and the deceitfulness to my parents, and going fishing without their knowledge, not to mention cutting up Dad's prized lumber. And I wanted to get baptized. But folks might think I was a real bad person if I got baptized, and I didn't want that either. And Mom might ask, "What kinds uf sins you been committin', son?" Of course, I'd have to sin some more by lying my way out of her noose. Seemed like a lose-lose situation to me. "Doomed if'n I don't; doomed if'n I do", I whispered to no one in particular. Mom gave me a sideways glance, and I averted her eyes by closing mine and bowing my head in reverence to the moment.

The sounds around us—birds chirping, a distant car approaching the curve around Bell Davis's house, and the crunch of a heel on a river rock— melded into a stillness you could actually feel. The quiet grew louder until the splashing of water shattered the tranquility as Coy Wells waded in for baptism. It drew no little excitement, except for his wife, Ellen, sister to my Aunt Georgie.

"It's Coy," somebody whispered.

"Agin?" another asked.

"He's been baptized so many times ever' crawdad in the riv'r knows'em," someone purported his wife to have said. I can't verify that statement, but I can vouch for the fact of his multiple baptisms.

Grandpa Charlie, kind as he was, always rebaptized Coy, and always added his name back on the church roll, alongside the same name he had previously scratched. I somehow came into possession of that list. Myself, I never got on the list, for I never did get baptized during the annual event. But it did cause me to spend an hour or so reflecting. I recalled church services I attended where the Spirit moved me to pray, and I thought of services where the carnal spirit moved me to play—especially the snake handling revival and the Bible cussing evangelist. My mind drifted in multiple directions: perhaps an unconscious way to avoid baptism. I pictured Daddy always praying before meals, Grandpa Charlie preaching up a storm every Sunday, and I even thought about Miss Nancy York, with her long, black hair (a bit wavy when she got caught in a rainstorm), dark eyes, and always happy. She must've been baptized to be so happy, I thought. Though I did catch her humming a sad song one time.

A crow cawed in the distance. My wondering mind returned. The baptism service ended. I watched as the participants waded out of the water to handshakes and congratulations from the congregation. Coy was grinning and crying at the same time. Folks patted him on the back and welcomed him back into the fold. He was a happy man, again, at least until his next nicotine attack.

Chapter Thirty-one

The Scare

Mom missed him first. "Does anybody know wher' Doyle is?" she asked.

"Hain't seen hide nur hair uf'em," Joyce answered.

By the time we realized his absence, a couple of hours had passed. Frantic set in rapidly. I searched under the house. Mom ran down to the river's edge and looked for signs of him there. Joyce ran over to ask our neighbors. No one had seen him recently. The community joined in the search. We spread out over the few acres surrounding the house, including bottomland along the North Fork, which reflected the biggest concern.

"Remember when that Lindberg child got kidnapped?" someone spoke up.

"Ever find'em?" another asked.

"Yeah, but he wuz dead. Right sad, ain't it?" the conversation continued.

This was not what I wanted to hear. Doyle had to be all right. "He just has ta be," I said, barely above a whisper. "But wher' in the world is he?"

"Been readin' 'bout some devil worshipers," another concerned but tactless searcher spoke up. "They like ta do human sacer'fices ta ther'gods. Like them phar'ohs uf Egypt in the Bible. That's the cause uf Moses' mother puttin' him in that basket. Lots uf killin' uf babies a'goin' on back then."

'Hain't no devil worshipers 'round ar' commun'ty ar' ther?" someone asked.

"Donno. But shore did have that witch, Matilda, yurs ago. Reckon she could've had some child'ern afore she died. Maybe one uf'um is a witch and's come back ta haunt us," some insightful person added.

The absurdity got more irrational by the minute, and the conversation continued in that vein of thought too long. The volunteers mentioned names and situations and recalled and evaluated as to the possibilities of some sinister plot going on in the community. They made no concrete decision; they just elicited a lot of hair-raising suspicions

The situation grew pricklier as everyone had an opinion, but Doyle was nowhere to be found, and desperation set in. Mom prayed, "Lord Jesus, hav' mercy. Lord Jesus, fergiv' me fer ma sins if'en I'm the cause uf ma young'ens harm. I'm sorry fer not servin' ya like I know'd I should've."

I didn't mind Mom praying, in fact, I liked to hear her pray, but not this way. It sounded too desperate. Too hurtful. Too hopeless. Too self-condemning.

Beulah Mae tried to comfort her. She gave Mom a handkerchief to wipe her eyes and steadied her as she walked through the house praying.

"We'll find'em, Fairlean. Jist ya wait and see," she said.

"We hav' ta find'em, Beulah Mae. Kain't live a thankin' his little body is floatin' somewhere in that muddy river."

Beulah Mae sensed Mom's pain like no other, having lost two children to sickness herself. Mom stood with her during those losses; now she stood by Mom.

I wanted to pray but realized I was a sinner and God was not going to listen to a sinner like me who sought His help only when in trouble. And I had refused baptism. And my unpaid for tins were stashed away underneath the house. I had all but sold my soul to the devil himself by taking the vow and cussing and participating in the secret club's sins. Then it struck me. The secret club … the sacrifice … the blood. Could that be possible?

I ran as fast as I could up the hill. Am I too late? I wondered. Would they really sacrifice a child? Surely not! On up the hill I scurried, darting bushes and jumping over rotten logs strewn along the path. I gasped for air but pressed on to the turn-off for Coffin Rock. I was angry. Afraid. Ashamed. My own chicken-liver cowardice had now come home to roost. It was all my fault, and I'd never forgive myself.

Then I saw them; simultaneously, they saw me. They were all there, in their ritualistic circle. A mass of blood and the remains of a sacrifice grotesquely adorned the center of the rock.

"I'm ganna kill y'all fer this," I screamed.

The club members jumped up like a bolt from the blue just hit them, totally set aback by my conduct. I grabbed a stick as I dashed toward the rock. The first swing, a crashing blow, hit the leader on the side of his head, knocking his mask half off. The second sent a couple flying off the rock.

"Why'd ya do this thang? I hain't told a soul 'bout yur club, and I've done ever thang ya asked 'cept wear one uf them stupid masks." I screamed at them like the possessed Gadarene tomb dweller, and I continued to swing the stick glancing blows, left and right, at whoever was nearest me.

The club members, disarrayed and confused, regrouped and came at me from all sides. They wrestled me to the ground. I struggled and clawed and bit, like a mad dog fighting for its life, but they subdued me. I could only lay there on my back, helpless: whimpering like a beaten dog chained to a tree.

I looked heavenward, beyond the masked faces, beyond the fluffy clouds, beyond the deep blue of the sky. I looked so hard that I could almost picture the face of the Lord. I saw him hanging on the tree with the Roman soldiers mocking Him. His bruised and bloodied face looked so pitiful. I tried to tell Him how sorry I was and how awful I'd been, but I couldn't get the words to come out. Just groans and more pitiful whimpers.

One of the masked members tried to console me. "What's a'matter, Larry?"

"It's all my fault," I cried. "All my fault."

Further struggle proved useless; they held me tightly on the rock. The leader approached with a thick stick in his hand, knotted on the end. He slapped the stick into his open palm over and over as he glared down at me. I closed my eyes and waited. I deserved to die, so I judged myself as harshly as I could, hoping that would ease the ache in my chest. I should've told someone what they'd been up to, but I was too chicken. I could've stopped all this.

The slap of the stick against flesh stopped. My heart pounded. I heard their breathing and mine. Otherwise, silence. The leader finally spoke.

"What'n tarnation's gotten inta you, Larry. You plum gone crazier than a loon."

"Crazy? Crazy? Who's crazy 'round hur?" I screamed. "You're the one done gone and kill't my little, innocent, baby brother. And I hope ta God He don't have no mercy on yur varmint soul."

My words echoed in the ensuing silence. Then the leader spoke again. My body quivered with sorrowfulness as I sobbed with regret. Their grasps loosened a mite.

"What cha talkin' bout?" the leader asked.

"Doyle. Ma baby brother, Doyle. Ya kill't him." I sobbed.

"We hain't kill't nobody," he spoke as if confused.

"Did, too. He's gone missin' and right thar' is the sacrifice." I looked again toward the carcass.

Silence again. Then laughter. My blood boiled. If only I had a pillar like Samson to pull down on their heads and mine, I would gladly do it in a heartbeat, I thought.

"Hain't kill't nobody, Larry!"

"What cha mean?" I questioned.

"Mean just that. Hain't kill't nobody. Just a chicken. Chickens don't got no souls. It hain't yur baby brother; it's just a dead old chicken we stole from a coop last night," the leader screamed at me.

Only then did I notice the chicken feathers tucked in the tops of their masks, just like Robin Hood and his merry men. And a nasty old dead chicken, looked like he'd been run over by a train, tail feathers plucked raw, lay there in the center of the rock.

I thought my heart would explode with joy. I looked to the heavens again. The Lord was still there beyond the clouds, beyond the deep-blue sky, beyond it all. He was there somewhere, and He was smiling down on me. I wanted to scream "Thank ya Lord," but nothing came out. Only tears.

They stood around me like surgeons over an operating table, masked and gawking, with a bit of empathy in their eyes. Seemed they wanted to help from behind those masks, but no one lent a hand. I arose and pushed my way through them. Stumbling along the path blurred by my tears, I ran, fell, rolled end-over-end down the hill but pressed on. My house grew closer. Shouts greeted me, and Joyce ran to meet me.

"Wher ya been? We've been lookin' fer ya ever since we found Doyle," she announced.

"Found Doyle?" I asked.

"Shore did. Curled up in the bott'm uf the cabinet on the back porch. Sound asleep, he wuz."

Chapter Thirty-two

The Music Teacher

Memories of Nancy York surfaced. I tried to get her out of my mind, but she appeared in my dreams. On occasion, my heart leaped as she silhouetted windows of the passenger train. I sometimes saw her face in the eyes of a nurse who came to our school to give us shots. She left wonderful memories, though I felt she, like all the others, had abandoned us. In the end, we represented just another project.

The move to the new school at Lost Creek possessed some advantages: a warm lunch program, a library with all kinds of interesting books, and a music teacher: Miss Circle. The name fit her for two reasons. One, she traveled from one school to another on a rotating basis, somewhat like the circuit riding preachers of yesteryear, making a weekly circle to assigned schools.

Further, her name matched her appearance—or at least we thought so. She measured as big around as she stood tall. She looked more like a ball than a bat, much more a circle than perpendicular. I don't mean to speak disrespectfully, for childhood observations aren't necessarily criticisms; they are merely immature perspectives.

I looked forward to Miss Circle's visits. She cared about us. Kids can tell. She possessed wonderful characteristics, and her personal interest in us excelled her interest in developing our musical skills. Also, she delighted in sharing her Christian faith. She, too, came to save us, but her salvation was a different kind of deliverance than the social workers or politicians.

Her opportunity to share Christ with me came one day while concluding a private trumpet lesson, though trumpets seemed a little out of place in our culture. Most hill people favored stringed instruments, like mandolins, fiddles, guitars, banjos, and jew's-harps, which as a child I thought was "juice harp," perhaps thinking it had to do with playing the instrument with ambeer running out the corner of your mouth. Anyway, Miss Circle asked me a question never asked me before—one on one, that is. "Do you know Christ as your personal Savior?" This one-on-one invitation to prayer was a lot different than when you have ten pews and a water bucket between you and the preacher, and especially when there are others in the room needing Christ worse than you.

Perhaps I should explain the water bucket. In our little, clapboard church, for some unknown-to-children, adult reasoning (and I question if some of the adults knew the reasoning), a bucket of drinking water, with a communal dipper, sat right in front of the pulpit. The dipper was not to pour water into a personal cup; it was your personal cup— and everyone else's. The drinking water, though ice cold when freshly drawn from a well, turned room temperature rather quickly; it also doubled as a swimming pool for all kinds of creepy-crawlers: beetles, centipedes, flies, and such. To get a drink of water, you simply walked to the front of the church, swiped away the critters, dipped the dipper into the water, and while slurping down the tepid water, stared up at the red-faced preacher thumping the pulpit or waving his Bible. We assumed he was red-faced from preaching; surely, it had nothing to do with us standing in front of the pulpit staring at him as we slurped down water. Still, another unknown-to-children adult reasoning was that the longer we stood drinking from the water bucket, the redder his face got, like he seemed upset. But why did they set the water bucket in front of the pulpit if they didn't want us to get a drink once in a while? That's like promoting a thief to bank teller.

It seemed like the preacher eased up a bit after someone

broke the ice by going forward for prayer. Though every once in a while we had an evangelist to whom this was a signal that he had picked up the scent of sinners, and being a hunter of the hell-bound, he determined to sic the bloodhounds of heaven on our trail. But usually, a sinner going forward meant that the rest could mostly watch, where before, you stared at the floor, or concerned yourself with an upside down centipede on the ceiling, hoping he didn't fall into the drinking water. Or you noticed that your fingernails needed cleaned. Sometimes you closed your eyes as if in contemplative thought and stared at the multicolored images floating on the backs of your eyelids—hoping that you did not have some incurable eye disease.

"Larry, do you know Christ as your personal Savior?" was a one-on-one pointblank question that demanded a yes or no answer. Miss Circle surprised me with her question.

"I kinda got saved at a revival once," I said. The "kinda" was the caveat that made the statement partially true. I had walked to the front of the church during the invitation to accept Christ. It was a sincere and moving moment, but like Coy Wells, my experience faded with time and temptation. Miss Circle was now asking me to get saved. Strangely, my emotions had callused a bit over the years.

I wanted to go into my eyeball stare, but she caught me off guard. I didn't even have time to check my nails. I knew about Christ, for Dad took me to church every weekend he was home from jobs that sometimes were a long way from home. And I somewhat resented that he didn't make time to take me fishing but always had two or three hours to take me to church. But somehow, I knew Miss Circle entertained a much more serious answer than one about church attendance. She challenged me to consider that realm I seldom ventured into, except during revival meeting time, or when an unconfessed sin crept into my dream as a huge, hairy monster dragging me, with fanged grip into a fiery furnace finality. I knew what she asked. Had I ever walked to the altar and confessed all my secret—and not so secret—sins and professed that I accepted Christ to take them all away? Had I experienced Christ through baptism? And had I let Christ's Spirit come to live in my heart? I never had, though I dreamed about it occasionally—dreams about getting saved left me with such a contrasting feeling compared to my hellion, monster dreams.

I played church many a time: it's a childhood thing we did, imitating (but not necessarily making fun of) adults. Often, I preached the sermon and gave the invitation. I especially liked to stare red-faced at my peers who dared take a drink during my sermon. You can do this if you hold your breath long enough. Even though I felt a little saved playing church, something inside told me it was a game that didn't count for real, though we were pretty good imitators.

Miss Circle wasn't playing chhurch. Her invitation to experience Christ remains vividly etched in my memory.

"Would you like to pray now or later?" She asked.

I opted for later.

Chapter Thirty-three

Underneath The Old Apple Trees

I wouldn't say I didn't like school; I simply liked my summer break more. For some, summer nostalgia is reminiscing about sitting along the third base line at Cincinnati's old Crosley Field; for others, it's a vacation to Mackinaw or Coney Island. Not so for me: no trips, no far-away places, and no grand adventures. Still, I have cherished memories of my summers. One such memory is how we spent many an hour underneath the old apple trees that bejeweled our yard in the springtime with fragrant and colorful blossoms, bowed low with apples by mid-summer, and served as a conversation piece all the time.

"How old ya thank she is?" someone would ask.

"Donno fer shore. Must be gittin' nigh on ta fifty yurs," another responded.

"Thank she'll have any apples this yur?" This question always came up. And all appletrees are she's: not he's.

"Donno for shore but no cause to thank differn't," the wise one among us responded.

Our miniature apple orchard was our version of the Roman Forum or the Athenian Pnyx. Stories were told and retold, changed and told again, all underneath our apple trees. Philosophies were formed and futures were fashioned as we lazily endured the dog days of summer. With heat and humidity contributing to boredom, many a tale, and some secrets, surfaced underneath these trees.

One of the factors that contributed to the monotony of summer was that Mom seldom allowed us to go swimming.

This was due to "just havin' eatin' and you'll git cramps and drown," or "the water's muddy and if you get it in your mouth it might cause an infection," or a hundred other reasons she'd come up with to assail her fears of us drowning. And she certainly didn't allow swimming during dog days. Mom reasoned, "If ya step on a piece of glass hidin' under the water and cut your foot, ya might go mad, just like a mad dog."

I think the dog-days' superstition was just another timely excuse because of her obsessive fear of water. It was a legitimate fear, for she had been taken under as a child and almost drowned, leaving her borderline thalassophobic— petrified of water. So, we lingered in the shade of one of the old apple trees, playing marbles or Chinese checkers, and praying that a mad dog didn't bite us, and hoping against hope, that some major adventure came our way.

Maybe that's why on no particular day, my brother, Roland, and I climbed on top the chicken-coop beside one of the apple trees—certainly a mad dog couldn't bite us up there. In addition, the height revealed a different perspective of the world around us. Our imagination grew keener from this pinnacle. The Alamo came alive with Davy Crockett clutching his flintlock and Jim Bowie sharpening his blade. It's amazing how BB guns and paring knives are transformed from the summit of such a vantage point. Then again, we savored these moments because they gave us easy access to the tantalizing apples dangling within arm's reach.

"Jim, y'all take the first guard and we'll take the last'n'," I said. We pretended as if we were the true characters of that ill-fated battle at the Alamo. "I'll fire one shot if'n it's Indians and two shots fer Mexicans," I continued.

"What'll ya do if'n it's Japs?" Roland asked.

"Wern't no Japs back then. They weren't borned yet," I said. Roland's knowledge surprised me, but then again, we wern't that far removed from the war daddy fought in.

We oiled our BB guns and took target practice, taking aim occasionally at a Cardinal. But Daddy had warned us, "Don't kill no Cardinal cause it's ur state bird." So, we just aimed at them, but accidents do happen, especially if you have a hair trigger.

Hours spent lounging under the apple trees weren't a waste of time, especially since apples were nutritional. We lived far enough away from Doctor Lewis' office in Jackson that our life gave new meaning to the saying "an apple a day keeps the doctor away." But every once-in-a-while we over did it on the green apples and wished Doctor Lewis would drop by—he never did. And Mom never took us to Doctor Lewis for overeating green apples; instead, she gave us castor oil.

We were in the habit of salting our apples, so we had sneaked a saltshaker from the kitchen and were enjoying the salted apples by the dozen. With my stomach stuffed and just minding my own business, for some unknown reason, the Morton "when it rains it pours" iodized saltshaker spoke to me. It wasn't an audible voice like a teacher or such, but a silent voice in my mind—kind of like I envisioned Grandpa Charlie sometimes hearing from the Lord.

"What makes me salty?" little Miss Morton, under her salt-soaked umbrella, asked me.

"I donno," I answered.

"Whad'ya say?" Roland asked.

"Nuthin'. Jist talkin' to myself" I said.

To be honest, I had never given much thought to what makes salt salty, so that saltshaker startled me, kind of like a rattle snake protecting it's turf, striking out without warning. I didn't have an answer. So, I pondered the query for a while and came up with an idea. Why not do some experimentation with salt? That's how Thomas Edison, Louis Pasteur, and others figured things out, or so said my elementary teacher at Marie Roberts. I didn't know how long it had been since

Mr. Edison came up with his invention of the lightbulb, but it took us a good while before we got electricity and was able to use his lights. And boy, did flipping a switch beat trimming a wick. And what a consolation Mr. Pasteur gave mothers when he discovered pasteurized milk prevented some common sicknesses associated with milk. But our milk, squeezed fresh from ole Maude, wasn't pasteurized, so we were still in danger. But the milk they served us at the new consolidated school was pasteurized. Teachers told us it was better for us, and we could buy a morning carton for two cents, which Mom always made sure we had. We were told un-pasteurized milk could cause diseases such as meningitis and tuberculosis, both of which our neighbors had. Still, that didn't deter us from drinking Maud's fresh milk. I never gave it much thought until a teacher told the class that Mr. Pasteur figured out if you heated milk to about a hundred and forty-five degrees for over thirty minutes and then chilled it quickly enough to about fifty degrees, the harmful, disease-causing bacteria, died. Mr. Pasteur found all this out by experimenting; no one told him, he figured it out himself. So why not experiment with salt?

My knowledge of salt was limited, though Aunt Fannie told me "If'n ya sprinkle salt on the tail feathers uf a bird, you kin tame it." I tried often but could never get close enough. Though unsuccessful, I still wondered how salt did that. Now here I was again, pondering the mysterious qualities of salt: wondering about what makes salt salty. It looked like sugar or sand, but sugar tasted sweet, and the sand along the North Fork lacked taste altogether. Oh, the wonder of salt!

"Wanna help me some, Roland?" I asked.

"Shore. Whadda I hav'ta do?" he asked.

Since he'd shed his diapers, Roland had followed me around. So I figured he wouldn't mind helping me a little with my experimenting.

"Close yur eyes real tight like and open yur mouth real wide," I said.

"What fur?" he quizzically asked.

"Fur a sper'ment. Don't you want ta help me out with a sper'ment?" I challenged him and shamed him for his lack of cooperation.

"What's a sper'ment?" he asked.

"It's how ya figure out thangs," I said.

Reluctantly, Roland opened his mouth.

"Wider!" I instructed.

"Kain't open any wider!"

He gave it a six-years-old's best shot.   I quickly unscrewed the bottom of the saltshaker and dumped the entire amount into his mouth. His eyes popped open; his face turned rather reddish, then bluish, and for some reason he just stopped breathing. I asked him if it might be the salt. He said nothing. I suggested he start breathing; he just sat there, like Lot's wife, stone still, mouth agape, just staring at me with his big, blue, naive eyes. I figured I better get Mom.

"Momma. Kin ya come out hur fer a minute?" I yelled.

Mom came running. By this time Roland had started breathing again, but the gagging continued a full five minutes, or so it seemed.

Mom compassionately, but suspiciously, inquired, "What'n the world wuz you a tryin' ta do ta yourself, Roland?"

Roland didn't say a word. Maybe he thought he would get into trouble for wasting good salt, or for being on top the chicken coup. Though feeling a bit guilty and a nudge to confess the whole ordeal—although Roland didn't seem too upset, and after all, he was a cooperating participant—silence won out. We just left Mom wondering. I never listened to Miss Morton after that.

Chapter Thirty-four

God's Gift

Winter is God's gift to children. There surely can be no other logical reason for it. Not so for adults. For them, it's shoveling snow, jumping car batteries, and scraping ice off windshields—all things they despise doing. For children, it's a wonderland of snowball fights, angel making, ice-skating, and sledding—not to mention some cancellations of school and the longed-for Christmas break.

And so that's how it was for us in the Cumberland. When the snow started falling, we started praying they would cancel school. Sleep comes hard when wondering if the snow is still falling—by morning, whether canceled or not, we were too exhausted to go to school. Six inches guaranteed a snow day. Three inches caused a stomachache until after the school bus passed. How amazingly swift we recuperated from sickness when snow covered the ground!

But the most wonderful thing about winter was the making of snow cream. When the snow started falling, we knew that snow cream wasn't far behind.

Snow cream predated Wendy's frosty like the dinosaur predated history. Wendy's eventually made the frosty possible any day of the year; winter made snow cream possible when Dave Thomas still wore diapers. Maybe that's where he got the idea for his frosty—from snow cream. Now, I'm not sure about Dave's recipe, but our snow cream consisted of a combination of sugar, canned milk, vanilla flavoring, and a pinch of salt, all mixed into a huge bowl of freshly fallen snow. And if you added chocolate, you had a facsimile of the Mr. Thomas' chocolate frosty.

Mom demanded we "Bundle up ta keep warm," before we headed outside with a washbowl to retrieve some snow.

"With yur Daddy way up north, if'n you take sick, I kain't git ya to Doc Lewis," she always warned.

And we surely didn't want to catch a cold, for at the first sign of a sniffle, Mom rubbed us down with warm camphor oil and forced Vicks salve up our noses. But our ordeal was a far cry from what our cousins went through. Their mother, our Aunt Marie, made them swallow the Vicks. It's people like Aunt Marie who probably caused some of the ridiculous labels we now read on children's products, like what I read on a bottle of cough medicine for children: Warning! Do not drive a car or operate heavy machinery after taking this medicine. As if a five-year-old needs warned about the dangers of falling asleep at the wheel! Or what about this one? Warning! Do not use snow blower on roof. Yes, sir, Aunt Marie was the culprit for such nonsense.

Knowing the penalty for getting sick, especially since Mom respected Aunt Marie's wisdom, and since Aunt Marie chaired a one-woman campaign insisting that swallowed Vicks worked better than Vicks smeared on your chest or stuffed up your nose, we readily complied with Mom's strict dress code of buttons buttoned all the way to the Adam's apple and hats pulled down over the ears.

We resembled Humpty Dumpty as we scurried outside and gathered snow to make snow cream. We scooped it off the porch banister and fence posts. We ladled it from off the well box and railroad tracks. What a tough decision whether to make snowballs to throw or to gather snow to go into the bowl for our snow cream. We generally did both. Once inside, we quickly mixed the necessary ingredients into the snow cream before it melted. What a treat! We lapped it up like pigs eating slop—kind of like the all-you-can-eat smorgasbords of today. Only better!

Perhaps the reason God chose to come to earth that first Christmas during wintertime was His way of showing that winter is God's gift to children. Now, I'm not sure we can biblically prove Christ was born during the winter, but can you imagine the children's Christmas lines otherwise: "And the shepherds came and found the babe, lying in a manger, stark naked, for the Judean night was too hot and sticky for swaddling clothes." Not good! God chose winter as the logical time for the Christ child. What better time could there have been? Swaddling clothes and snow cream! God's gifts, especially for kids!

Chapter Thirty-five

The Flood

With Christmas toys already broken, and no snow in sight, and with months to go before the Easter break, there seemed little to look forward to. Since we wouldn't have another revival or baptism until summer, we needed a change from the mundane. Well, we sure got it in the winter of '57.

This was a change we didn't anticipate. It came without warning. We didn't have the convenience of a meteorologist, though we had The Old Farmers' Almanac. But the almanac gave us generalities, not specifics: when to plant and harvest, when to fish, and when to expect dog days and Indian Summer. Of course, being a Christian community, we shied away from the Zodiac emblems. Still, we had our supertitions.

So, without a weather report, we wore a raincoat because it was raining, not because a weatherman said there was a fifty percent chance of rain. While truth dollars were fighting communism through Radio Free Europe, going behind the Iron Curtain and incriminating the Kremlin, we could barely get radio reception for the weather report in our community. And that sometimes caught us off guard.

It should have been a blizzard in January; ironically, it was rain: a Noah's day kind of rain. The flood took us by surprise. In retrospect, we call it the flood of '57. It was the same year Chevrolet "flexed its big, new muscles with the Sweet, Smooth, and Sassy" model. These vehicles became defining masterpieces in the coupe, sedan, and convertible. What a winning combination for Chevrolet; what a catastrophic year for us! The rain just wouldn't stop. At first it created conversation, like that year's Edsel, with "…

the same air of elegance, the same look of superb ability...,"
but as the water crept higher, and the rain kept coming,
conversation turned into concern. And just as Bing Crosby
and Frank Sinatra could not prevent the future sinking of the
Edsel, even with their "song and dance, live Edsel Show"
on CBS-TV, neither could we prevent the rising waters that
would sink all our futures.

This became the first weather catastrophe for my
family, though quite predicted by Dad. Dad had dissuaded a
potential purchaser from buying a piece of property owned
by Sid Allen. He convinced the buyer that the North Fork
would someday flood the house. The day the buyer backed
out, Dad bought that same piece of property, which included
a two-bedroom house, a chicken coop, smoke house, and
a one-seater outhouse (later made into a two-seater). Dad
wasn't "saved" just yet—that wouldn't come until after his
purchase, so his ethics were still a mite on the questionable
side. And he had quite a gambling reputation—Mom had
not saved him from that just yet, though she would, with
threats of using an iron skillet over his head. She actually
saved him from gambling before Jesus saved his soul. But
his gamble on buying the house was a poor hand, for Dad's
predictions of that "someday flood" had come true.

It rained almost continuously for some sixty hours.
The flood crept up the banks like a cat stalking a Blue Jay:
deliberately and relentlessly. Uncle Billy and I spent the
day checking our homemade water gage: a wooden stick
notched to indicate inches and stuck in the ground at the
water's edge. We kept a vigil on the rising water. Johnny
Cash's song, *Five Feet High And Rising*, would come along
a couple years later. We would have already lived it.

Dad was "way up north" working, but Uncle Verdie was
home, so he took charge. He went to Grandpa Charlie's to
borrow his mule and sled so he could move our furniture to
higher ground.

"Come to barr'y ole Jack," Verdie announced.

"What fur, son?" Grandpa responded.

"Need ta git Fairlean's furn'tur moved affore the water raises inta the house."

"Don't thank that's necessary, Verdie." Grandpa balked. "Hain't got that high since '37. No need ta thank differ'nt this time," he said, shaking his head. "I don't thank it's gonna flood that much."

Grandpa stuck to his gut instincts. Either he truly felt the water wouldn't get in our house, or he thought it would do less damage than Uncle Verdie turned loose with his mule. Anyhow, he refused to loan ole Jack to Uncle Verdie.

We went to bed that night in hopes the morrow brought sunshine. It didn't. Darkness fled the dawn of another glowering sky—more rain. Bill and Ida Deaton had slept calmly throughout the night, as if their house was a boat, secure from rising water. They awoke to a whooshing and tapping in their bedroom. Throwing back the covers, Bill bolted upright in bed, scared that someone was in the house. When his feet touched the floor, he realized it was wet. Momentarily blaming the dog, he reached for the lamp switch, turned it on, and swallowed down terror, for muddy water an inch deep covered the bedroom floor. The sound he heard was the sound of his shoes, floating like twin boats, bumping against the lamp stand.

Billy and Fred had spent the night with Shoog. They, too, awoke to the flooded house, but for them it was to the delight of adventure, escaping out a back window that opened to a hillside which stood higher than the rising water. A neighbor and his boat rescued Bill and Ida Mae out the front door. Ida was too heavy to climb through the back window. Even the boat rescue looked risky.

Reports of devastation squawked across the radio, until we lost power. And we observed such devastation with our own eyes. A house floated down the river, with a rocking chair swaying on the front porch and a rooster perched on the roof. Langley Davison tied a rope to a tree, paddled his boat into the raging current, and attached it to the floating house.

"Hooked me a whale," he yelled across the river to the neighbors.

"Whatcha gonna do with yur whale, Jonar?" someone called back.

"I'm gonna ride it ta Ninever."

"Better watch out or that whale might take ya some place worse than Ninever," another joked.

The rope tightened and the house swung toward the shore. Langley yelled jubilantly as the house bobbled up and down like a cork on a fishing line; the jubilation was short-lived as the rope broke loose, and the top of the house crashed into our swinging bridge, ripping off the roof and tearing our bridge apart. In a matter of a few moments, we were stranded. But somewhere upriver someone was homeless, or worse yet, dead. Being stranded didn't sound so bad in comparison. It's strange how other peoples' sorrows cure your own—immediately.

The Stanley Brothers gave their rendition of the flood in a song they appropriately called *The Flood of '57*. They sang to the melancholic rhythm of guitar, fiddle, and mandolin:

> This was different,
> And we suddenly realized,
> That the flood was raising,
> And we fought for our lives.

Each new day brought more calamities. Langley Davison kept to his rescue efforts. He yelled a constant barrage of messages to us from his side of the river. His voice skipped across the swirling, murky depths like a rock thrown into the water on its flat side. Though out of harm's way, his tone carried a certain element of alarm, and his reports predicted disaster. We interpreted one broken commentary to suggest that a car, left parked on the brim of the road, perilously eluded falling into the river, for the road showed signs of sliding into the raging current.

Considerate as he was, Saul Clay arose to the challenge. He climbed into a boat and pushed off from the bank into the raging current that immediately swept him downstream. Paddling hard enough to beat the water to death, dodging floating trees, bloated animals, and partially submerged logs, Saul finally landed the boat about a quarter mile downstream from where he put in. Staring from the shore, we all breathed a sigh of relief. Langley met him at the car, walking around it and signing like a deaf man, first at the car, then the river, then the sky, back to the car, and across to us. We waited. After they pushed the car to the opposite side of the road, Saul reversed the treacherous crossing. He commented little about the ordeal but simply shook his head in disbelief. We will never know for sure if the car was in danger, but the event, told and retold by eyewitnesses—present, and not so present—remained a lingering controversy. After all, it was Saul's silence against Langley's tall tale.

Langley stuck to his story that if it hadn't been for him, the car would have been swept away. I wondered if it would have gone all the way to the Gulf of Mexico, and if so, what it would cost to retrieve it. Saul, though tempted to refuse Langley credit at his store, felt a charitable responsibility to Langley's wife and five children. When asked about the misunderstanding, for months he still shook his head and refused comment, especially to Langley, who occasionally reminded him of the miracle, since the car wasn't washed away. Saul eventually mellowed a bit but not much. I think he harbored a slight grudge because he had endangered his life over what turned out to be an exaggerated reaction. Such a courageous act is the making of living heroes, but it is sometimes the martyrdom of others. Saul was close to the latter.

Saul, being the good-hearted soul he was, eventually reasoned that "Langley just overreact'd. After all, what fun is it a goin' through a flood if'n ya kain't share the drama with someone. That's like a preacher baggin' a dozen squirrels on the only Sunday he ever skipped church ta go hunting. Only he and God can share it, and it's questionable that God cares." Saul eventually told the story lightheartedly. It was good to see him laughing again.

We lost most all our furniture and all our year's supply of canned goods stored under the house. We moved into an abandoned shack until the water receded. Living on the side of the river opposite the road, we were cut off from most rescue efforts. Sid Allen, who sold Dad the house, and who also worked on the L&N Railroad, helped to orchestrate a train stopping at our community to give us food. Disaster makes us all neighbors.

The Red Cross assisted our community with some disaster relief. A self-appointed informant enlightened the Red Cross representatives as to who should and should not receive aid. Our family somehow made it on the "needs no assistance" list, evidently because Dad had a job. Dad worked hard and long prior to the flood to buy Mom some new furniture. So when goods were given away for free, in the eyes of some, we did not qualify, though we lost almost everything. When Fulton Noble, being a distinguished mason (that's "Freemason" as in funny hats, aprons, and secret rituals, but with some sort of powerful influence in the county), heard about the shenanigans going on, he made a personal trip to Jackson and spoke on behalf of those who were either denied or overlooked aid. Thankfully, we eventually received some assistance. Ironically, some neighbors, who prior to the flood had used furniture, got new; my family, who had new furniture, lost it in the flood, but we were grateful for the new mattresses they gave us.

Grandpa Charlie never did apologize. Though wrong in his decision, he must have felt right about his decision: not loaning the mule to Uncle Verdie. Uncle Verdie reminds me of the flood once in a while. "Ya know," he begins, "yur Grandpa Charlie wuz a purddy good man, but I'll nev'r understand why he wouldn't let me barr'y ole Jack when that flood wuz'a comin'. Yur Mom would still have her furn'ture if'n he had've," as if Mom is still mourning over the loss of her furniture that would now be close to, oh, perhaps Methuselah's age, that is if furniture is like dogs and ages faster than humans.

"And another thang," he always added, "he should nev'r have let them Thomas boys hold that reviv'l. Ya know 'twas yur daddy stopped it, dontcha?"

I answer depending on the mood I'm in—sometimes to hear the story again, for Uncle Verdie is a grand storyteller, sharing details of dates, names, places, and opinions. A negative nod, or silence, quickly brings the story to life—the snakes getting madder and multiplying in number each time he tells it. I miss Uncle Verdie; he was the communicator in the family that kept reunions alive. Now that he's gone, so are the reunions: such a tragic loss.

The river crested at forty feet, six inches. Once the rising water reversed, Mom took a boat and reclaimed our house, scrubbing out the mud as the water receded. She timed it just right so as to use the receding river water for scrub water. It's unbelievable the amount of mud left on the floors of a flooded house. Joyce worked by Mom's side and groused all the while about her irresponsible siblings. That would be Sue and me. Sue sat on the elevated railroad tracks that ran in front of our house, observing like a silent reporter and a camera-less photographer—just listening and watching but nothing to show for it. She still possesses incredible mental pictures of the flood, though she was only five years old at the time. Many families, mine included, lost precious memorabilia; our memories must suffice.

Uncle Billy and I paddled a boat round and round the house like we were in the America's Cup. Of course, we won every race. Since Noah's ark can be a floating barnyard or a floating carnival, we made the catastrophe around us a carousel of fun. We retrieved treasures floating down the river: balls, dolls, and lots of bottles. Surely the bottles were antiques and would be worth a fortune someday. Our biggest catch of the day was a decorative Jim Bean bottle, half full, straight from Bardstown by way of Perry County. Since our county was dry, the boys usually had to cross over the county line to buy booze, but the booze now floated across the line to us.

How strange that government busts small stills but approves large ones! How hypocritical the "healthier and safer for you" lie of the distillery companies. From a certified distillery or from a Cumberland still, liquor gives too little pleasure in return for what it takes. "Safe liquor" is an oxymoron; like, a pet rattlesnake.

Uncle Billy's better judgment kept him from trying liquor again, for he remembered the humiliation over Dad finding him and Fred wallowing in the mud like pigs drunk on sour slop. So, we found a more creative way to use the liquor other than drinking it. My tomcat had lazily occupied the bow of the boat most all day. Uncle Billy coaxed him into his lap, uncorked the bottle, and cajoled him into drinking the Jim Bean. Boy, did it take a lot of cajoling!

What normally was a docile creature, suddenly sprang to life. He let out a tiger yell and jumped five feet into a tree we were passing. He stayed there, like it was Noah's ark, 'til the flood receded. We never could rescue him from his perch.

Mom, out of concern for the cat, solicited an explanation. "What's a'going on with Tom?" she asked.

"Donno!" Uncle Billy said. "He just jumped right inta the tree after a bird, and we're mad as kin be at him fer killing that little innocent thang," I noticed Uncle Billy's hand behind his back, fingers crossed. That makes it okay, he later assured me.

Mom insisted, "He shore is actin' peculiar just settin' in that tree."

"Might be a feather in his throat," I suggested. "Serves'em right." I didn't know at the time to cross my fingers like Uncle Billy had, so I felt a tinge of guilt for lying to Mom.

Dad, still in Michigan, listened anxiously to the news reports of the flood. With no telephone in our community, he could not call; he hastened home that weekend to find the community distraught.

"Reckon we might start lookin' fur another place," he casually commented.

Routine is difficult to escape. We were pulled in different directions and knew we had to someday make a decision about moving. The flood seemed too devestating to remain, but Dad hesitated in making such a call.

Dad left for Michigan a few days later. Too many stood in line wanting his job. That was the way it was. Whether working on a railroad section gang, a "Happy Pappy" project, or way up in Michigan (where his brother had gotten him on at GM), Dad boarded for two weeks and then came home for the better part of two days. Leaving Michigan on Friday evening after work, he arrived home early Saturday morning and left for Michigan on Sunday after church. Trapped between providing for his family and clinging to his Cumberland roots weighed heavily on his mind. He bore a double yoke—the physical burden of hard work to provide for his family and the emotional burden of being absent from his family.

The flood tilted the scales in favor of a change of

location for us. Dad's dreams for our homeplace gave way to prudence. Mom resigned to the move. We kids fantasized about what our new place would be like. We waited. And waited.

And so life continued as it had for years. Birth and death. Joy and sorrow. Good and bad. While Preacher Charlie challenged us on Sundays to "change yur sinful ways," Elvis Presley entertained us on Saturday at the Jaxon Theatre with *Love Me Tender*. We had some decisions to make.

Going Away Party

Chapter Thirty-six

B reathitt county had a long history of patriotism. Ours truly was "the land of the free." We were a part of the land, for the "good book" had told us "from dust thou art and to dust thou shalt return." Our land was the United States of America, so we were Americans to the core. Political correctness be hanged! Canada was Canada, and Mexico was Mexico; we were The United States of America. And when The United States went to war, no matter what for, our community was at war. Young men made their way to Jackson to "sign up." We boasted a high rate of volunteerism into the armed services. During the First Great War, so many sons of Breathitt volunteered that the draft proved unnecessary—the only county in the United States to possess such bragging rights: at least a plaque stands on the courthouse lawn at Jackson as proof.

Kentucky boys may be accused of a lot of things: barefoot hillbillies, revenue-shooting moonshiners, or illiterate rabble-rousers. But let it never be said that they were unpatriotic—never! Dad served in the Pacific Theatre aboard the USS North Carolina. He was present at the surrendering ceremony of the Japanese. Two of his brothers fought in Vietnam. Five of Mom's six brothers served in the army. This was typical of our county. But wars made widows and sent young maidens, like Jephthah's daughter of Scripture, into isolation. My family was fortunate; all returned home safely.

When one of our young men "joined up" to serve his country, the family threw a going away party, with the whole community invited. Uncle Fred joined in '59. Uncle Billy got upset that Fred "run off and joined up" without telling him. It was the first time they had been apart. "We should have joined together," Uncle Billy contended. The army drafted him the next year. Both received assignments in Germany. They were two unknown country bumpkins missed by but a few. Another country boy was just leaving Germany, but his promoters made it a bit different for him. All the world knew when he arrived and when he left. For Billy and Fred, it was a chance for poor boys to travel the world for a song and a dance; for Elvis, it was a chance for the world to idolize a poor boy who transformed both song and dance into a fortune.

The going away party for Billy took place on a Saturday in May of '60. Family and friends came from all around. We downed Kool-Aid, roasted hotdogs, and played games. We welcomed occasions to have parties: bean stringing, hog killing, corn shucking, and such. Local cooperation not only accomplished the task at hand but made it fun in the process. Take for example hog killing time. A hog knows when it's killing time. He knows, for a crowd gathers in. "If'n it wuz only feedin' time" a lone figure would approach with a couple buckets of slop. It's safe, so the hog runs over to the trough "a gruntin' ta beat the band," allowing you to scratch his back and behind his ears. But when a crowd shows up, he knows it's bacon for breakfast they're after. Maybe it's difficult to kill a hog alone. The emotions get involved and one feels a bit inhumane, even though the family needs the sausage and bacon. But let a cheering crowd show up and it's a different story. The scene is sheer drama.

"Bet ya kain't git'em with just one shot," someone calls out.

The hog finds the farthest spot away from the crowd, facing them with his rump, not in disrespect, just wishing they'd go away.

"If'n I don't git'em with one shot, y'all just hit'em in the head with the sled hammer," the shooter responds.

There's a lot of frolicking that goes on at the hog's expense. Someone chases the fattened swine from his hiding place in the corner of the pin. A Kentucky marksman, probably a descendant of Daniel Boone and his long rifle, draws a bead between the pigs pleading eyes and gently squeezes the trigger.

"He's down. He's down. Ya got'em," someone shouts.

"Cut his throat so's he kin bleed," another offers direction.

The hog doesn't have a chance when the crowd shows up. And somehow the hog recognizes calamity in the crowd. So, he keeps hanging out in the corner, but soon the crowd uses the corner to their advantage, gathering around him like vultures to a kill, shouting until he runs into the open, and cutting off his retreat back into the corner.

Further, it's more than a one-man-job for "scaldin' and shavin' off the hog hair and hoistin' that hog up a tree fur guttin'." You need a crowd, and the occasion needs to be as much fun as it is work. So, the women folk cook a meal of fresh hog brains and corn pone, and the bloody project becomes a full-blown party.

But even the nobliest of parties can lose focus. A simple corn shucking party can swiftly turn into a cob-throwing brawl. Neighbors turn nasty and kinfolks vow revenge. So the host must keep the crowd focused. That's why an hour into the going away party for Uncle Billy we called for him so we could say some nice and funny things about him, to tell him we were proud of him, and to wish him well—before we got too unfocused and carried away with drop the hankie, spin the bottle, or post office. A thorough search came up empty handed. Uncle Billy had vanished, but someone spied him, a lone figure a distance off down the railroad tracks, walking swiftly away from us, suitcase in hand. He left without even saying goodbye. I couldn't understand why?

The frivolous chatter and vociferous laughter of a few moments prior abruptly gave way to intermittent whispers as the crowd meandered from the front porch and back yard to get a final look. Someone standing near Mom held her kindly but firmly. Aunt Fannie cried. Dad abruptly disappeared into the house, as if out of the blue he remembered an unfinished task that couldn't wait. The taste of departure seemed awfully bitter. I ran after Uncle Billy, calling out his name. He never looked back.

Chapter Thirty-seven

Revenge

Stars sparkled across a cloudless sky; lightning bugs flashed like Christmas lights, outlining a shadowy landscape. In the distance a coon dog howled a lonely tune—not an alarm, just a reminder that he was still on duty. A hinge squeaked and a screen door banged slightly as Kelly King slipped onto his front porch. He muffled his chronic cough with the back of his shirtsleeve. The glow from a match briefly revealed his gaunt face as he lit a cigarette in his cupped hands. I laid in bed missing Uncle Billy and wondering where and how he was and when he would come home. Otherwise, our community slumbered in the stillness of another repetitious summer night. But trouble was brewing, and some knew it, for the rumors had leaked out.

Harlan Chaney was out of prison. He was a bitter man; further, he was a mean man. Time spent in the penitentiary had not toned his malicious nature. He loathed our community, saying we had abandoned him when the county sheriff hunted him down. He hated us almost as much as he reviled the law. He vowed revenge.

Our tranquil summer night exploded with a thundering firepower. Harlan Chaney's revenge had begun. I bolted from bed and rushed to Dad's side where he knelt at the front door. A rowdy gang of men fired shots into the air as they approached our house, walking along the railroad tracks.

"It's him," Dad whispered.

Dad had a gut feeling something like this would happen. He had expressed it in days past, especially after news surfaced of Harlan's parole.

With lights remaining off, Dad retrieved his .12 gage shotgun from the closet and loaded a shell. Crouching motionless, he peeked through a slit in the white, sheer curtains that covered the front window. Mom clutched Doyle in her arms and rocked him gently. I knelt beside Dad, wanting him to hold me but feigning courage as he cautioned for silence with a hand gently touching my gaped lips.

A dozen more shots rang out; a glass insulator atop a line pole shattered into a hundred pieces. Baying dogs joined the ruckus, ready for the kill. I imagined the scene: parents clinging to frightened children and to one another.

Harlan Chaney was a happy man tonight: happy because of the crazed havoc he was creating in this turncoat community that had applauded his prison sentence. He was having the last laugh.

I sat in stunned disbelief as Dad simply waited, not even aiming his gun. What was he waiting for? For a shot to crash into our home? Was he afraid? Shouldn't he show these hooligans that we won't tolerate such mockery without a fight? We dare not succumb to such tyrannical intimidation! I can use these words now—as an adult—to describe my childhood emotions. And as an adult, I wonder how Dad must have felt back then, the anxiety that gripped him, being the sole protector of his family against a pack of drunken ex-cons.

The gang meandered past our house and down the tracks, their laughing, accusations, and obscenities slowly drifting into obscurity. The lights of a dozen homes blinked on, and we all breathed a sigh of relief. The night gradually returned to normality.

Dad sensed my bewilderment and disappointment. He sat beside me on the cold linoleum, gently placed an arm around my rigid shoulders, and spoke kindly but confidently. "Son, life will hav' plen'y 'nough conflicts without hanker'n fur a fight uf yur own makin'. Fight outcomes ain't always predictable even when yur'r in the right, and they usually leave lastin' grievances."

I did not want a lecture. I wanted to see valor. Harlan Chaney needed to be put in his place. Dad had really disappointed me with his lack of action. I said nothing.

He interrupted the silence as he continued, "Some fights you kin avoid by waitin' them out, others by talkin' it out, and some by just ignoring'um 'cause they ain't worth the bother uf a fight."

"But they wuz a shootin' at us, Daddy. And nobody stood up to'em," I argued.

"Select yur fights, son," he said. "Don't be too proud ta turn t'other cheek if'n it kin prevent a fight. Don't fight out uf anger nor out uf being a'feared someone'll brand ya a coward. Fight only because it's the right thang ta do, after all other means ar' exhausted. And then, fight with ever' thang within ya, till yur enemy says, 'I give.' Then hep'em up, and if'en he will, shake his hand and buy'em an Orange Crush and a bag of Planters peanuts."

Some things are hard for men and boys to accept, and we fight against it, no matter who the instructor. Turn the other cheek, Jesus taught, but Peter didn't buy it; he bought a sword instead. The writer of Proverbs penned: "... he that is slow to anger appeaseth strife ... he that is slow to anger is better than the mighty; and he that ruleth his spirit than he that taketh a city." But too often we lash out first and learn later. Revenge allows anger to roam unbridled, unleashing havoc as it journeys. My French ancestry could add: *ira furor brevis est*—anger is a brief madness. Will we ever learn?

Chapter Thirty-eight

The Fishing Contest

Tommy Lee Spicer held the bragging rights for fishing; primarily, it was because he fished all day most every day. Folks scattered when he entered the general store. Another tale by Tommy Lee was the last thing they wanted to hear and another fish story they could scarcely swallow. And so on a Saturday morning, when Tommy Lee came to our house for his monthly haircut and started in on how many fish he caught that week, Dad threw down the gauntlet.

"Tommy Lee, I kin beat you fishin' any day uf the week 'cept Sunday, and you know why I kain't Sunday, but you can count yur Sunday fish anyway."

"Betcha a dollar bill ya kain't," Tommy Lee countered.

"You know I ain't gonna make a bet, but if'n you win, Tommy Lee, I'll cut yur hair fur free fur the next six months," Dad challenged. "If'en I win, no more fishin' tales from you fur the next six months." Dad laughed at his own comments.

Dad enjoyed fooling with Tommy Lee, but Tommy Lee took him serious enough that he insisted Dad shake hands to seal the deal. He got a couple customers waiting on their haircuts to witness the challenge. They agreed the contest would last one week beginning that Saturday. Tommy Lee headed straight for the riverbank; Dad went back to his barbering.

News of the contest spread faster than a melting snow in April: two locals were betting for bragging rights. Someone stretched the facts a mite and the rumors became full-fledged truth that everybody was talking about. The truth is Dad quit gambling sometime after he married Mom. She encouraged him to give up the habit by breaking up a poker game with some strong threats of a frying pan, the corncrib, a shotgun, and such. But this time Mom turned a deaf ear to the existing rumors and said nothing against Dad getting involved in this fishing bet. To her, this was not gambling, for money wasn't at stake: it was the hope that Tommy Lee would have to stop bragging. She wanted to take that right away from him. She felt it belonged to one of the working men in our community.

Monday evening Dad came home from a long day in the mine, his blue eyes aglow—like a hoot owl in the dark—from the black coal dust that covered his face. What a surprise to find his fishing poles setting in a corner of the living room! That was a first at our house. Mom had put them there

"Ya might as well do a little fishin' before ya scrub up," Mom encouraged. "The kids'll carry yur bath water from the river while you relax a bit with some fishin'," she insisted.

Dad obliged her. Two hours of fishing produced three catfish, a gar, and a snapping turtle. After Dad's bath, we put the fish in the tub—after we'd retrieved some clean water—and harassed the turtle. The next evening proved to be a little better, but by Wednesday the fish just stopped biting. We busied ourselves keeping the fish alive in the washtub and hiding them from Tommy Lee. Dad kept fishing every night after work but with little success. Word was out that Tommy Lee was "slayin'em right and left."

Friday night Dad came home a tad more jovial than we felt he should be, him being behind in the fishing contest the way he was. He placed his black, metal lunchbox on the highest shelf on the back porch, an unusual storage place and a disappointment to us, for we liked to rummage through the pail for any scraps left over from lunch, or any candy that might just happen to be hiding out in the lunch box, especially on a Friday evening. By the look on his face, something was in the air, and we spent most of the evening guessing what it might be.

Next morning, bright and early, Dad took his lunchbox down from the shelf, picked up his fishing pole, and headed for the river. He said he'd be back by lunchtime with a mess of fish. How odd that he took his empty lunchbox! But then again, maybe he planned to put the fish he caught in it, but that surely wouldn't be enough fish to beat Tommy Lee. I wanted to go with him, but he adamantly insisted that he fish alone, since I might scare the fish away if I started talking too much. Joyce, Sue, and I trailed him to the riverbank and watched as he untied his boat, climbed in, and shoved off. We spied on him until he rowed upstream and out of sight.

The morning sun slowly chased away the mist rising from the river and cascading across the bottomland. Its radiance transformed the dew into a field of dazzling diamonds, but just as quickly it rendered them invisible. The sand warmed under our feet as we frolicked away the morning on the riverbank, awaiting Dad's return from upstream, and hoping against time that he would outdo Tommy Lee.

A sudden explosion shattered the tranquility of the otherwise perfect morning. A thousand birds took to the sky and a million crickets stopped their chirping in mid chorus, as if the conductor had abruptly stopped the orchestration in mid concert. The explosion seemed akin to the supersonic boom that caught our community off guard from time to time. Still unaccustomed to the phenomena, we had calmed somewhat from the first time we experienced the boom, for we thought either the Lord or the Russians were coming. The explosion jolted us from whatever it was we were doing. The bang came from upstream in the direction Dad had disappeared. What in the world could it have been? Was Dad all right? Should we get Mom? We didn't have to, for Mom came running, and of all things at a scary moment like this, she had the washtub in tow.

We waited anxiously, Mom especially. It seemed eternity passed before we saw an approaching object floating from upstream, bobbing sideways as it took on water. It was Dad's lunchbox, drifting towards us like the sole surviving flagship of a shattered armada. Our faces paled and our breath faded like the sun-bleached, windless sail of a helpless dinghy. Mom wiped her eyes with the corner of her apron, but we couldn't tell if she was crying or cleaning something from her eye. I waded into the water and retrieved the crumpled lunchbox. What seemed like a forever of horrendous apprehension passed before we heard the splashing of water, the scraping of wood against wood, and spotted Dad's boat rounding the bend. Dad sat in the stern, brandishing a victor's smile. The boat gunnels rode low in the water, and a stack of fish filled the center of the boat. Dad's fishing pole trawled behind.

The mess of fish packed Mom's washtub to the gills. We threw a hastily called fish fry, the largest our community ever had. Tommy Lee conceded the contest and chipped in several catfish to boot. Dad casually commented to us over dinner that Tommy Lee was probably the better fisherman, but quipped, "We never discussed the type fishin' we could use fur the contest."

A stranger stopped by several weeks later: on a Saturday morning during barbering hours. He waited until Dad finished the last customer before he settled into the cane woven chair Dad used as his barber chair. His official looking hat left a ring mark in his hair, but Dad smoothed it down with a little dab of Brill Cream. After the haircut they sat on the front porch for a while, just talking and such. Finally, the stranger put on his hat, firmly shook Dad's hand, and left, without paying. I suspected he was from the game warden's office. Then again, it crossed my mind that he could be from the Cloverine Salve Company, come to collect the debt I owed them. Dad never said.

Tommy Lee eventually got Dad to divulge the location of the fishing hole but tried it out and commented, "You fished her dry, Delmar. Ain't no fish left in that spot."

Dad straightened out his mangled lunch box as best he

could, but it forever smelled of dynamite. Probably from setting around in the coal mine all day. Mom bought him a new one for Christmas.

Chapter Thirty-nine

Decoration Day

On any given Memorial Day weekend there are two places you don't want to be stranded without a motel reservation: Indianapolis, Indiana, and Breathitt County, Kentucky. Both places host events that focus on a start and finish. In Indianapolis it's the Indy 500; in Breathitt County it's the commemorating of the start and finish of life. In Indianapolis the multi-tiered Borg-Warner Trophy displays the name, image, year, and average speed of every Indy 500 winner since 1911. In Breathitt County the birth and death of loved ones are etched on enduring stones dotting graveyards high on the hillsides, and they are memorialized annually.

Folks called it Decoration Day. Christian denominational boundaries vanished at the annual event. My family always met at the Nimrod and Fugate Cemetery where the service became a blend of singing Baptists and shouting Pentecostals; a friend nicknamed us bapti-costals. Saint and sinner sat side-by-side, indistinguishable, for the dead we memorialized, though they had attended different churches in life, or attended no church at all, were laid side by side at death. Kinfolks and neighbors, who argued the Bible throughout the year, broke bread together on Decoration Day.

Singing Baptist Ader McDaniel sat next to shouting Pentecostals, Chester Spicer, Preacher Charlie, and anyone else who had felt the call. A major difference between singing Baptists ministers and Pentecostal ministers was the uniqueness in sermon delivery. Singing Baptists sang their sermons; the Pentecostals shouted theirs. Preacher Ader McDaniel, with his hand cupped to his ear to keep on pitch, sang his meloncholic message, drawing out certain words for emphasis and climbing and descending the scale per how the Spirit moved and to the delight of the audience. "Welllll childernnnn, I want ya to knooooow, knooooow, know that ever'thang is gonna beeeeee allllll rightttt whennn Jeeeeesus commmmes…."

The Pentecostal preachers sucked in great gulps of air as they climbed the scale at break-neck-speed, then abruptly stopped, like a balloon exploding from excess air. The monologue started over after the brief pause for more oxygen. Baptist folks joked, "We ain't afeard you Pentecostals won't make it ta heaven, we're just concerned ya might run right past." The Pentecostals retorted, teasingly of course, "At the speed yur preachers deliver their sermons, they might not get ther' 'til the second millennium."

Preachers Lewis Arrowood, Buelow Noble, Melvin Tackett, Eddie B. Lawson, Doug White, Chester Combs, and more—all with a word from the Lord—awaited their turn, while the laity shared their testimonies. Lizzy Spicer, in her usual style, always went first. "Now I don't wanna git ahead uf nobody, I jist wantta be quick ta testify fer ma good Lord." Some spoke in tongues, and some tamed their tongues on this day. And the service lasted most all day.

Preparation for the service began weeks in advance. Oscar Strong cut the brush and repaired the log benches. He gathered up the weathered, plastic wreaths from last Decoration Day and lit a bonfire that sent black smoke billowing into the sky. Come Decoration Day, the appreciative slipped him a few dollars by way of a subtle handshake. He nodded his gratitude and discretely stuffed the money into his pocket.

Throughout the morning a stream of people filed across the swinging bridge at Copeland and walked down the railroad tracks, calling out to various friends of years gone by. They turned left off the tracks into Fulton Noble's yard where they rested a spell and exchanged pleasantries with the Noble family. Reinvigorated, they continued their pilgrimage through the wide-open, straw-strewn center of the Noble barn and climbed the steep hill behind the barn where a meandering path through the towering pines led them to a clearing at the top of the ascent. A sagging wooden gate guarded the entrance to the cemetery. A glance backward over the traveler's shoulder revealed a sweeping green valley of splendor, a colossal arena that had witnessed a few hundred real-life dramas. Each drama remained different, yet similar. Ofttimes the same tragedy repeated itself, simply stalking new victims. Another drama would unfold today.

Folks arrived from as far away as Michigan and as close as Sulfur Gap. Most families carried a bouquet of plastic carnations, or roses, some attached to a Styrofoam cross with a metal tripod. The flowers were lovingly placed on the graves of family and friends, and though artificial, the acts were real. And the flowers being artificial, would suffice until the next year.

The drab graveyard gleamed with the various decorations, hence the name, Decoration Day. And we sure did dress up on this day. The ladies wore white heels that imprinted the yellow clay, leaving a distinctive trail, not too unlike peg leg Elb's footprints. Their straw hats, with grosgrain ribbons, shielded them from the sun and gave them a dressed-up feeling, not unlike the derby ladies of Louisville. A suit and tie was as prevalent for this event as at a wedding; still, some donned tieless, white shirts with open collars. Very few men wore overalls to the Memorial Day service, but that's all some had, so it was okay. Most had handkerchiefs that dangled from the hip pockets of their britches. Young boys in white shirts with ties clipped to kinked collars pressed hard to impress the girls. The younger girls showed off their new gingham dresses, adorned with lots of buttons and bows. The teenage girls wore mail-order taffeta garments with matching crinolines underneath. The younger men had on the skinniest ties with dungarees and white socks, their hair slicked back into a ducktail. Cameras clicked as families and friends captured memories.

Friends, who time and circumstances had distanced, stood in huddled groups catching up on the year's news of jobs, cars, deaths, marriages, and births. A thousand books could not contain the stories shared at the headstones of the departed. A young woman stood at the grave of an infant. Tears dripped onto the tombstone but quickly evaporated from the sun-warmed monument, leaving stained evidence of her chronic grief. God knew best to make life but a few years long, while He made heaven eternal, for if the two were reversed, the mother's tears would have eventually worn away the headstone. Her young husband stood nearby, stiff and still, staring across the distance. He no longer shed tears.

Children played hide-n-seek among the markers, reprimanded often for stepping on a grave. Birds gathered in the treetops as if ready to participate. A curious cow from the Noble farm approached cautiously, its bell clanging with each step.

The service started about noon. The preachers sat on a crudely built riser, while everyone else sat on the log benches facing the pulpit. The funeral singers got the service underway with half-a-dozen hymns. The audience called out requests for favorites; the singers accommodated. The melancholic singing echoed across the serene valley, drifting heavenward upon the zephyrs of faith and sincerity. The stones need not cry out today, for mankind was in tune with his Maker. Each believed in that grand reunion in the sky with the Lord and departed loved ones, and some uttered their heart-felt wishes that the Lord hasten the resurrection. Today resembled a dress rehearsal. They sang of a better day, a brighter tomorrow, and a faraway land of endless peace and freedom from pain. Rapturous spirits soared with the angelic host encircling the small gathering of believers. In a fleeting moment, one sensed the attention of heaven on that lonely hilltop, most lingering as if not wanting to go back down.

Words of comfort abounded from the speakers. Scriptures came alive in the presence of the dead. On occasion, a preacher bellowed out a hellfire and brimstone message. But the dead, like trees, lie where they fall. No amount of preaching changed their status; I suppose the preaching was meant to change us. But hellfire sermons seemed rather abusive under the circumstances, like kicking your opponent while he's down. Some misrepresent the great apostle who spoke of the "foolishness of preaching" as being foolish in style. Conversely, the foolishness of preaching is the message of eternal life because of the death of the Savior; we find freedom by having a servant's heart; we gain by giving; we find happiness through mourning.

Not to discredit the numerous speakers at the Decoration Day service, but the most effective sermon came from the silent stones. They spoke to us a hushed but distinct homily that lingered as we descended the hill. Life at best is too short. Share your possessions, for you can't take one penny with you. Speak kindly, for some words cannot be recalled. Communicate often, for once you're gone, wishful words cannot be spoken. Abandon personal grudges. Mend bridges and tear down walls. Laugh at yourself and laugh with others. Love relentlessly. Hug tightly.

In Indianapolis, winners celebrated their conquest by guzzling a bottle of ice-cold milk at winner's circle: a tradition started by the first three-time winner Louis Meyer—though he drank buttermilk instead of regular milk. In our distant community in Eastern Kentucky, at days end, we slowed down a bit and sipped a cold soda as we sat on wooden pop crates on the porch of Saul and Mary Emily Clay's grocery store, contemplating the day's activities as we shared another splendid sunset at the close of Decoration day.

Chapter Forty

Silent Pain

His name sounded aristocratic: Glen Lawrence. He lived with his mother, in what today is quite common, but in the fifties raised eyebrows—a single-parent home. We seldom spoke of his father, but when someone did, it was in hushed and melancholic tones and always in the absence of children. His mother eventually remarried, so Glen Lawrence spent a lot of time with his grandparents on his mother's side, who were our neighbors.

Glen Lawrence epitomized the perfect child; he respected his elders and peers, was unpretentious and kind, and did not experience a doting single-parent, nor grandparent, household. He enjoyed simply being one of us. His one advantage, however, was his English racer. We all looked up to Glen Lawrence—almost envied him for this expensive bicycle.

His father was a WWII veteran. The phrase, "He never was the same after the war," applied to Glen Lawrence's daddy. His was a sad story, for in time, something shattered within, spilling out all the ugly, bottled-up emotions. We have a name for it today: post-traumatic stress disorder. But Glen Lawrence's daddy didn't get the help he needed, and rumor has it that in a battle of bewilderment, he killed his momma, Glen Lawrence's grandma. The irony of it was—other than the singular tragedy—his daddy showed exceptional love toward his momma.

For those of us too young to comprehend, the story unfolded through years of questions. The questions first surfaced because Glen Lawrence's last name differed from his mother's, who had remarried. Who was his real father? Was he dead? If not, then where did he live? Had he abandoned them? Why did he never come around?

Children's repeated questions sometime wear down the resolve of parents or elicit information from those prone to gossip. And so, the story slowly unfolded to our young ears, bit by mind-boggling bit. And we sometimes wished we had never asked, as if not knowing could cause the tragedy to have never happened.

In our isolated community local news came mostly by word of mouth. Other than Mr. Deaton, we none received a newspaper. Adults shared weeks-old news in huddled groups, as if to keep the children from having to fret over tragedies and such. And real bad news drew silence, like a time capsule to be opened at some distant future, when the wounds had healed, and the children had grown up and could handle it.

A letter sometimes arrived for Glen Lawrence. Its return address revealed an unfamiliar location, not like Flint or Cincinnati. Adults tossed awkward glances as Glen Lawrence cradled the letter and walked home; no one dared ask him about it.

Early on, Glen Lawrence and his mother sometimes caught the train and left for the weekend. They traveled light. Mom waved to them as they passed our house on their way to the train station. Our "Reckon whur' they're a'going?" fell on deaf ears. Mom guarded the secret with her silence. The trips eventually stopped. We never knew why. I assume Glen Lawrence's daddy died in the mental hospital.

Glen Lawrence bore the pain in silence. I've been told that over time he learned to share the silence with a bottle. I'm not sure if the bottle, or the silence, killed him. I wish I had talked to him about his pain, but back then I did not know what to say, and he was older than I was, and I reconned that if he'd wanted to talk, he would have initiated the conversation. At least that's how I reasoned.

Such silent pains were borne by many. I hesitate to

mention names, for to do so seems too invasive. Such is the case of another neighbor. Like all caring fathers, he loved his children more than life and looked forward to spending each weekend with them. He, too, worked away and came home on the weekends. The children ran to meet him and he to them. Tossing them into the air, he caught them to the squeal of delight. No one loved his children more; no children were happier.

"Do it agin, Daddy!" the laughing children begged. "Higher, Daddy!"

And so, he tossed the children into the air, over and over, until exhaustion took its toll, not on them, but upon him.

No one knows for sure how it happened. Miscalculated timing? A stumble? A slip of the hand? But in a flash, it happened. One moment the child was high in the air with mouth agape in exhilaration, the next moment he lay motionless on the ground. Like the crazed face of a catcher on a trapeze after a failed summersault, the father gazed upon the crumpled body on the ground. The sense of helplessness overwhelmed him. Despair engulfed him. Guilt clutched its fingers around his throat, wrenching tighter with each hopeless second. His thoughts spun round and round like a top that never stops. He picked up the unresponsive child and staggered into the house. They lived miles away from the nearest doctor and hours away from the nearest hospital. Too far and too late.

It was not a criminal act punishable by prison; rather, it was a foolish act for indulging the child in enthusiastic play, so the law made no arrest. But doing nothing wasn't enough for the father's guilty emotions. He felt responsible for the act that broke the neck of his own child. He must somehow pay.

Days passed in silence. Mental flagellation failed to appease the personal guilt. Self-blame reined. The mind succumbed to its own torture: guilt and grief tangled into a knot he seemed helpless to unravel. No one was able to save him from his self-inflicted, emotional wounds. Life grayed into meaninglessness.

Some sixty years removed, no one quite understands my response when they toss their child into the air in playful entertainment. "Please, don't do that," I plead, even to a stranger. The look on their face says, "Back off, bud," so I walk away, reliving the past and hoping for a better outcome for them than that which happened to my neighbor.

Chapter Forty-one

Moby Dick
and
Preacher Charlie

The bookmobile stopped weekly at the Marie Roberts School. I loved to walk the isle between bookshelves and feel the books. I wished all the information in print could by some process of osmosis seep into my brain. I finally succumbed to the art of reading but not without some complaining. It was Mr. Dickens' Great Expectations that conquered my resistance to the discipline of reading.

The one positive of riding the school bus the miles to and from school was the opportunity to journey a thousand miles by way of reading from the books we had checked out from the mobile library. And reading prevented a lot of mischief from idle time; however, I found it difficult to simply read the storybooks; I wanted to live them. And that sometimes got us—us being whoever would join with me—into mischief. And some of that mischief happened on one of my visits to Grandpa Charlie's house up on Lick Branch. He had moved from Copeland back to his small farm. My dad had helped him purchase the farm with money he had saved while serving in the navy. I had heard stories about a fish that lived in Grandpa's backyard well: a well that was covered by a four-foot tall, rough-hewn, wooden box. Per the accounts of some, the fish grew through the years from a minnow tossed into the well for a prank, to a monster with fiery eyes and razor-sharp teeth. We suspected there existed no fish at all, but curiosity must sometimes be satisfied.

It all started with Melville's *Moby Dick*. We sat spellbound through nightly chapter readings. The allegorical meanings passed over my head and the Archaic English sounded mighty strange, but the frightening escapades made my hair stand on end. When the lights went out, I hid my face under the covers, trying to veil the visions of the darkness. During the daylight, I sat on the bank of the North Fork, imagining what sailing with Captain Ahab would be like. I reflected upon whether he was crazy or possessed. Evidently, kids can't comprehend the term "fiction," or else adults don't explain the term correctly. So, for me, Moby Dick remained alive, living somewhere in the world, and for all I knew, he could be the fish in the well in Grandpa's back yard. Some families had aquariums for their fish: Grandpa had a well for an aquarium.

My fears somewhat subsided after the nighttime stories about Captain Ahab ended, that is until Grandpa Charlie chose for his weekly sermon: "Jonar and the Whale." His sermon took me back in space and time, where once again the waves crashed against the wooden deck of an endangered ship, crushing man and mast, spewing froth and seaweed, generating terror beyond reason. With fist punching skyward into the atmosphere, Grandpa punctuated the damnation of those who dare flout God's commands. It seemed he stared directly at me as he pronounced judgment to the defiant.

It took him a while to lay the foundation of the Bible story, but once he got toward the end of the sermon, it was like the afterburner kicked in. "Hell awaits the Jonars uf this day. The whales uf the abyss ar' on thur' way ta claim thur' prize. You ain't nothin' short uf whale bait if'n ya don't giv' yur heart ta Jesus."

A moment of silence passed as Preacher Charlie paused and gulped in needed air. The silence was broken by a supportive "amen" from the congregation before Grandpa continued.

"A fathomless sea uf red hot far' prepare't fur the devil and his angels awaits the dis'bedient, and the fated ship uf stubbornness t'will carry ya thur'."

Sweat coursed down Grandpa's face as I envisioned him standing on the deck of the sea-sprayed ship tossed about like a twig in a vortex. Moans from the audience simulated the hopeless state of the doomed aboard this hell-bound vessel. Suddenly, an ashen-faced Jonah sprang from the crowd and threw himself at the captain's feet. With lips quivering like a pin oak tree-leaf in a winter's breeze, he confessed.

"It's me. I'm the low-down scoundrel that's a runnin' from the Lord. I'm tar'd uf runnin', and I ain't gonna run no more. If'n God will furgive me now, I'll nev'r run agin."

I had my eyes shut tighter than tree bark and couldn't make out what sinner was repenting. I sneaked a peek as the audience reflected the response of heaven, rejoicing that one sinner had come to repentance, and they gathered around him to extend a hand of hope. Preacher Charlie placed his hands on the humbled Jonah's head and stormed hell with rebukes and demands for Satan to release this poor soul into the custody of heaven.

And so, a moonshine runner, gun-toting ruffian, with a criminal mentality, left the altar to stumble through a darkened, back-woods trail, with ax in hand, to bust up his hidden, moonshine distillery. He hastened back home to share the good news, smelling of whiskey, but clean as a whitewashed fence and kind as a kitten. Forever changed.

Some more-educated folks consider Christianity to be a band-aid to psychosis, a crutch for the weak souled, or a support group for the slow of intellect. I'll confess I've seen some laughable sights—even downright ill-mannered actions—at some church events. But the truth is, there are "Jonahs" everywhere whose only hope is a direct confrontation of their actions by the seething sermons from the "Preacher Charlies" of this world. It's delightful, no matter how unorthodox, to see an addict stirred to freedom by a preacher's challenge and the gospel message of deliverance.

Some folks respond to a gentle voice of persuasion, while others respond to an emotional appeal. Still, others need a foot stomping, finger pointing, and sin-naming delivery. That's just the way it is. Preacher Charlie was that kind of preacher. And since the hypocritical warnings of beer companies, and the small print from the surgeon general's office on packs of cigarettes, carry too little a punch, we need Preacher Charlies to herald the news of hope from the vices of evil. And though bartenders lend a sympathetic ear to the symptoms, but seldom confront the source, merely keeping it wiped off the counter, the Preacher Charlies make wonderful contributions to society. They deserve a medal for their grit rather than ridicule for their crass approach. Perhaps Jesus resembled such when He turned over a few tables and chased out the greedy merchants. He passed over gentle persuasions and emotional stimuli for head butting, butt kicking, confrontation. When a prison counselor does this to help inmates look beyond their excuses for criminal activity, he is using professional techniques for which we are grateful. But when a preacher does so, he is accused of using appalling and uncouth tactics. Personally, I like a preacher to challenge my sin rather than cater to my failure. The catering messages tend to rock me to sleep.

Now, kids don't always respond to sermons like adults do. Adults get mad and pout; kids get scared and confess. That said, with Melville's *Moby Dick* recently finished, and Grandpa's whale sermon, I should have considered some of my sinful ways; instead, I became curious about the aquarium in Grandpa's backyard. These back-to-back renditions of fish stories—the sermon about Jonah and Melville's novel—caused some psychological fixation to set in, and I couldn't get the visual out of my head about a whale in Grandpa's well. If it was true, I figured the well inspired that fathomless sea of fire Grandpa Charlie preached about. And a modern rendition of *Moby Dick* could well be living there. And if he was, Captain Ahab needed vindication, or at least I thought so. All this speculation needed to be figured out, or so it seemed to me.

The bright sunshine would give my accomplice and me ample light to peer into the well. With fishing pole in hand and mischief in heart, we tiptoed cautiously up to the well, wanting not to warn the supposed occupant of our intrusive approach. A water bucket set on the wooden cover, attached to a hemp rope threaded through a rusty pulley that hung over the well box. The excess rope dangled to the ground, coiled like a serpent on guard.

We carried a milk pail on which to stand, the smell of milk permeating our blue jeans, for we hadn't anticipated the milk pail atop the refrigerator to have anything in it when we tipped it from atop the frig. We had cleaned up the mess as best we could and wiped our milky-hands on our jeans. I positioned the upended pail beside the well, climbed onto it, and peeked through the opening at the top of the well's cover.

"Whatcha see, Larry?" my impatient accomplice whispered.

"Kain't see nuthin' just yet."

"Lemme try and see if'n I kin see anything," he said.

"Be patient, will ya? I'm a tryin'," I responded.

My eyes gradually focused to the darkness of the deep, which bit by bit took on a mirrored appearance. Nothing looked unusual: rocks lined the sides of the round, hand-dug well, a damp, green moss covered the rocks, and a long-legged spider figure-skated gracefully on the water's surface.

"Ain't nuthin' hur 'cept a spider," I reported.

Lemme see, will ya?" he pleaded as he tugged on the back of my shirt.

"Just a minute. I thank I see somethin' else," I said.

The mirrored surface of water showed a ripple, at first miniscule, but then the water exploded where the spider had been, as a mammoth fish burst to the surface, mouth agape and thrashing like a bucking bull. At that very instant, an unnoticed cat, following the smell of the milk on our jeans, responded to the surprise attack of a yapping beagle that bolted from its stalking. The cat shrieked a wild and hideous wail, leaped upon my back, dug its claws into my neck, and continued across the top of my head. The unexpected assault frightened me to wits end, whereupon I knocked the water bucket into the well, at which point the attached rope attacked my leg.

For a split second I saw the fiery eyes of Moby Dick with a harpoon plunged deep into his side. I felt his jagged teeth chomp onto my leg. I heard the deafening crashing of the churning sea as the monstrous fish plunged sideways down into the deep. And worst of all, I recalled the thunderous sermon of Grandpa Charlie: "The Bible says, Leviathan…is king over all the children of pride." No, those were not exactly his words, but the paraphrased childhood recollections were just as frightening. "Ya ain't nuthin' 'sides whale bait if'n pride sneaks inta yur heart."

Come Sunday, I sat on the front pew, close to the altar. Over time, my fears dulled to the point of taking the third row with catnapping during long sermons. But for weeks, any sudden rise in Grandpa Charlie's voice snapped me to attention. And I knew, sooner or later, just like Jonah, I was going to have to make my way to the altar and repent for my sinful ways.

Chapter Forty-two

Threats

With school out, life always drifted into boredom in a matter of days. Nancy York was a distant memory, and the flood was but a conversation piece. Aunt Fanny was busy raising a baby, and the club was hardly ever meeting. Still, it was amazing how quickly life could change. And so it did.

A note arrived about a secret meeting at Coffin Rock. I found it laying on my bedroom windowsill, held in place by a rock. I tossed the rock outside, unfolded the note, and read it:

> The club meets tonight at 10 aclock after dark on the rock. Everbody has to be thar. Don't nobody be late les you want to pay fer it with yur hid. And don't tell nobody bout this meeting.
>
> The leder.

Some things troubled me about the secret club. One, I was the only member who did not wear a mask. Why should I? They all knew who I was. Further, they refused to take their masks off in my presence. I almost knocked one off that day of the chicken incident. Finally, the way the letter demanded I be there sounded more like a threat than a club. I knew Mom wouldn't let me leave home that late at night, but they demanded I come to the meeting. I was in a quandary as to what I should do.

I pondered the letter all evening trying to make up my mind. When all lights were out, and a chorus of unharmonious snoring rattled the otherwise calm of the house, I slipped from under my sheet, still fully dressed except for shoes. I slid through my bedroom window into the darkness of the night, shoes in hand.

The moon remained hidden behind the hills, but that made the stars brighter still on the backdrop of the black sky. The Big Dipper seemed close enough to reach out and touch. A million crickets sounded like an orchestra warming up before rehearsal, but they stopped momentarily as I walked across the yard; they returned to their individual recitals once I passed.

I sneaked out the front gate, closing it gently, but cringed as the squeaky hinges sounded their alarm. Why had I not thought to oil them? I gingerly hurried across the cinder stones to the railroad track, where the crossties pricked my feet. I walked a good distance before I paused, sat astride the track, slipped into my Converse tennis shoes, and tied and double-knotted them.

The climb up the trail to Coffin Rock was more difficult in the darkness. The sounds and shadows frightened me as I felt my way along the path. Once atop the hill, the glow of the club's fire offered a momentary reprieve. The leader seemed annoyed that I was late, like they had waited on me.

The usual stuff took place: pledges, rituals, and the sharing of a cigarette. The smoking had started out with corn silks, but over the months had grown into full-fledged cigarettes: the butts of Winston Cools gathered from the yard of the local store. Surprisingly, though I coughed a lot, I enjoyed the mint-like taste the first time I ever tried one. Was the mint flavor coincidental? In retrospect, I think not. It was the bait for addiction.

"I thank we should start bringin' girls ta the meetin'," the leader announced.

"Hain't never done that afore," someone reminded him.

"But I thank we've been missin' out some by not lettin' the girls join," the leader argued. "We've run out of thangs to do 'cept get inta trouble. We could play some games and such if'n we let them join."

"What if' they don't wanna join? Whatta we do? Make'em?" another asked.

"They'll wanna come," the leader insisted. "They ain't got nuthin' better ta do."

I was confused. Why do we want girls? Why would girls want to come to a secret meeting of boys? My sister wouldn't want to come. And something within told me this was wrong. I couldn't figure out what they were up to, but whatever it was, I didn't like it. I stood to defend my sisters' honor.

"My sisters will nev'r come to a stupid boy's meetin' like this," I challenged.

Everyone turned and stared at me, like I had upset their applecart, or dynamited their group think; conversely, I was just being truthful, not defiant.

"Larry, girls like ta do stuff with boys. Yur sister Joyce'l come," the leader snapped. "You'll see."

"No, she won't, and I ain't gonna ask'er. And you ain't gonna ask'er either," I said.

"Son, if'n you wanna be a member of this hur club, you gotta do what we all 'gree on. Now, I sed we're bringing girls and we ar', like it er not. Nothin' you kin do ta stop it," the leader rebuffed me.

"Then I quit," I said.

"Kain't," he said.

"Why not?" I asked.

"Cause ya took'n oath. No man can take an oath and then just take it back, 'specially if'n he knows what's good fur him," the leader said.

"And what's good fur him?" I asked.

"Remember that dead chicken you thought wuz yur baby brother?" he asked.

"Whatta 'bout it?" I asked.

"Could be yur dead brother next time," the leaded said.

That about scared me into silence, but I continued to argue my cause. Finally, against my strong objections, they agreed that girls would be welcome at the next meeting. Disappointed, I slid from the rock and sat on the ground. My head ached, and my heart thumped in my temples. I must tell Mom, I thought. But that might only endanger our family. Maybe I could tell Dad—whenever he comes home—that the leader threatened to kill my baby brother, but he might just do like he did with Harlen Chaney, and that would be nothing, though his explanation to me made some sense. I had to think of some way to protect my family and at the same time to get out of the club.

I heard little they said the rest of the meeting. The adjournment startled me from inner thoughts. I hardly said goodbye as I turned to slowly walk home. I wished I could walk right on by my house and never stop going, for I had failed my family by becoming a member of the club. But I could not skip out on my family now, for I hadn't made enough money on my Cloverine salve sells to pay the bill, let alone have extra money to run away from home. And I had sold my bicycle to Loyd King and had already gone through that money. Retracing my steps, I slowly walked the train tracks toward home, kicking up gravels, and blaming myself for the whole mess.

The moon rose from its slumber just as I approached my house. I paused to watch it illuminate the countryside; I prayed for God to enlighten my mixed-up mind. I opened the squeaky gate halfway hoping it awakened Mom. I sat on the front steps for a long time, thinking. It was in those moments of deep contemplation that an idea came to me. Maybe. Just maybe.

Chapter Forty-three

The Trap

I invited most all the fellows I thought were in the secret club to join me "fur a game uf basketball on ma new goal." They all came. We played basketball until boredom set in. That was a good time to spring into action on a plan I had concocted, but I tried to act casual because I didn't want them to get suspicious.

"Want somethin' ta drink?" I asked.

"Shore," they all responded, almost in unison.

That was the signal. Joyce came out carrying the biggest glasses she could find and had them full of Kool-Aid. She served them up and went back for more.

We sat on the back steps of my house, slurped our drinks, and chatted between burps. "Wanna play post office or maybe spin-the-bottle?" I surprised them with the suggestion.

"Kain't play that without no girls," someone remarked. Everyone laughed.

"We got girls," I announced. "My sisters and a bunce uf her friends are in the house makin' cookies fur us right this minute."

"Yur're really somethin' else, Larry," someone said. They slapped me on the back like I was a renewed believer on a Sunday morning.

"Git'n line," I said.

A wild ruckus ensued as they scrambled to get at the front of the line. Right on cue, Joyce stepped onto the porch with refills.

"The fellers wanna play post office ur maybe spin-the-bottle. Thank the girls will join in?" I asked.

"Hain't got much else ta do," Joyce answered.

She set the drinks on the porch and retreated into the house. The fellows fought for another round of Kool-Aid but became anxious as time passed with no sight of the girls. Joyce finally reappeared.

"They wanna play post office," Joyce announced. Shouts of delight ensued. She held up her hand for silence. "Hur's the rules. Ever'body gits one chance ta answer a question one uf the girls will ask. And if'n ya git it right, ya git a kiss from the postmistress. Plus, ya git a cookie straight out uf the oven."

Cheers rose from the group, hats flew skyward, and more chaos followed with retrieving hats, shoving, and cutting back to the front of the line.

"Let the game begin," I yelled.

One by one the fellows shyly marched into the house to meet the postmistress as the girls took turns fulfilling that role. The fellows all answered the one question correctly, got their promised kiss, and came out of the house clutching their cookie and sheepishly grinning. The one simple question posed to them all was predetermined by me. "Whur' did ya git the chicken y'all kill't up on Coffin Rock?" Greedy as they were to get a kiss from the postmistress, no one denied killing a chicken, and they all gave the same answer: from Lani Peters' chicken coop.

The last kiss was delivered and Joyce came out of the house holding a piece of paper which she handed to me. I took a quick glance, folded it, and stuck it in my shirt pocket.

"You didn't git a turn, Larry," someone said.

"No use, 'cause I don't know the answer ta the question. Only those in the secret club who participated in the killin' uf chickens knows the answer ta that question. I only saw the chicken after it wuz kill't. But all uf you knowed the answer 'cause you were present when you stole the chicken. Y'all can keep wearin' yur masks, but yur names are recorded hur on this paper, and I know who you are." I patted my shirt pocket. "And furthermore, I hur and now quit the secret club."

"We wuz just makin' up like we wuz a part of the club, but we ain't," someone yelled. The others shook their heads in agreement."

"You ain't got no names in yur pocket," another said.

I took the paper out of my pocket and held it up so they could see the list but not so close they could grab it.

"Ain't fair, cause ya tricked us," someone yelled.

"Now, if'n anythang happens to my family, yur names are all recorded right hur on this paper, and all these girls know about the intar' plot, so the law will come lookin' fur ya," I said.

The girls giggled, shaking their heads in the affirmative, pleased with their work.

The party ended rather abruptly. The boys strolled off down the tracks, kicking gravel, and fussing up a storm. Only then did I notice Dad sitting near an open window.

"Good job, son." He smiled.

"Got'em real good, didn't I, Daddy?" I bragged.

"Real good, son. But you prob'ly should git on down ta the store and buy'em all a bottle uf pop and a bag uf peanuts," Dad said. He smiled and tossed a five-dollar bill out the window.

Chapter Forty-four
The Move

Though droughts come in increments of about two or three every decade, the floods were less predictable. A second flood came in '62. We waved to the school bus as it passed by on the other side of the river. Mom thought it best we stay home. She was right. The rain kept falling, the water kept rising, and for the second time in five years we relinquished our residence to the invading floodtide.

Dad was away—again—working, but this time he was closer: Cincinnati. It pleases me today to think about him away working, not that he was away, but that he was working to make a living for us. I suppose he could have stayed home and collected the dole and fished our fishing hole, but he chose to leave home to find work. This second flood did something no other calamity had done: it sealed Dad's decision to move us.

Dad's immediate task in '62 was saving his family from the peril of a third flood. Though a war veteran himself, he hardly noticed the news that United States Army units landed on South Vietnam soil. He was tunnel-vision focused on his family. To him, the Bay of Pigs sounded more like a farmers' quarrel than the losing conflict it became. Reports by McCarthy that Russia harbored missiles in Cuba registered far down his worry list. John Glenn's solo orbit in the heavens did not excite him. He needed to relocate his family to a safe haven on the earth—safe from another flood. He did.

Dad broke the news at the supper table. "We're gonna be movin'," he abruptly announced.

I looked at Mom, not knowing what to say. Her expression showed relief. "To Cincinnati?" she asked.

For years she wanted to be near his work. She delighted in fixing his meals, packing his fried bologna sandwiches, and doing his laundry. She felt less a wife when he had to do these things for himself but less still when the elderly woman he boarded with did them.

Dad hesitated in answering Mom.

"Wher'r we moving to, Delmar?" she asked again.

"Dry Bread," Dad said.

"Dry Bread?" We kids looked at each other, puzzled, and repeated Dad's answer almost in unison.

"I've found us a place at Dry Bread. No more floods fur us," Dad said.

Mom tried to act happy, like a child excited about opening a present, to find a pair of used socks. Dry Bread was a tiny community a few miles from where we lived. I'm not sure how it got its name.

We moved into the house at Dry Bread, but this time on the right side of the river: no more need for a boat or swinging bridge to cross over to our house. Dad could park his car in the driveway. Best of all? No more floods.

We hoped for an upgrade in housing, but the house we temporarily rented in Dry Bread, like our house in Copeland, also lacked indoor plumbing. Further, it didn't have a well at all, which seemed a downgrade. We had to carry water from a spring down the road. The fresh, spring water tasted great, but it had its drawbacks, for it housed crawdads and some other unidentified, multi-legged swimmers. It was almost as intriguing as Grandpa's well but lacked a Moby Dick. And it was quite a chore, carrying the water to the house, as one bucket never sufficed for the daily needs—it took several trips a day and more so on laundry day.

I'm not sure how Dad sold our house along the North Fork. Maybe he used another one of his real estate pitches: "This house has paid its dues. It shouldn't flood in another hundred years." He always was a good horse trader. You learn that when life depends on your own ingenuity and not someone else's. Letch Bellamy bought the place. To my knowledge the house never flooded again, but it burned down some years later, perhaps an electrical fire—I'm not sure if Dad discussed the wiring. That was probably to our benefit as the sellers.

Dry Bread was short lived, as Dad knew what he needed to do, but he was slower than usual making up his mind. All the while, we were growing up without him and getting used to it. I think he sensed that, so he rented a place for us in the Cincinnati area—on the Kentucky side of the Ohio River, on a street named Liberty. Perhaps still living on Kentucky soil on a street called Liberty made the move less painful for him, having to say goodbye to his Cumberland roots. And he definitely missed his garden.

We were packing again but this time for the real move up north. Neighbors came by to ask questions about where we would be living and to wish us well.

"We're movin' ta Newport," we explained.

"How fur is it?" they asked.

And before we could answer, "Don't thank I would like it, livin' way up thar," they concluded, their comment somewhat in the form of a question more than a statement. I experienced a bit of personal guilt for not feeling sad: seems I should have been sad, saying goodbye to my friends, grandparents, and cousins. But I was excited. It was an excitement in a frightening way—somewhat like Halloween at midnight or fishing for Moby Dick in Grandpa's well.

The day finally arrived. My family was leaving the Cumberland Plateau. For years others had come to save us from poverty and ignorance, to turn our sadness into joy, and to make the plateau livable. But they were too late in many ways. Ofttimes we had saved ourselves. Other times we accepted the loss and prayed for strength to go on. Through floods and drought, through sickness and sorrows, in death and pain, and most times without a doctor, we had made it. Without Billy Graham or Ed Sullivan. We made do with Preacher Charlie and created our own entertainment (though we could have done without the snake handlers). This is not to brag, for we didn't feel like victors; rather, we were survivors. Maybe we needed saving, and maybe life would have been easier with their help; it's just that they were too late for my family. And maybe we needed what they offered, but we did not want their pity, as if we were poor hillbillies destined to die without happiness unless they rescued us.

The White House was the last to attempt our salvation. I'm not sure why our community even mattered; we were so few that even McDonalds hadn't discovered us. We were still eating sizzling burgers off the grill at the local White Flash. But even without a fancy eating place, Breathitt County made it on the itinerary for the wife of POTUS—Lady Bird Johnson. Someone must have told her about "those pitifully poor families living in the hills of Kentucky," so she came to see for herself: to see the shabby little shacks sitting on reeling stilts on the hillsides, to peer into our sad, aching eyes and view our scrawny ashen faces of hopeless hearts. What she found were blue-eyed and rosy, corn-fed faces of shy children: curious, but shy. Shyness is a far cry from hopeless.

The media came first, sending back pictures for the masses to gasp at our plight, and surely the powers that be wanted the world to recognize the compassion being shown by caring politicians. Then came the tour buses, right on schedule as the news of the time of their arrival had spread by word of mouth. What a grand occasion! The local folks came out, by cars and truckloads, to get a glimpse of the president's wife. It was a rare occasion for a lady of such distinction to set foot on this native soil. But she came, and the event will be told again and again down through the generations to come.

All the politicians that could get an invitation came, and some came that didn't have an invitation. No one wants to be on the outside looking in when the agenda of "saving the poor" is on the table. They came to see us, like we needed them; local folks came to see them, mostly out of curiosity. The reciprocity drew a pretty good crowd. Flags waved and horns honked. A vendor or two reaped the immediate benefit. No one seemed disappointed. The politicians received credit for caring about the poverty stricken in Breathitt County, and the town of Jackson eventually got a new school called the LBJ Elementary.

But were they too late? Many had already made their escape. Or too early? Would the locals accept them? Hill folks have unique ways of viewing things. Survival helps you formulate philosophies; for us, *c'est lavie*—that's life—answered a thousand and one otherwise unanswered questions. Many of our beliefs were of a religious nature. We still considered the Bible to be "the book" worth reading. Our teachers read to us from its pages. Though some were not churchgoers, most could still quote from the Bible. So, we had our philosophies—wives' tales mingled with Scripture. Our *Deus vult* attitude, God wills it (the rallying cry of the Crusaders), mustered the strength for us, not to conquer, but to endure another graveside departure. And though we were considered by many to be simple hillbillies, we lived true to our philosophies. These philosophies formed our code of honor. Whether right or wrong, engrained principles are difficult to cast aside, and sometimes dangerous. Jumping without a parachute is equally as dangerous as riding out a crashing plane—or worse.

The government associated happiness with money, things, and conveniences—as if happiness remained impossible void of these. We perceived it differently. Honor was above wealth; one's honor was his value. When we weighed money in the balance beside honor, we didn't feel poor. And a family that loved each other as much as ours did would never die as paupers, alone and forgotten. You can't take a dime with you out of this life, but you can take love; it's stored in the soul.

Happiness wasn't too complicated for us. Jesus taught (and Preacher Charlie reminded us) that the poor, the meek, and the mourning could still have happiness. And we had found a measure of happiness. So, the offer of strangers seemed a gamble, where our "present happiness" versus their "promised happiness" turned out to be the stakes. Should we trade what we had for what they promised? To hear them talk, the right vote suggested happiness would be sent in by the truckloads. We were trapped in the game of political statistics: the more people, the more votes, the more resources sent your way. With our meager population, we were unable to compete with the world around us because we had so little to offer. We had no assurance for their promised Eden, but we had experienced happiness. We didn't want to chance losing what we had.

They all came to save us. They came with social programs to get us through the impending night, a long night in which we dreamed about their promised tomorrows with uncertainty. Such grandiose hopes had long ago vanished. The logging companies had offered us treasures for our trees. They took our trees and floated the treasured timber down our North Forth, leaving us a few pennies and a whole lot of stumps and wasteland. They failed to mention the erosion to our soil, creating barren hillsides. The coal companies promoted the advantage of selling mineral rights—immediate cash and lasting jobs. But idle tipples and rusted, iron tracks were reminders of worldwide troubles—not too encouraging to our world, which already lagged way behind the rest. They failed to mention the dreadful scene of hundreds of dead fish floating in the muddy North Fork, killed from the runoff of poisonous mine-water. Their improved road system brought promises of a better life, with jobs for all. The roads came in; ironically, businesses did not follow. Instead, our men followed the roads in search of work elsewhere; eventually, entire families left.

Yes, they all came to save us, but in the end, it is my caring mom and a hard-working dad who get the credit. Their love never faltered; it was rooted in something deeper than dreams. Mom encouraged us to strive for the best, while Dad worked two and three jobs to see that we had the opportunity to succeed.

It was June of '62. Dad made the decision. He beat Mrs. Johnson's visit to save us by a couple of years. We traveled State Route 15, snaking north over Dead Man's Hill out of Jackson. I sat in the back seat, right side, next to the window—being second oldest to Joyce Marie. She sat on the left side, next to the window, right behind Dad, holding our one-year-old sister, Sherry—simply Sherry, no middle name—on her lap. Brenda Sue and Roland—simply Roland, like Sherry, with no middle name—had already gone ahead with Uncle Fred. Roland's name was an afterthought, for he was supposed to be called Gary, after my friend, Gary Clay, but a cousin got the name first.

"We kain't have two Garys in the fam'ly, 'specially months apart," Mom explained.

"But why Roland, Momma? Who in the world do we know by the name uf Roland?" We teased her abundantly.

"I like Roland fur a name," she defended her choice.

"But why not a middle name, Momma?" We continued the foray to her dismay.

"Cause I couldn't thank uf one at the time. By the time I thought uf a middle name, Doc Louis already had'es birth certif'cate made out."

Doyle Eugene and William Freddie—oh, how he hates that name, Freddie, so we call him Fred— squeezed in between the rest of us, front and back. At about five-minute intervals Doyle asked, "Ar' we ther yit?"

"Not'chet, Doyle," someone snarled.

"We'll tell ya, Doyle, when we git thar," Mom consoled him. "Might try'n go ta sleep so's the trip'll pass fast'r."

I noticed Mom wiping a tear. She was leaving dear friends behind, but life had been hard the past fifteen years. The move promised to make her life a bit better. Perhaps the tears were from a combination of joy and sadness.

Estel Gambrel followed us in his coal truck carrying our few pieces of used furniture. We preceded the Beverly Hillbillies, but we had no "black gold" in our coffers and no mansion awaiting us. Our only mansion was the one Preacher Charlie reminded us of every Sunday, and hopefully that was a good way off.

We traveled north through Campton, Winchester, Paris, and Cynthiana. These were Kentucky towns we had heard about but never visited. Our mouths gaped and we stared bug-eyed when we viewed the rolling fields of the horse farms at Paris. The houses stood majestic, like we imagined heaven's mansions they sang about in church. Each had manicured yards lined with stone fences that resembled row after row of dominos.

"Slaves built them fences a long time ago," Dad said. He explained the history like he had been there, though research suggests that the Negro workers were freemasons at the time, who had acquired the trade some years prior as slaves. But that "long time ago" of slavery amounted to only about a hundred years. Some folks were still alive who were born into slavery. I was born into poverty, but the two, slavery and poverty, were far apart. I pondered the idea of slavery. Word was the Negroes were still being mistreated down south, and the new president, John Kennedy, was inclined to correct that, but I didn't quite know whether to believe all the rumors or not. Dad said some black folks lived where we were moving. I'd never seen a black man in real life.

My thoughts drifted across the grassy fields where the grandest creatures I had ever seen idly grazed on the luscious, thick grass. The mules I was accustomed to didn't quite measure up to these splendid animals. But the white horse that pastured near our house, the one nobody ever thought about telling me belonged to my dad, had somewhat the same elegance.

Dad told us they called this part of Kentucky the Bluegrass. "Cause of the color uf the grass," he said. Was that the color of the ocean? I'd heard the ocean was blue also. These fields seemed more green than blue, but I tried to imagine them as being blue. Though I had never seen the ocean, I tried to imagine it looking like those rolling fields.

Our white Impala hummed a consistent but off-tune melody as we sped along the blacktop. The intermittent white lines painted down the middle of the road reminded me of the countdown at the beginning of a film on the big screen at the Jaxon Theater—a scene I had not often witnessed, for it was a luxury we could seldom afford, and per Dad's strong Christian belief, a vice we could live without.

I felt secure thinking about Dad coming home every night, but I wondered what the big, city school would be like, and if I might be in a class with a Negro. I wondered if they would accept me as a friend or perceive me as an enemy. At the time, I had no way of knowing a black schoolmate would become my best friend, and I would worship with many people of color in years to come. And I had no inkling that I would become a minister and one day pastor a multi-cultural congregation.

I was glad to be shed of the secret club, but I didn't consider that their equivalent—or worse—awaited me in the big city.

The scenes of the countryside swished by much faster than when you are lying flat of your back on a grassy knoll, swatting flies, and counting cotton-candy clouds drifting across the wide-open sky. The wind from the open window made my burr haircut stand straight on end. I closed my eyes and tried to imagine what lay ahead, and I suddenly remembered something Nancy York had said about Newport: "… a rowdy river town opposite Cincinnati." I'd be living a stone's throw across the river from Nancy York.

A smile crossed my face. Life was beginning to speed up a little.

Chapter Forty-five

The Letter

At the Marie Roberts School I was leaving behind, Miss Circle had used gentle persuasion to get me to join the school band. With her influential position, she convinced— or maybe manipulated—Mom and Dad into purchasing a used trumpet so I could develop what she called "innate musical talents." Mom and Dad seemed a bit skeptical of her handwritten note expressing "unusually gifted," but more so, the cost created a hardship for them. Still, they gave it consideration in the budget.

"Don't see how in the world we kin afford it," Dad reasoned to Mom.

"Don't want'm ta miss out on opp'tunity," Mom injected. "I kin wait fur ma new couch if'n we kin buy'm one uf them trumpets so's he kin practice."

"Will make an awful lot uf noise round hur," Dad argued. But he was slowly losing the discussion.

Miss Circle's most convincing line in her note to Mom and Dad was her rationale that if it did not work out, she would find a buyer for the trumpet: a no-risk purchase.

"Why don't we just try it fur a while and see how's it works?" Mom finally asked.

They did. My siblings tolerated it. The neighborhood regretted it. The dogs loved it. And I was committed to it.

But things did not work out. With our upcoming move to Newport, I had returned the trumpet to Miss Circle, who, true to her word, accepted the trumpet with the promise of payment as soon as she found a buyer. I gave her my new address so she could mail the money, and we parted, forever.

Weeks passed, which seemed like months, with no word from Miss Circle. Time for a child has little reference points;

it seems Christmas or a birthday will never arrive. Age reverses this process; events of fifty years past seem like only yesterday, and we count what time we—hopefully—have left. Life ceases to beckon us to go; rather, death beckons us to come. I learned to speak the words in a despised freshman Latin class, but the true meaning of *vita brevis* I would not understand until about age fifty—life is short. The last half of a century is downhill and slippery at best.

I waited impatiently for the money for the trumpet to arrive from Miss Circle. Frequent trips to the mailbox proved futile: not a word from her. I concluded my parents had been swindled. This made me angry—angrier than when Sidgel Diddle sucker-punched Uncle Billy. I had to find a way to fight back. I could not let a deceptive schoolteacher, hiding behind the cloak of religion, cheat my parents out of much needed money. There had to be a way to get even.

With pen in hand, I unleashed my attack. Dear Miss Circle, I began, but quickly got to the point and held nothing back as to my feelings for her: hypocrite, cheat, con artist, swindler, fake, liar. My bold handwriting screamed my disappointment in her lack of compassion for a family of seven children, whose mom and dad sacrificed their own needs to purchase the trumpet, in good faith that if it did not work out, she would make it right with us. I closed with "I know I will never hear from you, but at least you now know what I think about you."

With emotions satisfied by the taste of vented venom, I signed, sealed, and sent the letter to her last known address. By this time, she had probably skipped country, disguised herself as a missionary, and was teaching natives in some foreign land that they were the world's next wonder, "if they purchased her used instruments," of course, my trumpet included.

As I dropped the letter into the mailbox, I chided myself for wasting time and the money for a stamp. She would not respond even if she received the letter; conversely, the next day a letter arrived in the mail, addressed to me, and the return address bore the same address I had used for Miss Circle the day before. How could she respond so quickly? My better judgment told me she could not.

With trembling hands, I tore open the envelope. A check fell from the letter and floated to the floor. My heart skipped as my mind replayed the words used yesterday in my scathing letter to her. I reluctantly read aloud her letter to me:

> Dear Larry,
>
> It has been some time since I have seen or heard from you. I have missed not having you as a student. Your love for and grasp of music was a great reward to me. You are a prized student, and I will always remember our times together. I hope you continue your studies in music. Enclosed is payment for the sell of your trumpet. I am sorry it took so long to find a buyer. This week I finally found a student whose parents were able to afford it, as I gave it to them on credit. The student, like you, has potential.
>
> Thank your parents for entrusting me with your musical potential. You have blessed my life in ways that you do not yet understand. I have but one regret, that I did not lead you to Christ. But I pray for you still that someday you will find Him as your Savior. I remain your loving teacher,
>
> Miss Circle

I sat for a long while staring at the letter. If tears could recall my impetuous wrath of words, I would have cried a river. I did not cry, but a part of me died. I found solace only in the thought that when Nancy York had abandoned us, I had not written a letter to her.

Chapter Forty-six

Indiana Migration

Though mountain folks never get past the magnetic pull to "go back home," I probably should mention that I have ended up living in Seymour, Indiana, a wonderful community sixty miles south of Indy and fifty-five miles north of Louisville, where I-65 and Route 50 intersect. My journey has had a few crooks and turns along the way: Minnesota, Ohio, and even taking me back to Kentucky for a couple years, but eventually leading me away for good—at least I assume it is for good, but then again, one never knows for sure.

The migration to Indiana began with my Uncles Billy, Fred, and James. James was much older, while Billy and Fred were twelve months apart, and the two were inseparable in life. Both went into the army a few months apart, as Fred sneaked off and enlisted, and Billy was drafted shortly thereafter. Both trained at Ft. Knox and were stationed in Germany. After their stint in the service, they married in a double wedding ceremony (Billy to Wilma Noble and Fred to Judy Cope, who were cousins), and both couples moved to the same small town of Westport, Indiana. Both found careers and eventually retired from Cummins Engine—only a few months apart. Their primary difference was in their hobbies: Uncle Billy collected model trains (Why am I not surprised?), while Uncle Fred took up golf—I was surprised. The contrasting hobbies separated them somewhat, but they still lived only a couple blocks from each other in the same little community until both passed away.

Westport is about twenty miles east of Columbus, Indiana. Columbus is an impressive city renowned for its unique architecture, Cummins Engine, and the 48th vice-president of the United States, Michael Pence. Unlike the progressive city of Columbus, unless you are looking for Westport, you may drive past without realizing it—it boasted one flashing red-light back then, but even that has been eliminated. An ambitious town counsel put up a sign along the main highway, evidently in a futile attempt to generate growth. The sign brought a smile but no increase in population, which peaked at the turn of the century and has been in decline since. It was a hand painted sign of a Revolutionary War Minuteman, sharply dressed in a blue and white-trim uniform, clutching his flint-lock rifle, ready at a minute's notice to go into action. A caption boldly proclaimed: Westport, Progressive and On the Move. More recently, they have changed that sign to a more modern appeal. But the population is stuck at below 1,400, though my cousin has opened a prosperous pizza business in the heart of the town.

Uncle James lived in a much smaller community, Sardinia, located a few miles from Westport, but eventually he upgraded to Westport. It's believed that Sardinia was named after the second largest island in the Mediterranean; ironically, this Sardinia is in the middle of a cornfield. And Westport? Likewise, in the middle of a cornfield. There is no river, but there might be a creek running through it, so I am usure of what kind of port they had in mind when they named the town.

After we moved to Newport, life proceeded full and fast, unlike the long and lazy days of the Cumberland Plateau. I busied myself playing tag football and strikeout with my brothers and newly acquired friends. I made the basketball and football teams. My sisters spent a lot of time on the telephone, a novelty for us, for we had never had a telephone in the mountains. School activities consumed my time. Latin class was horrible. I was "jist learnin' ta speak like city folks" when I up and "jined a Latin class."

Mom loved having Dad home every day. She enjoyed a routine of packing his lunch and getting him off to work, preparing breakfast for the seven of us before we left for school, and cleaning a house that was triple anything she had ever lived in. Supper always awaited us. Dad worked however many hours—or jobs—it took to clothe and feed us and occasionally buy Mom some new furniture.

Newport was good and bad for me; I quickly realized it had all kinds of secret clubs, each one beckoning. Dad found an alternative for me—a church similar to Grandpa Charlie's. For the first time we attended church together on a regular basis. One by one we all got baptized—in an inside baptismal instead of the sometimes muddy and swift flowing North Fork of our past. I'm sure Mom preferred our baptism in a tank instead of the river, as afraid as she was of us drowning.

Nancy York remained a lingering memory. I searched for her in my dreams, but she was always a block ahead, and I always lost her in the crowd. I graduated from Newport High School and left in the fall to attend college in St. Paul, Minnesota. That's where I finally found her. Walking down the hallway of the college, I saw her standing on a balcony overlooking a stairway; she was pretty as a picture, innocent as a lamb, but for some reason sad of countenance and humming the song *Paper Roses*. For her birthday I anonymously ordered her a dozen, red roses minus one. She somehow figured out the anonymity, thanked me graciously, and hesitantly divulged that the florist shorted the order by one rose, not that she minded, for they were beautiful and all, but she knew they had to be expensive, and it wasn't right for the florist to cheat me that way. I explained that she was the missing rose in the flower garden of my heart. Two years later we married, I finished college, but she dropped out to have a baby, and after graduation we moved to Seymour, Indiana, about twenty-five miles southwest of Westport. I was excited about being close to my uncles Billy, Fred, and James.

Seymour doesn't have a Minuteman sign, but we have had a VFW V-J Day Parade every year in August since 1946: that is before COVID. At one time it boasted being the only continuous VFW V-J Day parade in the country. But the floats and the crowds dwindled. It's now a celebration by a few. Death of the veterans happened before the organizers caved to the parade being considered politically incorrect due to the kind and industrious Japanese families who live in our community and are good neighbors and have invested millions of dollars into our town. The subject became an ongoing debate in the local newspaper. Those for the parade argued we were honoring the brave boys who fought for us, not insulting those who fought against us. I can't imagine anyone ever forgetting the horrors of that war or any war so long as there are wartime pictures of Pearl Harbor and Hiroshima and Nagasaki—solemn reminders lest we ever forget. Still, somehow we do, for wars continue to be the answer over diplomacy. And Hitlers continue to pop up around the world.

Anyway, Uncle Fred's hobby is why he and I (without Uncle Billy) met for a round of golf a few years ago at the city-owned, nine-hole course in Columbus, Indiana. Residents of the city receive a dollar discount—we, of course, didn't qualify. He was a resident of Progressive-and-On-The-Move Westport; I was a resident of Seymour, home of the V-J Day Parade.

The clerk asked, "Are you city residents?"

"I am," Uncle Fred declared without hesitancy. He received his dollar discount and placed it in his pocket with satisfaction. "For a candy bar later," he said, prompting a grin from him.

Mischief tempted me to ask him, in front of the clerk and just for the fun of it, if he had recently moved from Westport to Columbus. Since I was his guest, I didn't, though I did give him a sideways glance. For a brief moment, a mirror in time, I saw him standing by the railroad tracks in the plateau, a scrawny orphan, clutching a willow pole and waving to the engineer, a victor's smile caressing his face.

Chapter Forty-seven
Tabby And The Big House

Before you jump to an assumption that this chapter is about a relative sent to prison, I'll alleviate any such concern. No, Tabby never went to prison. And no, Tabby wasn't a relative; conversely, Tabby was our cat. The timeline for this chapter was two sons later and multiple moves. Nancy and I had lived in Indiana, Kentucky, Ohio, and back to Indiana. Unlike my childhood, we moved rather frequently. And we had lived mostly in basements, second floors, or not too desirable small houses. But this time we were fortunate to live in one of the grandest homes in Seymour, Indiana.

The owner of this mansion was the former governor of the state of Indiana, whom by some fortuitous circumstances we had met. Over time, Mr. Whitcomb took a liking to us and rented us his house at an affordable price.

Mr. Whitcomb introduced us to one of the neighbors and explained that he was going to be doing extensive travel, and we would move into his house. This was an intimidating experience, meeting the neighbor, as her family name was plastered on the local hospital signage, which I'm told had to do with their benevolence. Her response to the introduction was a question: "Moving into the carriage house?" I was embarrassed to think that her perception of us was that of caretaker, but the governor replied quickly and graciously, "No, they're moving into the big house." With that introduction we became neighbors; further, we became close friends.

We always referred to it as the Whitcomb house. It boasted three floors, a basement, and a tunnel that ran from the basement to the carriage house. The carriage house had an upstairs apartment for the caretaker—a caretaker which we could never afford. But Nancy's mother payed a student from the local Indiana Bible College—where I worked—to wash the windows. This was a never-ending job, for there were an unbelievable number of small, lead-paned windows throughout the house.

Over time, the big house became the neighborhood-animal-control clinic. I lived by the philosophy "no child should be denied the companionship of a pet," eventually expanding the philosophy into "parents should be awarded a trophy for caring for the pets their children were not denied," and ultimately adding to the philosophy "shoot me on the spot if I ever bring another animal into this house."

I suppose my tenderness toward animals stemmed from my childhood, for as a child we always had animals. My favorite was a fat and furry, tiger-orange tomcat we uniquely named Tom. He was quite independent and routinely climbed through a hole near the top of our corncrib to catch mice. Uncle Billy and I took care of the orphaned mice left unattended by Tom's aggressive nature. Billy made miniature harnesses for them to wear, and he built miniature sleds from cornstalks, which he tied to the harnesses. This established our own twenty-mule-team of mice. To our delight, the wee mice pulled the sleds along the yellow brick roads we paved with corn kernels. Not having television, our entertainment required stretching the imagination, especially on rainy days. We harnessed up the baby mice and sent them toiling along our toy roads. I suppose in our politically correct world, our antics bordered on animal cruelty: though I don't recall a society for protection of mice. How cruel, some probably lament! Maybe so. We didn't necessarily mean to be cruel—though I must admit that using them for target practice after they had toiled all day might have bordered on some inner savagery. Still, we never used Decon or mouse traps, like city folks. And we didn't allow Tom, no matter how hungry he might have looked, to attack our baby mice. We were, to some degree, their protector from Tom, at least until we got bored paying with them.

Tom was rather adept at supplying his own meals. Mom added one delicacy to his otherwise wild diet: she routinely gave him a bowl of milk for breakfast. But the routine was broken one morning when he didn't show up for the milk. So, she went searching for him. And that's why she, instead of me, found Tom—dead.

Mom awakened me with the heart-rending news. "Larry, yur Tom is dead." She managed the words through quivering lips and downcast eyes as moist as when she peeled one of the onions we raised in our garden. She wiped her tears with the corner of her apron and continued, "Reckon it wuz his time to go."

Tom, dead? That seemed impossible. Caught in a muskrat trap maybe. A mite cut up or clawed up maybe, but dead? Surely not!

Mom had found him that morning hanging lifeless from the same hole he had crawled through a thousand times. Evidently, even animals get careless. I cried, kind of like I did at Grandma's funeral. It seemed the right thing to do, especially considering the demeanor with which Mom broke the news. It resembled the way she broke the news about a cousin or neighbor dying—not necessarily the words, but the tone of her voice, and the expression on her face.

Having gone through that experience as a child, I should have been more sensitive to my youngest son, Aaron, when he lost his closest companion—his tabby cat—whom he appropriately called Tabby. But I wasn't the least bit sympathetic to Aaron's pain. One less mouth to feed was my initial thought, since cat food can be expensive.

Though Tabby had disappeared for a couple of weeks, Aaron wasn't overly concerned, for the tomcat had strayed before but always returned. However, driving down the street a few blocks from our house, I spotted a cat lying motionless along the curb, evidently hit by a vehicle. Curiosity and concern, mostly curiosity, compelled me to stop and investigate. My investigation identified Tabby as the victim of a hit and run. I stuffed the stiff into an olive-green garbage bag and dropped him off in a garbage can by the alley behind the carriage house. As a child, country living offered a more respectable burial for our animals, but now, living in the city, our Tabby wasn't so fortunate. The garbage dump would be his eternal tomb.

Being a logical father, I called a conference with Aaron, and matter-of-factly (without any facts, just emphatically) announced Tabby's death and that he would not be returning home, today, tomorrow, or ever—of course I withheld the where-a-bouts of the deceased. Aaron took the news in a rather resentful way, as if I had messed up his day or that I should have been more tactful at my presentation. He immediately went into the usual stages of grief: shock, disbelief, anger, but got hung up in the denial stage. All through the evening, his mother, my usually sweet wife—who to my surprise joined in with Aaron in resenting my straightforward manner of fulfilling my fatherly role—tried to console him. She hinted of an animal heaven, and Tabby—being the saintly feline he was—surely made it to the animal afterlife and wouldn't want to come back even if he could.

"Right now, he's probably enjoying a meal of Swiss cheese and warm 2% milk, surrounded by a host of cat cherubim waiting on his every whim," she comforted, justifying such a far-fetched falsehood because of the pitiful face of her distraught son. "Would you want to deny Tabby that reward?" she challenged.

"I just want my Tabby back," Aaron insisted.

Nothing worked. No amount of reasoning, consoling,

or manipulation changed his demeanor. Aaron refused to be comforted. He held to a couple Sunday School lessons about Jesus raising His friend Lazarus and a little girl from the dead—placing emphasis on "friend" and "little" and talking as if it happened yesterday. "And," insisted Aaron, "Jesus can do that for my Tabby."

The entire household felt a bit tense at bedtime. Aaron's older brother, Andrew, shook his head in resignation; he had been here before with Aaron and knew of his indomitable resolve. We bid Aaron goodnight and left him clutching his sheets and his faith. A night of sleep brought some resemblance of calm for me, a calm shattered early in the morning by muffled sobs coming from the back yard.

Bolting out of bed, I quickly donned robe and slippers and bounded downstairs, all the while envisioning the inevitable—Aaron had found his dead Tabby in the garbage can. Throwing open the back door, sure enough, there he stood cradling his cat, tears streaming down his cheeks. But something was amiss. The muffled sobs were not from sadness; rather, they were sobs of joy! Like a hallelujah chorus, "Christ is risen!," or, Mary Magdalene's tears of delight at an empty tomb. Aaron possessed the biggest smile a child can offer. Never before or since, except cases like Lazarus and the little girl Jesus raised from the dead, does a child smile so. Tabby remained cuddled in his arms, reminiscent of the prodigal's son, which was dead, but now alive, and come home. And Aaron exclaimed, through euphoric tears and sniffles, "Jesus did it, Dad! Jesus raised Tabby from the dead!"

Aaron rushed past me eager to share his rewarded faith with his mother and brother. I, like a combination of the prodigal son's angry brother and Jesus' doubting disciple, Thomas, headed straight to the garbage can. Happy for Aaron, yet angry. Wanting to believe, yet doubtful. Relieved, yet wondering. I opened the still snug lid. My hands quivered from adrenalin, and my mind raced with emotion as I worked to unknot the plastic garbage bag. Apprehensively, I peered inside. Just as I thought! The cat was still there and still very much dead. It hadn't turned over, let alone resurrected, and by now, *haut gout*, a little on the decaying side. How confusing! How can this be? It was then that an impromptu autopsy revealed "he" was actually a "she"—not Tabby at all. I had brought home the wrong dead cat.

Retying the knot, I closed the lid and walked slowly toward the house. Now, I knew I couldn't let Aaron spend the rest of his life believing, even reveling in—and reciting—a false story about a modern-day resurrection of a cat. The full picture must be painted here; reality must be redeemed. As I strolled across the back yard—collecting my thoughts for a logical explanation for this untimely return of Tabby, on the very morning of an all-night, prayer vigil by a distraught child—a little sparrow darted in front of my path and landed in an aged, flowering Redbud. I paused for a moment as it leaped from limb to limb, head cocked as if to say something, but never did, though by this time nothing would have surprised me. As it flew off, a message lingered in my heart. A reprieve, like a gentle breeze, consoled my fretful emotions. Even the little sparrow, not worth a dime a dozen, doesn't fall to the ground without God seeing and caring. Further, except you have childlike faith, you can't perceive the miracles of Scripture or the hope of heaven. Let it be, I thought. Let it be. In later years, when reality is more tolerable, I will tell him the full account. I have told him, but I am unsure he believes my version over his own childhood memoirs. After all, he's the one who stayed up all night praying.

Very early that first Easter morn, Jesus did what adult reasoning struggles to comprehend but childlike faith simply accepts.

Chapter Forty-eight

Genealogy

A long journey of at least a millennium had landed my family in the Cumberland Plateau. Around the time Leif Eriksson set sail across the Norwegian Sea to discover and plunder, my forefathers navigated the channel from France to England to expand and conquer. But for us, such information was long ago lost in the annals of memory. No one alive in my family could remember, nor did they seem to care. So, born without papers of pedigree, we never made much of a mark in the big picture of things. Outsiders considered us paupers, but that was by their standards. If we were indigent, one good thing (probably the only good thing) about it was that we didn't know. With sows' back and pork rinds as food staples we could always count on, we considered ourselves living high on the hog. And most all of us were in some way descendants of Daniel Boone or Davy Crockett or Simon Kenton or honest Abe. And these had certainly left their mark, so that must have left us somewhat significant.

As a child, I once asked Mom where I came from. She went into a short story about the rabbits that ran around on the hillside overlooking our house, without homes, and looking for their mommies. "You wuz one of them rabbits," she concluded, "but yur Daddy and me took ya in and raised ya." How enlightening!

We call it the "birds and the bees" today, back then I suppose it was the "rabbits and squirrels," different critters, but the same concept—avoidance of a child's curiosity about procreation. Even though a child, I expected a different explanation than the one Mom gave, but I let it be. In later years I felt compelled to override her condensed version, so

I delved into a bit of research. I doubt, unless you are a relative of mine, that my genealogy is of much interest to you, nonetheless, here goes.

To date, the research of the Arrowood lineage has turned up a great-great-great grandparent, Nathan Lewis Arrowood, born in 1818 in North Carolina. It seems uncertain who his parents were, but a family history, written by his grandson, states that he was the son of William Anderson and Susan Arrowood. Before jumping to conclusions, they may have been married to each other. The story goes that Susan, a full-blooded Cherokee, enacted a tribal tradition and gave Nathan her surname of Arrowood. This story sounds much better than the alternative, and I love this connection—a true American, with forefathers standing on the banks of the Atlantic, waving to the approaching ships of the first white settlers, who could well have been my relatives on Mom's side of the family—the Brewers. And the Cherokee blood gives meaning to the migration of my forefathers into the highlands of Kentucky, where Nathan died in 1905 in Breathitt County.

The Brewer lineage has been easier to trace. Progenitors of the Brewer family in America came from the coast of Flanders. A member of the Brewer family, Drogo de la Bruviere, married a cousin of William the Conqueror, and followed him in the invasion of Britain and the defeat of the Saxons in 1066. His name is listed on the Roll of Honor Abby in Hastings. I would like to see that someday.

I shy away from the dark side of Drogo de la Bruviere, but his descendants (the Brewers) were no small potatoes. The argument goes that Thomas Brewer married Nancy Drake, relative of Sir Francis Drake. Their son, John, sailed with Drake on his circumnavigation of the world, and was sent to inform Queen Elizabeth of their triumph. The sad note is that another son, Thomas, was captured and eaten by cannibals on that same voyage.

John Brewer II immigrated with his father to America in 1622—two years after the Pilgrims—and first settled in Isle of Wight, Virginia. He served in the House of Burgesses. Brewer's son, John III, may have played a role in Bacon's Rebellion in 1676, when followers of Nathaniel Bacon, property-owners in the western part of the Virginia Colony, defeated an Indian invasion—probably my descendants on my Dad's side of the family. The farmers accused Governor Sir William Berkeley of acting too slowly and of favoring friends. When the governor accused the landowners of being rebels, to prove him wrong, they captured and burned Jamestown. The innocent victors ousted Governor Berkeley which led to some reforms in the Virginian Colony. This rebellion may well have been the first blow for liberty from England a hundred years before the Declaration of Independence, but it got my ancestors into a heap of trouble with the crown. They moved farther into the colonies' interior, from fear of reprisal from former Governor Berkeley who had been reinstated by the English crown. That's how the Brewers eventually ended up in Breathitt County, Kentucky, by way of North Carolina, poor as Job's turkey. And that is why I ended up a Kentuckian instead of a Virginian.

Families often fail in communicating such salacious tidbits of ancestry to their children. I shared this thought with Uncle Fred while he was a captive audience in the hospital after surgery—it is sad that too many of our visits take place in hospitals (when the center piece is drugged) and in funeral homes (when the conversation piece is dead). That's when Uncle Fred shared his personal story.

"When I was a lad, my mom took me by train to Jackson. While there, we met a little man on the street corner, and she stood and talked with him for a long time. I remember he was short, and his hands trembled as he gestured. I wondered, how odd that Mom would talk so long with a total stranger! After this little man left, I asked Mom, 'Who in the world is that strange man, Momma?' With surprise she answered, 'Why son, that wuz yur Grandpa.' And that was my first and last time to see him."

When Uncle Fred told me this story, I could have cried, but he wasn't, so I didn't. But it certainly piqued my interest of my genealogy. Where did I come from? I wanted a better answer than the one Mom gave me—or that Darwin suggested, but Aunt Fannie disproved. And I'm eager to share my research with family, friends, and anyone who will lend an ear. This over zealousness needs some boundaries though, before my friends start running when they see me coming.

Somehow, most subtly I'm sure, I once worked a bit of my genealogy into a conversation with a friend at a birthday party—especially the part about the Brewer family being married to relatives of William the Conqueror. My friend expressed his interest in genealogy, for which I was pleased, but then he added, "Amazing about your family being associated with William the Conqueror. We may be slightly related."

"Oh, really?" I asked. Whereupon I continued to share more in-depth information about my famous, and infamous, family association. I was about ready to switch into the Arrowood clan when he interrupted. "My grandfather, a few times removed of course, just happens to be William the Conqueror." I detected an emphasis on "just happens to be" and sensed a conqueror's smirk materializing on his face. I retreated to the punch bowl.

Chapter Forty-nine

The Last Ride

Until the day illness stopped him, Dad worked long hours in his blue-collar job. It was not an illness caused by riotous living; it was a rare disease doctors at first struggled to diagnose and later could not cure. He had barely turned fifty-nine. It left him disabled and chronically in and out of the hospital for thirteen years.

The sounds of beeps and hums filled the hospital room. We kept a vigil around his bedside. The door slowly opened and Doctor Cohen—dressed in his usual casual attire—stepped inside the room. He never was into vogue, but he was into attacking infections with a vengeance. He briefly made small talk with Mom but then abruptly got down to business.

"Not good news, Delmar," Doctor Cohen reported. "I'm starting to think this line's beginning to sound like a broken record," he continued.

"Whatcha mean, doctor?" Dad asked.

"Another rare staph infection. No approved medication available."

Doctor Cohen was single, Jewish, and devoted to his work. We felt fortunate to have him doctoring Dad, him so devoted and being a descendant of Abraham in the Bible, making him kind of closer to God than many. He brought Dad back from the brink of death (on more than one occasion) and became a trusted friend to our family. He stayed by Dad's bedside beyond expectations, sometimes remaining at the hospital all night because he cared.

"There is an experimental drug I can obtain from a research center in Philadelphia. I'd like to try it," Doctor Cohen said in a questioning tone.

Dad consented.

The treatment was scheduled to last thirty days, with close monitoring and evaluation. Doctor Cohen stopped the treatment prematurely because the side effects terrified Dad, whose body had a history of reacting negatively to drugs. With this reaction, Dad's options had dwindled.

But not to be deterred, Doctor Cohen pushed on. "I've been in contact with Philadelphia," he explained. "We have a recommendation."

Dad listened without commenting.

"We feel almost positively we know what went wrong, and if we correct it, I believe it will cure you. In retrospect, the dosage we gave you was too much for your system. We have recalculated and want to repeat the procedure, with your permission, of course," Doctor Cohen explained.

"Thirty more days?" Dad asked.

"Yes," Doctor Cohen said.

"It wuz tough going, doctor," Dad whispered.

"I know, Delmar. I'm sorry, but we're doing the best we know. Got the finest working on your case." Doctor Cohen rested his hand on Dad's shoulder and waited for his response.

Dad remained silent as he considered the request. He looked around the room at each of us, closed his eyes, and finally spoke. "I trust yur judgment, Doctor Cohen. Do whatever needs ta be done."

Doctor Cohen repeated the entire procedure, with favorable results, but it only cured the infection. Dad never shed the disease that ravaged his body for years: Vasculitis, an inflammation of the blood vessels that restricts the blood flow, especially to the extremities of the body, and for Dad, it also attacked his lungs.

Not being able to work was almost as frustrating to Dad as the disease. Working and providing for his family was a responsibility he embraced with honor, never a drudgery.

But his ability to work ended abruptly. By then he couldn't drive, so I drove him to the government office where he applied for limited Supplemental Security Income until his Social Security benefits kicked in. We waited in line until his turn. An impatient clerk fired questions that he answered in a whisper, due to his shortness of breath.

"First name?"

"Delmar."

"Speak up please."

"Delmar," I responded.

Dad dropped his head in exhaustion.

"Middle initial?"

"None," Dad beat me to it.

"No middle name?"

"No."

"Surname?"

Dad hesitated.

"Your last name," she barked.

I suspected she had gotten her government job through some special program for the underprivileged. Surely, she should understand, I reasoned, but she showed no compassion for the sick or poor. How odd! I wanted to scream: "Lady, he is one of your own. He is a common laborer like yourself. Your income right now is from taxes paid by working people just like him!" But too many like her had already parted from the working principles my dad had strongly supported and truly trusted.

I wanted to walk away and take Dad with me, to shield him from her barbed arrows of cynicism and critique, to tell him we had made it before without their help, and we would somehow make it still, but that wasn't fair to him. He had earned this right with the amount of taxes he had put into the system. I was angry with her and embarrassed for Dad. But he had seen enough hard times to be shed of the cloak of pride still worn by many of us. He had worked hard for over forty years—never taking a dime he hadn't honestly earned. No, Dad is not like her, I thought. His is a dying breed.

Death stalked Dad for thirteen, exhausting years—maybe that's what finally got him. He was tired. He fought and suffered through six amputations, colostomy procedures twice, long hours of dialysis necessitated by kidney failure, and extensive lung impairment. He never sought a Black Lung pension—though he probably could have gotten it for the years he worked in the Kentucky mines. Dad believed his sickness came from something else; his character prevented seeking compensation otherwise. I've heard some who never worked a day in their lives in the mines applied; conversely, Dad would not.

They called us to the hospital the eve of the New Millennium. Dad had taken a turn for the worse. All seven kids and Mom stayed by his bedside. Relatives came from as far away as Michigan—Appalachian people, though far removed and somewhat shy in social settings, know what it means to pay respect and give support.

A love for life consumed Dad. The day before he died, he revived when they removed the ventilator, and he told us all—especially Mom—how much he loved us. He lived into the second night of the new millennium before he gave up. Unconsciousness followed more quickly than we were prepared for; death's claws would not let go.

We heard the train coming before we saw it rounding the curve. Dad hesitated in boarding; I think that was mostly because of leaving Mom behind. But she had adjusted to his long absences down through the years; she would adjust again. And in his condition, it was not fair to him for us to dissuade him boarding for the last ride.

I leaned closely, hugged his unconscious body tightly, and spoke firmly into his ear. "It's all right Dad. Get on board. It's your journey home. We'll take care of Mom."

We huddled at the station watching the huge steel engine

strain as it began the final destination. We stared longingly after it, until it was but a distant rumble.

Heavy clouds hovered low at the cemetery. Family and friends huddled close in a lovely, little chapel. My brother's pastor spoke encouraging words. A sparrow landed in an oak and jumped from limb to limb. A ray of light pierced through a tiny opening in the clouds, and surprisingly, the clouds parted, separated as if brushed apart by the hand of God. The sun burst forth with a brilliance and grandeur seldom witnessed by mortal man. Dad was finally home.

Chapter Fifty

Save Yourselves

Perhaps I should elaborate on the title of this book: Save Yourselves. My family was born poor, as society considers poverty; however, we were blessed to be born in the United States of America. That blessing gave us the opportunity, resources, and the liberty to dig our way out of poverty. It didn't come easy, but each generation dramatically improved their lives. We saved ourselves, kinda. That's not to contradict the Bible teaching of salvation through grace: salvation and succeeding in life are separate issues. Only Christ can save our soul; however, though I'm a firm believer that Christ's blessings help us along life's journey, most of our accomplishments are up to the time, energy, sacrifices, and decisions we make. I'm talking about pulling ourselves up instead of expecting—even demanding—someone else, especially the government, do it for us. I'm inclined to believe that if the government sustains us, to a great degree it owns us. That is anything but a democracy.

It's been over two decades since Dad passed. Mom outlived him by 14 years. My sister, Brenda Sue, lived with her for years and watched over her daily needs. Mom's health finally dwindled into needing 24/7 care. It pained us that the nursing home was our best option; I couldn't break the news, so Joyce, being the eldest sibling, accepted the task. As she sat in the living room, across from Mom, mentally formulating her presentation, Mom looked at her and stated, "Joyce, I thank I need ta go inta a nursing home." To which Joyce responded, "Mom, why in the world would you think that." Mom listed all the reasons on our list. A couple days later she moved into the Lutheran Nursing Home in our community. They took excellent care of her, for which we are forever grateful.

Unexpectedly, the nursing home called with the news that Mom was dying. The family gathered in, expecting the worst. To our surprise, she was happy as a bride on her wedding day. We assumed the nursing staff had made a mistake in their medical evaluation, as Mom communicated with the family throughout the day. To my nephew, she asked, "Steve, do ya know where I'm goin'?" To which Steve responded, "Grandma, is this a trick question?" She delightfully answered, "I'm goin' ta see yur grandpa." A few hours later she went to sleep and never woke up this side of heaven.

Yes, the good Lord saved their souls for eternity, but Mom and Dad fully understood and accepted their responsibilities on earth. Though both only finished the eighth grade, they worked hard and did a good job seeing to the needs of their family. They sacrificed and saved, and by their example they encouraged us kids to do the same. "Nobody owes ya nothin'," seemed their philosophy, and the double negatives don't change the meaning one iota. We knew what they meant. They even left us a small inheritance from their labors.

My parents had life better than theirs. I've had it better than mine. My sons have the same privilege. And, hopefully, their children will have the same. Let's call it the stairway of succession: there's the opportunity to climb or descend. I believe this process can continue, unless we only measure success by a bank account, and if our society doesn't cave to the craze that we have to make life equal for all by giving to some and taking from others. "All men are created equal ..." is followed by an explanation of the equality: " ... life, liberty, and the pursuit of happiness." This is not something our government is to give us; conversely, it is an opportunity they should never take away from us.

In considering the absurdity how we might make life

equal for all, let's start with sports: basketball. I've never been beyond five feet, six inches tall, but I loved basketball. I did okay until after middle school: that's when it seemed that overnight everyone outgrew me. Shouldn't the system have created a level court, allowing me equal opportunity against six footers and above? Shouldn't they have made each team have at least one player my size? Well, there goes the NBA down the tube! The reality? We must accept certain disappointments about life. We all live with some underprivilege when compared to others. There's always someone smarter, richer, better looking, naturally more aggressive, more likable, born into a wealthier family, or from the right side of the tracks. The list is endless. So, we can protest because of where we are and demand to be placed at the front of the line, or we can do our best to progress from where we are and advance as far as we can. This doesn't mean we'll end up the champ, but we can always improve our score. How? That's where the title of this book comes into play: you can save yourself, kiinda. Study harder. Make more friends. Finish high school. Enroll in college. Value fulfillment over fortune. Sacrifice the present for a desired future. And as one of the greatest preachers of all time wrote: "… I have learned, in whatsoever state I am, therewith to be content." Simply put, learn to be happy. Period.

I'm more than a little concerned with the current, cultural trend: tear down the old establishment and build a completely new one. Tell the poor it's someone else's fault and they were never given a chance to be otherwise. Demand that the government give them everything for free. Pay the teenage hamburger-flipper what the seasoned plumber is making. Control every aspect of life with government regulations. Turn this horrible place called the USA into a political equity farm so no one is above another.

Nope! I'm not buying it. I've been poor, but because I had options, and seized upon such, I have made a difference for myself. No, I didn't get wealthy, but I did get enough. My choice of career placed limitations for material wealth, but I'm grateful it was my right to choose. And the benefits of the right to choose a career far outweigh material possessions I may or may not acquire. Then again, I've seen some of my friends from mediocre backgrounds become quite wealthy. I'm happy for them. It didn't happen because they were handed life on a silver platter. It was a combination of choices, hard work, personality traits, and sometimes just a whole lot of luck. But the common factor in all the scenarios I know always boils down to one thing: a multitude of opportunities. These opportunities can't be replicated by rules of equity, but they are made possible by living in a land where one can choose, and plan, and persevere. This is made possible by the structure of an incredibly-unique country: the United States of America.

Author's Final Comments

This book is a work of fiction with anecdotes of my childhood. A few things are true: dates, historical events, some names, and some places. But I've used writer's privilege to color the black and white tales of yesteryear's momeries.

The stories contain obvious heroes and insinuated villains—not necessarily because they were villains, but because my child mind perceived them as such. I apologize to anyone who may insert themselves into this work of fiction and be offended. I do not intend to insult; rather, I'm telling stories as I perceived them over sixty years ago while trying to find my place in a picture that was like the sands along the North Fork, ever changing and being reshaped by the forces that existed. The footprints have long since vanished; the memories remain, though sometimes murky.

I vacillated between using characters of my past versus creating a whole set of new characters, and I eventually settled on using some real personalities of my past. No one in the stories is my enemy, and I have no animosity to vent, only a heart full of memories that I have enjoyed putting into print and now share with you. Those in the stories, though fictitious, are a part of a fuzzy memory—a part of a past that I cherish with each dawning day, recognizing that I, too, will someday be only a memory in another's heart. And I shudder to think how I may be perceived by some.

A real Nancy York existed in my life but only for a couple weeks; she was the replacement for Mr. Deaton when he retired from teaching and moved away. After what seems like a few weeks, the authorities closed our school, transferred her to I know not where, and bussed us to a distant school. Nancy represented the numerous people that made a positive influence on our lives, easing our burden, pointing us toward progress, and challenging us to improve. But then, like many others, she moved on. She was all those that ever helped to make life a bit easier for my mom, though no one could completely remove from Mom the many struggles of life raising a huge family in the Cumberland Plateau while Dad had to be away for weeks at a time. Nancy York represented the missionaries who brought simple programs to our schools and handed out Bibles as rewards for the memorization of verses. She symbolized the social workers who handed out food and clothing during the disastrous times, the nurses who administered vaccinations, the teachers who taught us to read and write, and the various ladies' guilds who raised money to give us conveniences we would otherwise not have had.

Though representing a fictitious role, Nancy York remained the missing link in my life; I searched for her for years. I eventually found and married her. Her name is Nancy Rae Baldwin. She was born in Virginia, a stones-throw from my colonial ancestors. She grew up in Ohio. We met in Minnesota, and we currently live in Indiana.

The secret club is allegorical. It represents the struggle between good and evil that embattled our community. While parents prayed in their living rooms, offering their homes as a haven, the powers of evil tugged at the hearts of their children as they made choices in the back rooms. Vices know few barriers. Evil was a strong force even in our isolated community. I can personally attest to that but choose not to elaborate.

Coffin Rock was an actual place, though I doubt the locals still call it by name. Legends abounded about this unusually shaped rock, but it isn't near as large as it appeared from my childhood memories.

When I left the Kentucky Plateau, I experienced a travelers' thrill, an adventurer's approval, and a wanderlust's liberty. For me, it was full throttle ahead with no looking back. I had not yet learned of the annual return of the swallows to the old mission in San Juan Capistrano, but I would visit that place some fifty years later. I could not yet perceive that the monarch butterflies—in our back yard—migrated all the way to a thirty-acre mountainside near Mexico City, to a location their ancestors of three to four generations prior came from, but to where they had never been. I, too, would eventually make it to Mexico City. As a child, I thought my tomcat was huge, but I would someday see what a huge cat looked like when I journeyed to Africa. And my fishing hole? I had not yet heard of the salmon's incredible two-thousand-mile journey from the open ocean to the isolated mountain streams far inland where they were born, nor had I read Jack London's Call of the Wild. I would one day visit the Yukon, and see the huge floating salmon canneries, and our taildragger would be fogged in, forcing us to stay with strangers—who became new friends—until the fog lifted and we could fly back to Anchorage. But with all my adventures to these and to numerous other places, the passing of time brings with it a persistent pull, an unrelenting urge, an inexplicable desire to go back to something left behind, back to our roots, be they ever so small.

Memory, like a magnet, draws one back to where he was bred, born, and played away his childhood. Like a chronic dream, memory keeps calling. Dreams have a way of inserting faces, places, and events from years long past. And so, you say to yourself, I must go back one more time, and each time you go back, you swear that this will be your last, for nothing remains there for you; friends are gone, and houses have vanished, leaving little trace that they ever existed, except for an occasional wooden box covering a hand-dug well with a rusted pulley and weathered rope still intact. A trailer replaces a burned-out house here and there. The valleys have shrunken from their gigantic proportions of childhood memory. The raging river of childhood is but a lazy stream. Still, childhood memoirs appear in dreams from which you always awaken before they end. And the graveyards, perched high on the hillsides, house tombstones—some are rugged and weathered sandstone, while others are polished granite—with names and dates that keep calling us to discover our roots.

There seems no logical explanation, but who knows when the internal body clock might kick in, not only for you and me, but for the millions of Highlanders who have relocated elsewhere over the last century, or are associated with some creek, branch, or hollow because of a relative who lived there? And if the sleeping urge to return awakens with galactic magnetism, perhaps some singular Memorial Day weekend we will have a grand reunion. Until then, our dreams must suffice.

I am honored you would read my reminiscences. I hope they bring back cherished recollections of your own and cause you to reflect upon your past, your heritage, and your childhood experiences and adventures. Though they may not always be pleasant, they are yours, and they are what make you unique in the entire world. We all have a story to share. Thanks for reading mine.

www.ingramcontent.com/pod-product-compliance
Lightning Source LLC
Chambersburg PA
CBHW060907250626
7159CB00008B/2907